TWISTED GENIUS

FAMILY GENIUS SERIES, #5

PATRICIA RICE

Book View
Café

Twisted Genius

Patricia Rice

Copyright © 2017 Patricia Rice

First Publication: Book View Cafe, October 2017

All rights reserved, including the right to reproduce this book, or portion thereof, in any form.

Published by Rice Enterprises, Dana Point, CA, an affiliate of Book View Café Publishing Cooperative

Cover design by Mandala

Book View Café Publishing Cooperative

P.O. Box 1624, Cedar Crest, NM 87008-1624

http://bookviewcafe.com

ISBN **978-1-61138-691-2** ebook

ISBN **978-1-61138-692-9** print

ALSO BY PATRICIA RICE

AUTHOR'S NOTE

THE FAMILY GENIUS SERIES WAS NEVER MEANT TO BE POLITICALLY CORRECT. I poke fun at everyone on an equal opportunity basis, including our fearless heroine. Please feel free to be offended by anything my characters think, say, or do, then learn to laugh at yourself and me. My only intent is to give readers an enjoyable read and maybe make you think a bit. And if you don't want to think, that's good too, because sometimes we simply need to escape reality for a few hours.

The timeline for Ana's stories takes place over a period of roughly a year —a presidential primary election year. Unfortunately, I'm not capable of writing fast enough to produce an entire series of books within that same interval. So the series will not take place in real time. Current events (Maryland's death penalty was repealed in 2013, for instance) and technology will remain in 2011 even though changes have multiplied since I conceived the original concept—and occur rapidly every day that I write.

Anyone with a modicum of political knowledge will realize that ten years after 9/11/01 does not correspond with a Senator Paul Rose—or anyone similar—running for office. All characters are fictional and entirely the product of my warped imagination.

CHARACTERS

MAGDA'S FAMILY:

Rathbone Maximillian — Magda's father, a meddling Hungarian-American billionaire, poisoned by the secretive cabal called Top Hat.

Anastasia Devlin — age 30; self-employed as virtual assistant and self-appointed family caretaker; daughter of Magda's first husband, Brody Devlin, an Irish revolutionary never long for this world.

Nicholas Maximillian — age 25; educated in Britain and has a dual passport; works for British embassy in DC; Magda's illegitimate son by Lord Terence Arbuthnot, British explorer who took too many risks

Patra Llewellyn — age 23; works for DC newspaper; father Patrick Llewellyn, English journalist who embedded in one too many war zones.

Alexander (Zander) Khosi and Juliana Aneke Kruger — twins, age 20; educated in South Africa; illegitimate children of Phillip Kruger—late diplomat in a country known for violence before diplomacy

Tudor Bullfinch — age16, educated in Britain, has 3 passports; father is traveling English and Australian merchant currently on third or fourth wife

Elizabeth Georgiana Maximillian (EG) — age 9; illegitimate daughter of cheating Senator Ewell (Tex) Hammond; half-sister of *Eloise*, Tex's legitimate daughter

ADDITIONAL CHARACTERS:

Amadeus Graham — alias Thomas Alexander, head of Alexander Security; Maximillian Rathbone's protégé; father is Dillon Graham, friend of Brody Devlin and Hugh O'Herlihy;

Sean O'Herlihy — political investigative reporter for DC newspaper with Patra Llewellyn; father is Hugh O'Herlihy, friend of Brody Devlin and Dillon Graham

CHAPTER 1

IN HIGH-DEFINITION TECHNICOLOR, GLOBS OF WHIPPED CREAM SLITHERED down the candidate's artificially bronzed cheek. The stretched skin of his facelift froze his usual stiff smile with horror. The cream dripped off a movie hero chin onto a Harvard-maroon tie.

Gleefully, I clicked the remote control to go back and watch again as the fat chocolate cream pie splatted squarely on Senator Rose's patrician nose. Aides rushed to hurry him off camera, but not before I caught a glimpse of the snarl curling his lip to reveal his capped incisors. I'd seen his high school yearbook—even his teeth were fake these days.

I happily clicked to the beginning of the clip again. Whoever was behind the pie-throwing clown disguise had a good throwing arm and fabulous timing. I watched Rose descend the stairs on a wave of mob enthusiasm after a gun control rally. The female clown with a bright red smile stepped out of the crowd as if to hand him her county-fair prize-winning confection.

Splat. I giggled happily and punched the clicker again. I couldn't get enough of the smug smile turning to cursing snarl. "I love TiVo," I said in contentment, rubbing my bare toes over a long masculine leg.

Graham was probably the reason for my unusual contentment, but I wasn't ready to let him know that. I wasn't prepared to acknowledge it myself. Six months from bitter enemies to lovers was moving much too fast. I could handle friends with benefits, though.

Graham crushed his muscular thigh over mine, trapping my teasing toes. Then he took my toy away.

"If there were no TV news, we wouldn't have to worry about the state of the nation," I complained as he switched from my fun recording to boring live TV.

"You're the reason I'm in bed instead of at my desk," he said in his low, spine-tingling baritone. "Want me to go back to my computers?"

"The house is blessedly empty," I pointed out, as I had an hour ago, right after I'd packed EG off to her father's. Graham had been quick to comprehend the message. He was smart like that.

My nine-year-old sister had been invited to a sleepover with her half-sister. The two were worse than magnesium and water, and I expected a report of a neutron bomb in the vicinity of Senator Tex's Georgetown home at any moment. I grabbed the momentary respite in the best way I knew how.

"Having all your family out of sight is what worries me," Graham said, proving his thoughts followed mine. He switched to his favorite news channel.

Graham bears a strong resemblance to the late Christopher Reeves as Superman, except for the puckered red scar from his temple to his eye. His thick black hair had been artfully styled to conceal the worst of the injury, except he sported bedhead at the moment, thanks to me.

He'd once been an up-and-coming politician, a presidential aide, and his pretty face would have assured that he'd go far. 9/11 had ended that, in so many ways that I had yet to uncover the depth of the damage—another reason I was wary of a relationship. The man did brooding and dangerous better than any movie super-villain.

Not that I couldn't keep up with him in eccentric territory. I'm Anastasia Devlin, granddaughter of the late multimillionaire, Rathbone Maximillian. I'm learning I have a lot in common with that wily old man I'd barely known. Unfortunately, I probably inherited the worst deviousness from his daughter, my mother, Magda, as did my many half-siblings.

So admittedly, Graham had a point about worrying over an empty house. When my tribe was loose upon the world, anarchy was obliged to happen.

"My family is not currently under my control. I bear no responsibility for what they do under the influence of others." I tried to sound dignified, but I was tickling the hairs on his broad chest.

Graham might be an agoraphobic hermit, but that didn't mean he didn't work out. He had muscles on top of muscles, built through sheer frustration in his private gym.

"You are looking for distraction because you *can't* control them, hence the remote control." He zoomed up the image on the enormous flat screen on his bedroom wall. We live in the same house, but we maintain separate quarters. We both like our privacy too well.

"You do not qualify as a psychologist." I grimaced as Senator Rose, no longer covered in the prior day's pie, strode down the stairs accompanied by his Evil Minion, also known as his campaign manager, Harvey Scion.

The TV announcer was reporting the defeat of a landmark health-care bill that the Senate, led by Rose, had worked hard to kill. Rose, as usual, looked smug and triumphant. Scion, as owner of a pharmaceutical company who would have been adversely affected by the bill, simply looked his usual dour self. Politics as usual, yawn.

I leaned over to hit the mute button and solemnly intoned as if I were Rose, "Far better that poor people go without medical treatment and die so our taxes don't have to support their uselessness into eternity."

Graham snorted and wrenched the clicker back, holding it out of my reach. "Solves over-population," he countered cynically.

I never knew when he meant that crap. I kicked him, just in case. "Privileged prick," I muttered. "Really, the pigs ought to be made to wallow in the same sty with the rest of us if they're going to represent us. Let them know how we really feel."

"You're not poor anymore," Graham had to observe.

Caught by an image on the enormous screen, I ignored him. "That's Nick." I tried to snatch the remote but Graham held it so I'd have to climb on top of him to reach it.

At some other time, I might have, but I wanted to know what my brother was doing in the same vicinity of the man I hated with all my heart and soul, for excellent reason, none of them political. Nick worked for the British embassy. He had no interest in health care reform.

"He's with the whistle-blower who wanted to present his paper on pharmaceutical company collusion to Congress before they voted. Rose stalled it in committee." Leave it to Graham to know everyone and everything.

I studied the whistleblower as he tried to escape the rush of TV cameras and microphones shoved in his direction. He was a scruffy but not bad-looking geek in a rumpled suit.

I wasn't a news fanatic and despised politics, but even I'd heard the rumors about the report revealing massive fraud and collusion between the drug and insurance industries. Jaded as I am, I figured collusion was nothing new. Drug lords got to be drug lords by physical and financial coercion in every corner of the world I'd ever lived in. Big Pharm might hide behind corporate legality, but only because they had more lawyers than the gangsters on the corner or the Afghans in their fields.

"What does the whistle-blower have to do with Nick?"

Graham gave me an odd look but didn't reply. That meant he knew something I didn't, which irritated me. A few of the more intelligent reporters abandoned Rose to delay the whistle-blower, whose name was apparently Guy Withers, *Guy* to rhyme with "me." Leave it to my gay brother to find a fancified Frenchman to pal with. Guy was just Nick's type—

Which was when I rolled my eyes. Nick had mentioned him in passing. I'd thought the name sounded familiar. Guy was probably a Brit, not a Frenchman, hence the involvement of the Brit embassy and my half-brother. Drug lords were international these days. And if Guy were as gay as Nick—I'd tease Nick to his dying day. Gay Guy—almost as good as EG, our baby sister Elizabeth Georgiana, the Evil Genius. We could call him GG for short.

The camera returned to Rose expounding on the benefits of private health care, apparently under the impression that the underemployed would choose health insurance over groceries and rent. Since our family had barely managed roofs over our heads until recently, I'd learned basic Band-Aids and Neosporin and then simply terrified everyone into staying healthy. Only recently had I coerced EG's father into covering her under his family plan, so I didn't have to threaten her into avoiding dangerous playgrounds.

As Nick and Guy continued down the concrete stairs and off screen, I grew restless. It was a Friday night. I didn't have any interesting cases to work on. I'd either have to get up and find something to eat—or arouse Graham to another round of hide the sausage.

A thunderous roar and shouts from the TV pumped my pulse into over-drive. I jerked my attention back to the screen and saw smoke billowing from behind Rose and his cohorts.

Graham cursed and rolled out of bed, hitting the ground running.

On the screen, Rose and his aides scurried off in a phalanx of police and bodyguards. Rose had refused to pay for Secret Service protection at this early stage of his presidential race. My guess was that he wanted no official record of his private meetings with his cadre of money-sucking vampires and two-legged wolves.

My mind was still in stun mode. My family was supposed to be safe here. People did not bomb the United States. That was for other countries.

9/11 had proved otherwise.

Nick and his friend had gone off in the direction of that smoke swirling up the steps.

My heart stopped. I took back my promise to tease Nick until the day he died. As children, we had survived the ruined streets of Sarajevo together. Surely he had not come this far, finally found safety and satisfaction, only to be killed by bad gas pipes.

Because it had to be gas pipes, right? DC was one of the most guarded cities in the universe. There had been no airplane this time.

Graham tugged on his black jeans and talked into one of his many phones.

I needed my phone. I flung back the covers, yanking my unbound braid into order as I fled for the hidden stairway in Graham's office. I nearly broke my leg running naked down the steep dark steps to the secret door in my grandfather's old bedroom.

I'd been contemplating moving my things into this dim tomb, but inertia had left everything untouched, just as it had been for the last six months. I'd been sleeping in the connecting office and storing my clothes in file cabinets.

I made silent promises to any deity listening as I grabbed the phone from my grandfather's immense oak desk and hit Nick's name.

"We're safe," was his curt response before I said a word.

I nearly expired of relief that he was alive, but I couldn't stop shaking. Nick didn't do frightened, he got angry. He was definitely not happy.

"Use the burner," he ordered and cut me off.

He was in trouble. Frantically, I scrambled through drawers looking for the burner phone we'd acquired during a bad episode involving our twin half-siblings before Christmas. I found it in the top drawer.

Nick's number was programmed into everything I owned. Closest to me in age, he'd been my right-hand man since birth. We'd been inseparable for years, even when his father had sent him off to school, and I was left behind. Communication was what we did.

Fear roiled inside my head as I waited for him to answer. I put the phone on speaker and began digging for clothes and a rubber band to contain my braid.

"We need a safe house," he said, when he finally responded. That he knew I could come up with such a thing spoke of my relationship to Graham and not necessarily Nick's confidence in me. "Guy's car was in that garage. We were supposed to be in that car, but we were running late and had only reached the entrance."

I could point out that he was being overly suspicious, that he wasn't the center of the universe, and with corroding infrastructure, gas pipes exploded all the time. But he was there and I wasn't and I had to trust his assessment, which didn't make me any happier.

"I'm on it. Are you in a safe place now?"

"Back alley, heading for the Metro. It will take time for them to sift through the garage debris to determine that we aren't buried under there." He sounded on top of the situation, but Nick hated skullduggery. He could do it with finesse, just as he could rob a casino of a quarter million bucks with card sharping. But my tall, handsome, brother came from a long line of British lords, and even if he was illegitimate, he'd been influenced by his family and was all about gracious living and charm. He hated the ugly side of life.

I conjured up the earlier TV image of Nick and Guy on the stairs wearing suits and nothing warmer. It had been unseasonably mild for January, hence Nick's abandoning of his usual cashmere overcoat. He'd regret that now that the sun was going down.

"Put your coats and ties in your briefcases," I ordered, because Nick liked stylish clothes that stood out, and he'd gone soft these last years. He would never think to disguise himself. "See if you can find a place to grab sweat-shirts and caps. Better yet, buy windbreakers. You'll freeze."

"Will do," he said curtly. "We'll take the first train that arrives and wait for you to call back."

I didn't want to believe anyone would intentionally harm my cosmopolitan half-brother. Why would they? He was a harmless embassy wonk. The whistle-blower had failed to stop the defeat of the health care bill. He was irrelevant now. It had to be a gas leak.

Graham would know. He had contacts in the offices of every bureaucrat and civil servant in DC, maybe the world. The *don't ask, don't tell* policy worked well when it came to where Graham got his information, but I needed his help now.

I'm short and don't fit well into jeans, so I don't own any. I dragged on my usual denim dress and draped a heavy fisherman's sweater I'd been given for Christmas over it. With my long black braid in some control, I tugged on leggings and boots and ran back upstairs.

Graham was back in his office with multiple monitors flashing scenes from every security camera in the vicinity of the explosion. "Suspected car bomb," he said before I even asked. The man had eyes in the back of his head. "It took out a gas pipe. The garage is wasted."

"Nick's okay," I gasped. "He and Guy need a safe place."

Without questioning, Graham grabbed a piece of paper off his desk and handed it over his shoulder.

That he had a safe house ready said more than I wanted to hear. He suspected Nick was a target of foul play as well.

CHAPTER 2

Using both his burner and mine, I texted Nick the instructions to the safe house, including the key code. Part of my *don't ask, don't tell* policy concerned Graham's ability to summon hideaways at an instant's notice. If we were to further our relationship, I'd have to start asking, and I didn't think I wanted to hear the answers.

Since I'd removed the GPS from my burner phone, I had to look up the safe house address on my computer before I headed out. Then I found the Metro that would take me there. The place appeared to be a small tower of condo flats in a nondescript area northeast of Dupont Circle, where we lived. I doubted that it came equipped with everything needed, so I threw some essentials from Nick's old bedroom and some of my own supplies into a knapsack.

I donned my new black leather jacket filled with necessities the police wouldn't like to know about and set out. Black leather fits in anywhere better than my old army coat, and it smelled delicious. I wasn't used to owning high-end luxury items unless I bought them used. I wasn't certain I approved of conspicuous consumption, but I loved this coat. Nick had given it to me at Christmas, understanding me only too well—one of the many, many reasons I couldn't lose my brother. No one else understood my dangerous insecurities the way Nick did, including Graham.

Out on the street, the general populace seemed unstirred by the news of a bombing of a parking garage. Media sensationalism has desensitized us to tragedy. We needed Rambo riding a Humvee shooting weapons of mass destruction before we woke up to the violence around us.

That philosophy didn't keep me from shivering as I got off the Metro and hurried toward the street where I hoped Nick would be safely ensconced. I'd almost lost my *brother*. I couldn't wrap my head around it.

Therapists had tried to explain my need to internalize and control as a result of my childhood. Explaining didn't prevent me from making it my goal to see that all my half-siblings were safe and well cared for at all times —an impossibility even I recognized. So maybe I had a Sisyphus complex.

As an example—with the help of my half-siblings, especially Nick—I'd spent these last six months fighting to win back our grandfather's inheritance against impossible odds. I'd moved mountains to provide a safe haven for my family.

As a result, we now had a multi-million-dollar mansion and a fortune in the bank. Only none of us had really accepted that we weren't still one step away from starvation and homelessness.

Nick had come closest to reaching normality. He had a posh job at the embassy, his own sweet little house, and apparently, a boyfriend. Or maybe I misunderstood Graham's look and Nick's accompaniment of the whistle blower. That remained to be seen. I wanted Nick to be happy, but I'd never met this Guy, and nearly getting Nick blown up was not a promising start to any relationship.

I approached the safe house indirectly, verifying no one followed me. I hoped it was an exercise in excess caution, but life had taught me that there was no such thing. I studied the empty apartment house lobby as I entered —no guard on duty but security cameras in every corner and two easily accessible exits.

I buzzed the suite Nick had been given and it buzzed back. I'd feel relief, but I needed to see his face first.

Not until the solid-looking suite door cracked open and I saw Nick's eye above the chain did I allow myself to relax a fraction. "Are you going to introduce me to your boyfriend?" I asked. If he punched me out, I'd still be happy just knowing he was alive and in one piece.

He unchained the door and looked more relieved than peeved. We weren't a family that hugged, but he squeezed my shoulders. "Squirt, meet Guy."

Huh, so he wasn't denying the *boyfriend*.

Withers looked a little worse for wear. Dark stubble accented high cheekbones. Brownish-black hair fell across his brow and into his deep-set black eyes. Nick had most excellent taste in companions. But Guy was attempting to staunch blood from a cut on his cheek, and his trousers looked as if they'd been rolled in mud and cut with scissors. He was still wearing what appeared to be a brand new nylon windbreaker with a Redskins logo on the back, but the white dress shirt beneath was filthy.

Despite his obvious disarray, Guy made a cordial bow. "The sister, I assume? And not really called Squirt? Pleased to meet you."

"I'm Ana. Sit down so I can reach that cheek." I dropped my knapsack on an ultra-modern chrome and leather chair and rummaged for the first-aid kit I'd thrown in. "Any other injuries? Do I need to call a doc?"

"Just flying debris and throwing-ourselves-into-the-gutter injuries," Nick said with an air of exhaustion, dropping into a gray leather lounge chair. "Nothing a good hot shower and clean clothes won't fix."

I pointed at the knapsack. "Not stylish, but the best I could dig out of your closet in a hurry."

He nodded but didn't get up. Instead, he watched me administering to Guy's wound.

"Does anyone care to explain why you believe it was Guy's car that exploded? I'm sure there were others in there." I dabbed the wound with antiseptic and rummaged for a bandage, pretty much the extent of my first-aid knowledge.

"I have received threats," Guy admitted. "They seemed foolish. I just have a single exposé that I have already given to the committee. There are copies in the cloud and my lawyer's office and countless other places. Blowing me up will not make it disappear. And since the committee has rejected it, it is essentially worthless."

I looked at Nick, who shook his head in disagreement. "Once the media digs into the information he and his partner have collected, it will blow the pharmaceutical and insurance industries into particles of atomic dust."

I was contemplating the meaning of "partner." Nick *wasn't* his boyfriend?

But I let the comment pass by and snorted at his naiveté. "If the writer of the report isn't available to verify the facts, the drug lords will sue the pants off any third-party attempting to make it public. You didn't really think

Rose's cabal of greedmeisters would allow that information to see the light of day?"

Guy lifted an inquiring eyebrow as I packed up the first-aid kit. "Drug lords? Cabal of greedmeisters?"

"Ana has a theory that Senator Rose is bought and owned by a cadre of wealthy industrialists who mean to control the presidency and Congress. So far, she's only been able to make a few powerful men furious and bring down some corrupt CEOs. Rose remains lily-white," Nick explained.

"I know nothing of Senator Rose," Guy said apologetically. "My paper applies to the price collusion among various pharmaceutical companies and a profit-sharing agreement with the insurance industries that allows both of them to pocket the difference between cost and price. There is also a chemical analysis of various popular drugs to show they do not justify their cost."

Which made little sense to me. I looked to Nick, our resident math genius. "I thought insurance companies fought to reduce the prices they have to reimburse to patients."

Nick shrugged. "It's complicated. Companies with a patented drug can charge anything the market will bear, no matter their actual cost to produce. But once the patent expires, generic companies collude with some insurance companies to keep the same high price by giving kickbacks. And because consumers are used to paying the cost of the patented drug, they do not understand that they're paying the same price for a cheaper drug."

"And as Nick says, companies *with* patents can raise their prices sky-high if people must have the drugs," Guy explained, sprawling on the black-cushioned couch. "Nadia is a chemist who works for Scion Pharmaceuticals. She produced the cost lists for a hundred different popular drugs. The profit-making in this country is unconscionable."

I recognized *Scion Pharmaceuticals* even if I didn't understand profits and losses and collusion. Harvey Scion was Rose's chief campaign strategist and one of the major contributors to the dangerous Top Hat cabal. He'd been there on the steps with Rose when the bomb went off. That's all I needed to set my worry cap loose. Top Hat had killed my grandfather and at least half a dozen others I knew of. They were ruthless.

And Guy and this Nadia had dared to try to expose Scion's evilness?

A shiver ran down my spine as I regarded the two men slumped on the furniture—two men who had nearly died.

"You have facts and figures supporting the accusation of collusion? And this Nadia can confirm them even if you're out of the picture?" I asked. My worry gene escalated.

At Guy's nod, I added with urgency, "And where is this Nadia now?"

"Picking her kids up at daycare, I imagine. She's a single mother who prefers to work in the background. I am the one who is trying to put our evidence in front of people who must *do* something about this travesty of injustice." Guy's dark eyes flashed with the fires of a flaming radical.

I glanced at Nick and noticed his admiration. My brother was a sucker for flaming radicals. My bad, I suppose.

"Have either of you thought to call Nadia and tell her to move her ass and her kids into hiding?" I suggested.

"I tell you, she is not—"

Nick was already pressing numbers on his burner phone. Nick understood danger as this pretty numbers wonk did not. Guy frowned, shrugged, and waited for Nick to talk to Nadia. And waited. Nadia was not answering her phone.

"She will not answer if she is driving," Guy explained. "She does not have the blue tooth in her car."

"What's her full name?" I was punching a text to Graham as I spoke.

"Nadia Kaminsky," Guy said with a puzzled frown. "She is divorced and has not lived here long. I doubt she is in your directory."

With the directional devices removed, the burner phones' search engines were a little less intuitive. Graham was faster. As soon as he received my text, he shot back a link to a news site. By this time, Nick had given up on calling Nadia and watched my face.

I tried not to be expressive, but my stomach sank to my boots as I opened the link. I handed my phone over to Guy, and he turned pale.

"This is not possible," he whispered. "It must be coincidence. She had the children with her!" he said, as if children were a magical protective shield.

He pulled out his own phone, but Nick leaned over and took it away. "That could lead them directly to us. Keep it turned off."

Nick took my phone to read the story. "Hit and run. It could be coincidence. The drivers in DC are reckless idiots. This happens a dozen times a week. The driver could be drunk, an illegal, driving on an expired license. . . She's probably fine."

Not if it was on a news site.

Graham texted a hospital phone number. I had a really bad feeling about this. Normally, I would have handed it to Guy to call, but I was cluing in on his emotional state. Hysteria would be detrimental to his safety.

I dialed and asked for Nadia Kaminsky. They put me on hold. Ten ages later, with Nick and Guy watching me as if I were hawk prey, I got an impatient female voice asking if I was a relation.

I put her on speaker phone and did what I usually did in these situations. I lied. "I'm her sister. Please, you must tell me how she is, and the children? Please? Shall we come for them?" I unintentionally imitated Guy's slight accent. It was a protective device left over from my childhood living in multiple unfriendly countries. Cursing in foreign languages was also useful.

The nurse spoke more soothingly. "The children have been sedated. You may visit them, if you wish. Our visiting hours are until ten tonight."

"And Nadia?" I demanded, raising my voice hysterically. "How is my sister? Is she with them?"

"She's in ICU and can't have visitors. Why don't you come in and talk to her doctor? We cannot give out more information on the phone." She made a few more reassuring noises and hung up.

Dead silence. She had said what needed to be said without saying it. Nadia wasn't going to make it.

I'd say Guy and Nick looked horrified, but petrified might be a better word.

CHAPTER 3

"Nadia has no relations in this country," Guy said in a shocked whisper. His big eyes were almost round with grief. "I must go to the hospital."

"*No*," Nick said with more force than I had. "If the accident wasn't coincidence, then Ana is right—Nadia was targeted as well as you. Going there will just get you killed."

"I am the children's guardian if anything happens to Nadia," Guy said in an urgent voice. "I promised her. She was thinking her abusive ex might come here and kill her, but not *this*. I do not want to believe it is my fault. . ."

"It is *not* your fault if she chose to reveal mass fraud and corruption. She took her chances, just as you did. We don't know for certain that she won't recover," I said. "Now it's time for others to step up. I will go to the hospital and talk with the doctors for you. Unless she's conscious and talking, they have no way of knowing if Nadia has a sister or what her sister's name is. The children might be a problem if they're awake. Do you have a nickname that might reassure them if I use it?"

"They are so very small," Guy said somberly, rummaging in his pocket for his wallet. "Nadia is such a good mother. . . I cannot believe. . ." He took the old-fashioned handkerchief Nick handed him to blow his nose and hide his tears.

I wanted to cry with him, if only for the sake of those two children. I hadn't known Nadia, but I knew kids, and their fate was breaking my jaded heart.

Guy finally pulled out a photo of two dark-haired toddlers hanging off his arms. "Vincent will be six in a few days. He is in school part of the day, but Anika is just four. She calls me Kiwi for reasons only known to her."

"May I take this with me?" I studied the photo of two adorable brown-eyed children and swallowed a lump. "I need something familiar with which they can relate. They'll be terrified."

"You know children well?" Guy asked with good reason.

"Ana essentially raised all of us," Nick explained so I didn't have to. "She may look and act like a Hell's Angel, but she's still a child inside."

I glared at him for the insult. I'd been hardened by the fiery furnace of reality. I was no marshmallow—okay, except maybe when it came to kids. "I know enough not to terrify them any more than they are, hence the photo. We'll need to verify that Nadia's house is a safe place to take them if they're well enough to be dismissed. Get started on that."

Everyone was carefully avoiding the subject of whether it would be safe for Nadia to go home with them. ICU meant she wouldn't be going anywhere soon, if ever.

I really, really wanted my fear to be paranoia. I wanted to be proved wrong that Nadia's accident had been more than that, but life had taught me otherwise. Coincidences didn't happen, not when a billion dollar industry was about to be hit with corruption charges and lawsuits. As far as I was concerned, Rose and his supporters were homegrown terrorists who thought people were as expendable as cockroaches.

As I rode the Metro to the hospital, I started making phone calls. Once away from Nick and friend, it was safe to use my own phone, thank goodness. I didn't like keeping my contacts in a throw-away phone.

Remembering Nick's snark about my thuggish look—he bought me the black leather, for pity's sake!—I stopped at the hospital gift shop before making inquiries at the information desk. I didn't think a short female in denim and leggings looked like a gang member, but I'm not a style maven. The clerk in the gift store didn't look the least surprised at my choice of a cuddly stuffed shark and monkey, so there, I could too look motherly.

"We have biker dolls too," the gray-haired clerk suggested, gesturing at a selection of big-eyed dolls sporting motorcycle helmets and riding Harleys.

I refrained from beating her over the head with the shark. I shrugged off the jacket in the hall outside the shop, but I felt naked without all my weapons easily at hand.

Unless the police were involved, hospitals had no reason to be suspicious of visitors bearing stuffed animals. Once I asked after Nadia Kaminsky and her children, the information desk told me how to find the pediatric ward but didn't mention ICU.

They didn't want me seeing Nadia. My throat closed, but I nodded, and headed for the elevators—and intensive care. All the way up, I fretted over those two beautiful children having to grow up without a mother because some asshat with a two-ton mobile weapon thought all life was expendable.

I wasn't the praying sort, but when I stepped out of the elevator into the formidable ICU floor, I tried to think positive thoughts.

There was only one patient behind the window, and all the nurses were in there with her. An urgent Code Red blared overhead. From what I could see, I was watching Nadia succumb to her extensive injuries. Her head was buried in bandages. More bandages covered her upper body. The nurses could do little more than check IV lines.

This was when prayer might help, if I believed in it. Still, with tears in my eyes, I whispered *Fight, Nadia, fight*, and hoped that would reach her.

Then, as I had much too often, I hardened my heart against death and went in search of terrified children.

I returned to the elevator and took it to the pediatric floor. For whatever reason, hospitals made me belligerent. My shields went up, and my obnoxious came out. But usually, I was visiting suspected villains. This time, the patients were innocent victims, and I was walking on quicksand.

My brother Nick was mixed up with a radical flake with a target on his back and whose partner was dying. And said flake was now responsible for two young children, which meant my brother was the next best thing to a father. I think my brain exploded.

The nurses on the pediatric floor were overworked and overwhelmed, but they took time to sympathize and hug me when I asked after the children—which meant they knew Nadia was dying or already dead. I didn't like strangers in my personal space, but I endured for the sake of my cover. It wasn't difficult to summon tears.

I'd come a long way from the agoraphobic nerd I'd been six months ago. I was still a nerd, but I was developing a shell that allowed me to function in public without the use of knives or fists—most of the time. Tears were new. I swiped them away as I reached the room to which I'd been directed.

Vincent and Anika were watching a cartoon on TV. Looking at them lying pale and listless against the pillows, I sure hoped Nadia had had an insurance card in her purse and the hospital had found it. I wanted Scion Pharmaceuticals paying for this. Vincent's leg had been plastered past his knee, and it was being held up in an uncomfortable-looking contraption to reduce the swelling. He wasn't laughing at the cartoon. He had gorgeous dark curls, much like Guy's, and huge brown eyes.

Anika had a big fat bandage on her forehead and part of her lovely dark hair shaved. But she was sitting cross-legged on the bed and sucking her thumb when I entered with the nurse. She looked at me suspiciously, but she studied the stuffed animals with interest.

Here was the hard part—passing myself off as an aunt they didn't know.

"Uncle Kiwi told me you were here," I said in a tone I hoped wasn't frightening. "He can't come right now, but he'll be there when I take you home." I turned to the nurse. "How soon can they leave?"

"If all goes well, in the morning, when the doctor signs off," she said, checking charts and pulses. "We need to keep an eye on them for swelling and signs of any internal injuries. But it looks like they should be just fine." Her voice oozed sympathy, knowing their lives had been turned upside-down.

"I want the shark," Vincent said grumpily.

I raised my eyebrows in my best maternal manner. "Is this how you ask for a gift?"

"I want Mama," Anika said defiantly. Nadia hadn't raised weepy wimps, thank heavens.

That was the cue for the nurse to run, as I'd hoped. She closed the door behind her.

Taking a deep breath, I bopped sulky Vincent on the head with the shark. "Give me a please."

He looked truculent, as only a tired, frightened six-year old can do. I'd seen my siblings look like that often enough growing up, and I really didn't want to deal with any more of the kind of life-changing disasters that had caused that look. But I wasn't in a war zone this time, I told myself.

When he didn't respond, I held out the monkey to Anika. "Your mama can't come right now. That's why Uncle Kiwi sent me. I'm Ana." I held up the photo he'd given me. "Want to send him more pictures? I think he'd like that."

"Thank you," she said politely, taking the monkey and hugging it, but still looking suspicious as she examined the photo. "That's me as a baby!"

That was her maybe a year ago.

"Let me see," Vincent demanded.

I applauded his suspicion. I needed to demand his respect. I turned and lifted one eyebrow again—it's a good intimidating trick. Kids were usually fascinated. My siblings had tried to imitate the arch. Only Nick came close, but he's fair and I'm dark, and I fancy my quirk is better than his.

I waited. The boy squirmed. With a huge sigh, he finally said, "Please."

Nadia had taught them good manners. I approved. I handed over the picture and the shark as a reward.

He hugged the shark and sniffed it, then examined the photo. "That's my Orioles cap! I lost it."

"You've grown since then," I sympathized. "You probably need a bigger one."

Male ego—they're all the same. He puffed up and nodded importantly. But then he turned those too-wise brown eyes on me and asked, "When can we see Mama?"

I wasn't much on euphemisms, but these were little kids in a strange place occupied by strangers. Hysteria would not be conducive to healing was what I told myself. "She was hurt pretty bad," I warned them. Not a lie, you'll notice.

"Like us?" Anika sniffed, on the verge of weary tears.

"Even badder," I told them. "That's why your Uncle Guy can't be here right now." Now I was lying and committing grammatical homicide as well.

To be honest, I wasn't totally certain how I got through the next hours. I think I burned up the burner phone's minutes sending pics to Guy so he could send silly videos back to them. They didn't like hospital food, and I was hungry, so we ordered pizzas. Eventually, they fell asleep, and I collapsed in the lounge chair provided for tired parents.

I am a virtual assistant, not a babysitter. I wanted to be tracking the monsters who had probably tried to murder Nadia and blow up Nick and Guy. But I simply couldn't abandon two children to the nightmares they were facing. So while they slept, I employed my regular phone to arrange what I could.

I was slipping into an exhausted doze when a figure dressed in black slid into the room. I reached into my jacket for my knuckle dusters and truncheon, but her perfume gave her away. My mother, the Hungarian Princess, Magda the Mysterious, and a thorn I couldn't remove from my side.

"Visiting hours are over," I informed her, wishing for a nice cup of tea to endure whatever insanity she was about to perpetrate. "I thought you would have left the country by now."

Don't get me wrong. Magda is probably an intelligence genius—aka spy. I was pretty sure she'd blown up a weapons warehouse and an illegal arsenal before Christmas. But she'd risked her children one too many times, and I'd lost patience with her single-minded superwoman sense of justice.

"No, I can't leave now, not with Nick involved," she murmured, perching on the edge of Anika's bed. "They're desperate if they took out a powerless chemist like Nadia. The final game is in play. I want you and Nick out of it."

As usual, I had to read between the lines. I didn't know the *they* she was stalking, but I could take a wild guess. As Max's daughter, Magda had grown up around the powerful men of the Top Hat cabal. After a lifetime of lies, Magda seldom said what she meant—but *she knew Nadia.* I figured that was a bad omen for Guy.

"Now is a fine time to start worrying about your children," I said in scorn. "Nick is an adult. He makes his own choices."

"Pursuing Scion is a wrong one," Magda said in disapproval. "Nick almost died today. That should be enough to convince him. Let him play house with his boyfriend. Don't help him investigate."

Coming from Magda, that was truly ominous. But I was operating on fumes and didn't have the strength to dig into her rationale. "If Scion was involved, he's going down," I informed her. "Give us a better way to do it."

"People like that don't play with fire. I just don't want you involved, understand? Stay home and take care of the children." Magda didn't wait to see if I agreed. She produced two small, neatly wrapped gifts from the pocket of her fur coat, set them on the nightstand, and walked out.

Stay home and take care of the children? She'd gone completely bonkers.

~

GRAHAM WATCHED THE SECURITY MONITOR AS THE FUR-COATED SHADOW slipped out of the hospital exit and slid into a waiting car. He shot a rubber band at the screen. *Magda*. Why had she been antagonizing Ana this time?

He understood why Ana was babysitting two scared children instead of returning to his bed. Ana had a mean streak a mile long, but when it came to the helpless, she put that streak to good use. She was sitting there, loaded for bear, should anyone try to harm those kids.

If Ana hadn't taken up guard dog position at Nadia's feet, it meant she didn't expect Nadia to live. Neither did the physicians, as far as he'd been able to ascertain. While Nadia was in ICU, she should be safely surrounded by nurses and interns. He'd order a watch on her if she survived the night.

Nick and the other whistleblower were safely ensconced in their hidden apartment and didn't need his help at the moment.

So to amuse himself and keep Ana occupied, he one-upped Ana's twisted genius of a mother. He punched his keyboard and sent Ana a copy of the document Nadia had risked her life for. The congressional committee had buried it, but it was available for those who looked. He'd leave it to Ana to decide what to do with it. He was an observer and sometimes a guardian. He did not interfere unless asked—although he knew perfectly well what Ana's reaction to the document would be.

So, sometimes, he was an instigator.

He'd given up self-analysis long ago. He'd surrendered common sense when Ana had invaded his territory. But the upside was that life was no longer tedious.

Ana texted a string of exclamation points and question marks Graham didn't attempt to answer. It was enough to know she'd received the document. She'd be asleep before she dug three pages in.

His computer security alarm sounded—one he seldom heard, for good reason. He frowned and diverted his attention to the suspicious activity battering his dedicated server.

Who the *hell* would try to crack his network? He wasn't a major player like Sony or WordPress or Boeing. Hackers had no good way to know that he existed. And even if someone stumbled on him, his defenses were top of the line, better than the Defense Department's. But other than swatting spam, they had never been truly tested.

As a precaution, he shot a cyber block at Tudor's ISP. Ana's computer genius sibling knew about the network and was capable of testing his defenses for reasons unknown. It had to be early morning in the UK. Teens generally weren't up at this hour. He got back a robo-response equivalent to a snarl. Kid wasn't stupid, but he wasn't online either.

The attack continued. Alarms flared, and his IT people had been jarred awake and were frantically shutting down to prevent any damage.

This had to be a deliberate, targeted attack. By whom? And why?

He'd have to sort through his recent cases and see who might need his information most.

In the meantime—if the hacker wanted war, he'd give the bastard a dose of his own medicine. Graham typed Code Orange and watched his bots eat theirs like an ancient Pacman game.

Given that he'd just sent Ana a copy of a report that had got a parking garage blown up, he hunted an interior security camera in the hospital to keep a closer eye on Ana. He knew he'd cleaned the file he'd sent her, but if someone was after it, had he just sent her an explosive booby trap?

CHAPTER 4

"GRAHAM DID WHAT?" I ASKED FROM THE HOSPITAL CORRIDOR AS DOCTORS examined the kids in their room. I was pretty exhausted from sleeping in a chair all night and not certain I was hearing right.

"He's had Nadia's house swept from top to bottom for bugs. There aren't any. If her accident was deliberate, the killers were only interested in taking out *her*, not whatever might be in her house." Nick sounded equally puzzled. "Guy has ordered security cameras outside. We probably need to update the burglar alarm; it's antiquated. But Guy wants to take the kids home, to their familiar surroundings."

"I'm still wrapping my head around Graham getting involved," I admitted. "If he thinks the house is safe, then let's go for it. You don't want to be confined to a room for long. We just need to make arrangements so that no one knows Guy is living there."

"From what we can tell, it should be easy. There's an attached garage. Nadia's car won't be in it. We just come and go through the garage. As long as they don't realize Guy is alive and believe Nadia is out of the picture, the killers have to think their job is done."

I was uneasy about him hanging around a man with a target on his back, but we all had to live in our own comfort zones. "The kids need their own rooms and they need Guy, so I guess this sort of makes sense. I don't like it, but Guy's the guardian. Get that burglar alarm updated pronto. Just because no one tried to break in before doesn't mean they won't try now."

"We're on it. Weekends just aren't the best time for ordering anything. First thing Monday, I promise. Do you think they'll be releasing the kids today?"

"I'm clueless. I'll text you when I know."

"Have Sam drive them in a car with tinted windows."

I grimaced and agreed. Safety was paramount, but transporting kids in casts would be a bear. And it looked like it was up to me to handle it—Guy couldn't appear in a public place. "Guy will have to fax the hospital office with his credentials," I warned. "I can't bust them out."

"Then we'd better pray our killers aren't smart enough to check the hospital billing office to see who's taking the kids, and the hospital doesn't know they're talking to a man who is presumed dead," Nick said ominously before signing off.

He had the British embassy to verify anything he wanted. I wouldn't worry about details—the big things were overwhelming enough.

Machines were keeping Nadia alive. She was still in a coma and not expected to live. Watching the kids struggling to dress after the doctor approved their release, I gritted my teeth against the anger boiling beneath my surface calm. I had too much to do to explode, so I applied my energy to tasks I could actually perform.

For now, my main task was overseeing transportation. I'd once disapproved of the conspicuous consumption of Graham's limo service, if only for the danger of a licensed car being easily tracked. I'd since learned that Sam, his driver, could be creative.

The kids transformed from whiny, fretting little monsters the moment the nurses wheeled them out to the tinted-window, long black Lincoln waiting at the curb. Even little kids can be impressed by cars. I was impressed that Sam had summoned a vehicle with no identification other than a license plate from Colorado. My *don't ask, don't tell* policy kicked in.

Sam and the nurses got them strapped into the back seat along with all their gifts. Magda, the ultimate gift-giver, had provided them with hand-held game boxes. They'd been chasing the equivalent of Pac-men and Tweety birds all morning. Right now, though, they clung to their stuffed animals and watched me with huge eyes. I prayed they wouldn't ask about their mother.

While Sam loaded the wheelchair Vincent would need, I climbed into the rear-facing seat. The kids didn't look entirely reassured. Since I was still wearing yesterday's clothes and not my happiest smile, that was understandable.

But as the car pulled away and the shield between front and back seats opened, they transformed into beaming, bouncing normality.

"Unca Kiwi!" Anika cried.

Vincent was a little more circumspect, but he relaxed and held up his shark for inspection.

I didn't know how Nick would handle this new development in his life, but I was good with it. Let the guardian guard. It was better than holing up in a safe house—and it got me off the hook.

Stay home with the kids, indeed! My mother had mincemeat for brains. Someone had almost killed my brother. That someone was going down.

Guy had dark circles under his eyes, and his smile looked strained, but he told the kids that they were going home, and yes, they could have peanut butter and apples. When they asked about their mother, I was afraid he'd pass out.

He just said they'd talk about her when they got home and asked them questions about school. Excellent save. He'd be a good parent.

Guy had the remote to Nadia's garage. Sam pulled the limo inside, and we closed the door before letting the kids out. Keeping neighborly questions down was a good idea. Unless Guy had notified someone, no one had a reason to know the kids had been hurt. The parking garage explosion filled the local headlines. I didn't think Nadia's condition had made any news reports yet. One traffic accident out of hundreds every day might make a back page, if the police made a big deal of the hit-and-run aspect.

Until then, we didn't need nosy neighbors stopping by with tuna fish casseroles. As long as the bad guys thought everyone was dead, Guy and Nick should be safe. How long would that last?

Sam set up the wheelchair, and I let Guy take the children inside to have The Talk. I took the coward's way out and holed up in Nadia's office with her computer. I'm not a tech geek like Graham or Tudor, but I work with computers and know how to back up files. I'd had Guy bring me the biggest thumb drive he could find, and I copied everything I could for my own curiosity. Then I called Graham so he could do his magic trick by downloading an app and slurping up the insides.

He didn't sound happy to hear me, but I'd learned that Graham got grumpy when otherwise occupied. He saw the necessity of wiping Nadia's files clean after he grabbed the contents though. While he did that, I went in search of laptops or other evidence.

The children were weeping in what I guessed was the family room. My bet was that Anika didn't understand half of what she was being told. It would take time for them to grasp the gaping hole in their existence. I could pray their mother would recover, but she had a long fight ahead if she did. Fighting my own demons, I fixed peanut butter and apples and left them on the counter, along with glasses of milk and Oreos.

I didn't find any laptops or tablets. I was afraid if Nadia had any—and tech geeks always did—they might have been in the car. I texted Nick my concern. I wasn't certain what he could do, but I didn't want to bother Graham again.

Nick texted back that he would be over soon. And then he sent me a link to a video. I wanted to be gone before Nick needed the concealment of the garage, so I didn't immediately follow the link. I hugged the teary-eyed kids goodbye and told Guy that Nick was on his way. He almost looked relieved, but then the complications hit him, and I could see his eyes glaze over. My brother is a good guy, but he isn't exactly the nurturing sort.

I told him I'd be in touch and left him that way. In the limo, I opened the video Nick had sent me.

I couldn't figure out what I was looking at, at first. It was just too weird. There was arch-fiend Rose pontificating from a grandstand, his fake tan glistening with sweat from the spotlight. I guessed from what I could see of the banners that it was a political rally in South Carolina. The camera panned over a crowd of mostly older people, burly truck drivers and balding men in baseball caps, ladies in gingham and denim and everything in between. They bounced red, white, and blue Rose political signs alongside of handwritten ones espousing conservative causes that made my socialist soul wince.

That was all normal. What wasn't normal was the eerie white balloons with painted faces rising from the floor and dropping from the ceiling, startling and distracting the audience from the speaker.

And the really bizarre part? They all looked like a scary caricature of Harvey Scion, of Scion Pharmaceuticals—Rose's campaign strategist and financial backer.

I stopped the video and zoomed up. That was the drug lord's distinctive V of bad hair implants receding across his balding dome painted on top of the balloons. He really did have an almost round head and a narrow jaw, so the balloons were perfect in that respect. The caricature made his eyes smaller and closer together and exaggerated the heavy bags under them. The nose resembled a snout more than the broken flat thing it was in reality. The thin lips were pinched, and his perpetual day-old beard completed the effect. It was a danged scary balloon.

People dodged the strange orbs as if they might be bombs. *And then the balloons started popping.*

Women screamed. Men pulled guns. Rose's bodyguards dived for their fearless leader, shoving him down the stage steps and out of sight. He must be growing tired of these interruptions to his speechifying.

I could swear, after that, men started shooting the balloons before they could pop—as if inflated rubbers were truly terrorists. Smarter people dived for cover. It was utter chaos—and made no sense in any world I knew.

Except one, I realized in panic. *Magda* had a love of caricatures. She collected them—which meant she knew the names of the best caricaturists in the world.

I called Nick to ask about the video link, but he was apparently already in his car, headed for Nadia's house. He didn't answer. I sent the link to Graham. He didn't respond.

Maybe my journalist sister Patra knew what the video was about.

I'd been planning on calling her about Guy's explosive allegations. The information needed to be made public if Nadia wasn't to suffer in vain—although having Graham warn me last night that the file itself could be explosive, on top of Magda's less specific threat, made me cautious. I hadn't sent it yet.

Magda had used Scion's name and warned "they" had reached the end game, whatever in heck that meant. After years of being a doormat beneath my mother's feet, I tended to rebel against anything she said. I decided it was unfair for me to treat Patra in the same way that made me resent my mother.

Patra was young, but she was smart. And she was living with Sean O'Herlihy, an experienced investigative reporter for the *Times*. I couldn't trust the material in the hands of two better people.

I hit Patra's number and only got voice mail. Rats. I hung up and pondered whether or not to expose her to the same danger as Nick was in.

From what little I'd read, Nadia and Guy's report focused on tedious data that proved price fixing and profit mongering in the entire U.S. pharmaceutical industry. But buried in it was an exposé of Scion's sprawling pharmaceutical firms, revealing them as the fraudulent blood-suckers they were.

Scion was Rose's closest political confidant, a man certain to be appointed to the White House should Rose win, a man who was providing funds to *ensure* that Rose won. Power and greed made for a ruthless combination, and the Top Hat cabal supporting Rose had proved the extent of their determination.

I'd lived under corrupt foreign governments. Once tyrants claimed power, there was no stopping their depredations because bullies had no conscience. Rose with a drug lord steering him could not possibly be good for any country.

The fate of the nation was my justification for leaving voice mail for Patra, then shooting Nadia's hot potato to Patra's mailbox.

Information just wants to be free and all that.

～

THE SECURITY CAMERA OVER THE MANSION'S FRONT DOOR TOLD GRAHAM when Ana returned. She normally strode through the house like a general off to war—a true disturbance in the force. For the introvert she claimed to be, his black-braided genie knew how to make herself known.

It had irritated him at first, then amused him. Now. . . he was stupidly admiring her attitude and achievements and sitting here anticipating her return, as he'd told himself he'd never do again.

She was slight, but she trudged up the stairs as if carrying the weight of the world, so he knew she was weary. Since she'd covered up all the cameras that invaded her privacy, he could only see her on the landing. After that, he had to assume she went to her room for a shower and sleep.

He'd been on contentious terms with sleep for years, but he relaxed now that Ana was safe in this fortress her grandfather had built.

He played the video of the balloons Ana had sent him on one monitor, the pie-flinging episode on another, and tracked Rose's campaign schedule on a third. Then he opened up files on Ana's mother and Harvey Scion and began tapping his keyboard.

The hacker interference last night had slowed down his search, but his resources were far and wide. With any luck at all, he'd soon have the recent itineraries of all the parties involved.

He doubted Ana would appreciate what he suspected he'd find. He just hoped it would distract her from the grenade he'd tossed to her last night, until he'd found the terrorists who wanted it.

CHAPTER 5

After a long nap and a shower, I dressed and jogged down to my basement office to check my incoming. I opened Nick's text first. FOUND NADIA'S CAR. NO LAPTOP. CLAIM COP REMOVED CONTENTS.

I have a suspicious mind. I didn't believe a cop searched the contents of a car towed after an accident. They didn't have time for that, unless there was reason to believe a crime had been committed.

I'm a virtual research assistant by trade, not a detective. I have a wide field of resources but no technical training to investigate bomb splatter or accident scenes. I left that to the professionals. I can often provide the missing pieces officialdom needs to solve an investigation, but generally, the cops didn't appreciate my aid. TV detectives have it so much easier. My script writer is worthless like that.

So hunting for whoever tried to take out my brother and Guy by examining an exploded garage was an impossible hurdle. The coincidence of Nadia's accident was not.

Graham's security network was so vast that if I dug deep enough, I could access files inside computers that shouldn't have back doors but do. Not my fault if they leave them improperly guarded.

Nadia's name got me into the accident report database. As I suspected, no detective had been assigned to clear out her car. The contents supposedly awaited a family member to collect them.

If I needed proof of skullduggery, a fake cop collecting family posses-sions was sufficient for me. I didn't have the facilities for finding a hit-and-run driver. The police would make standard inquiries for videos and match car parts, but a trained assassin would have that covered. The cops weren't thinking in terms of a killer. I was.

I texted my cyber-genius half-brother Tudor and asked if he could trace the location of the laptop using Nadia's e-mail and other information from her computer. He's A-level in a Brit public school, buried in work and play, so I didn't expect an immediate answer.

I opened an e-mail from Zander, the male half of my twin siblings. He had returned to South Africa to persuade his brokerage firm to give him a position in the DC branch with our family money as his starting point. He's really young but exceptionally smart, and I wasn't surprised that he reported he would be returning soon to start sorting our new-found wealth.

After a lifetime of near-homeless poverty, I wasn't entirely certain how I felt about my grandfather's millions. I feared they'd been acquired in ways I wouldn't approve, but he also meant the money to take care of his family. That part, I could appreciate. Ambivalence-is-me, and I didn't get to be dictator. Money decisions belonged to everyone.

Out of wicked curiosity, I asked Zander if he had any way of tracing Harvey Scion's investments. Yeah, I knew financial records were supposed to be confidential, but they never were. I tapped whatever resources were available, and it would be faster if Zander dug than if I had to. He'd learned the dangers of too much money in the hands of the wrong people when he'd been here last. He knew how to dig deep to find what we needed. He would have copied my resources, and he was better at interpreting financial state-ments than I was.

Since I had no reply from Patra, I went online to read more about the Scion/Rose balloon incident. The left-wing media was positively gleeful about the gun-toting Rose supporters shooting each other up, but no one could explain how painted balloons had suddenly bounced all over the school gym where the rally had been held. Or why.

The articles were amusing but didn't help in finding connections to Nadia's murder attempt, even if the balloons looked like her boss. The report she and Guy had written on Scion Pharmaceutical was my biggest lead—unless her abusive husband had knocked her off. Just in case, I sent off a few inquiries to determine his name and location, but it was likely he'd show up to claim the kids and insurance if he was involved.

Balloon caricatures and exploding garages and hit-and-run assassins didn't necessarily connect. I just didn't like the coincidence. If the cops did the footwork and covered their bases, I would do my best to find connections behind the scenes.

While I pondered the best approach to finding a hit-and-run driver, I poked through more unofficial backdoors to see what was being done about the garage bombing. Explosives had been found, so they had real detectives on the case, not to mention the FBI and the KGB for all I knew. So Guy could be right—the bad guys were after him as well as Nadia.

Of course, it could be terrorists, but even the most stupid terrorist has better places to blow up than a parking garage—unless they had a specific target.

I didn't dare dig too far if the FBI was paying attention, so I just scanned the police file and slipped out again. Hacking the FBI wasn't happening. I'd leave that up to Graham.

But my snarky thought about the KGB churned up a memory about Scion Pharmaceuticals. I rummaged around on normal search engines until I had a small file of business articles about Scion expanding the manufacture of their popular pain-killing drug, Mylaudanix, to Eastern Europe. The business news was more excited about expanding markets than in the patients or the drug itself.

But now I remembered Mylaudanix being in the news recently, so I rummaged some more. Research wasn't as exciting as running bomb-sniffing dogs through a burned-out garage. It was tedious and time-consuming, and I was starving since I'd missed breakfast and lunch. Did I really care if thousands of people were hooked on pain-killers? People since the beginning of time have done drugs and alcohol for reasons unfathomable to me. I need my brain sharp and in control. Others apparently don't.

The front door over my basement office slammed.

The intercom spoke at the same time. "Guess who's coming to dinner?"

Once upon a time I used to fling the speaker across the room when Graham did that. Now I stupidly thrilled at his deep chocolate voice. Maybe he felt safer with mechanical communication, except I knew he wasn't waiting for a reply. I also guessed who the door slammer was. I'd been half-waiting for this since yesterday. Time for a break.

I jogged up the stairs to confront EG before she disappeared into the black hole that was her Gothic tower room. "I thought you were spending the weekend with your father."

"Helloise had a headache." EG is pretty much a shorter version of me—long black hair, short, slender, with our mother's elongated, long-lashed green eyes. She narrowed those deadly eyes now. "We were supposed to see *Beauty and the Beast* in 3-D. It's a dumb movie, but I wanted to see how the glasses worked."

Helloise was *not* her half-sister's name—it was EG's opinion of the ten-year-old brat whose real name was Eloise. Before he ran for the Senate, EG's father had separated from Eloise's mother and took up with Magda in some resort in Spain. I tried not to understand our mother's intentions, but I suspected she was not beneath wielding influence over a wealthy man on the brink of political power.

Whatever, Senator Tex headed back home to make nice with his family, abandoning EG to my youthful, resentful care. When EG had showed up at my door last year—all by herself—I'd gathered my rage and headed straight for DC and her father. Parents ought to be responsible for the offspring they flung into the world.

Except some people just weren't cut out to be parents.

I followed in her stomping path across the foyer to the impressive staircase that adorned our Victorian mansion. "Couldn't Tex take you to see the movie?"

"Mrs. Tex was supposed to take us, but now she's nursing her poor achy baby. Tex is busy taking calls about drugs," she said sourly.

Drugs? But my sister's disappointment came before research. Tex had left EG hanging like an unwanted extra appendage. "And what did you do to give Eloise a headache?" I knew my sister too well to sympathize totally.

She snickered, looking a little less disgruntled. "It was almost worth missing the movie. I told her about the billions of bugs living in her fancy princess bed, then showed her pictures on the computer when she didn't believe me. She had a screaming fit and demanded a new mattress and all new princess pink frou-frou to go with it."

That was the Evil Genius I knew and loved. "I shouldn't reward you for meanness, but pink frou-frou was obviously irresistible," I admitted. "I'll take you to the movie. Find the nearest theater. Just give me time to eat."

I wanted to know more about the Senator and those drug calls that were keeping him busy, but I wasn't grilling EG about her father. I despised Tex and his backward thinking, but he's her dad.

At my promise, she perked up and pulled out her phone. I know she wanted to be with her new-found father, but she would learn the same way I had—family are the people who love and nurture you, not necessarily the people who brought you into the world.

"There's a showing at four, on the other side of the Circle," she cried triumphantly as I trotted for the stairs to tackle the basement kitchen.

"Put on your princess costume," I called back. And then, just because I knew he was listening, I texted Graham: DOES THE BEAST WANT TO GO TO THE MOVIES?

NOT NOW was his only reply.

Given his hermit nature and our prior relationship, I actually considered this a positive sign.

"You do know Beauty is not a princess?" Mallard said as I invaded his kitchen.

Mallard was the epitome of a perfect butler, starched shirt and all. But he was once a revolutionary general in Ireland and probably a spy, so I never underestimated his ability to starve us to death if we didn't step in line.

"I will catch up on my fairy tales in my next life," I informed him. My education had been in the school of hard knocks and not in libraries.

I would have reached for the massive refrigerator door, but he handed me a plate with a wheat bagel loaded with eggs and goodies, plus a fresh cup of my favorite tea. I guessed that meant taking EG to the movies met with his approval. He normally scowled when I entered his private domain.

"Scion Pharmaceutical has its headquarters in Ireland," he intoned solemnly. "It employs hundreds of people who would otherwise have no jobs."

"So do weapon manufacturers," I agreed between mouthfuls. "That doesn't mean they shouldn't be making aspirin and toys instead."

"They have stockholders to pay."

I knew the old revolutionary was merely playing devil's advocate. Yeah, he loved guns as much as any military man, but guns and drugs disseminated like candy on street corners were death to civilization as we knew it. "They have gluttonous CEOs to pay," I countered.

"Your grandfather was once one of them," he reminded me.

"Yeah, and Max paid with his life. So don't tell me not to cut the greed-meisters where it hurts, and I won't tell you how to make coq au vin."

"Respect," the refrigerator intoned in Graham's deep baritone.

I finished chewing, sipped my tea, and stuck my tongue out at the security camera in the corner. *Respect* was a word I reserved for those who earned it through living an honest and honorable life—which meant maybe a monk in Tibet, a very young one.

"Does Scion headquarters hire Irish ex-revolutionaries as security guards?" I asked, heading for the door.

Glancing back, I saw a tiny smile of approval cross Mallard's stiff expression as he replied, "Or their descendants, naturally."

Once upon a long time ago, the Irish Revolutionary Army had characterized the universe of car bombers. I should know, my father was one—and that was how he'd died.

I hunched my shoulders against a shiver. I didn't want Nick—or anyone —dying as my father and his friends had. My father's friends had included Graham's father and Sean O'Herlihy's father, so we formed a very special club. If Scion was hiring ex-car bombers. . . The imagination freaked out.

I frantically checked my email as I dashed up the stairs again. Patra's reply to the dangerous report I'd sent her was all in the new idiot-glyphic faces I wasn't about to translate. I guessed they meant hair-raising surprise. I wanted to yell at her *Use your words!* But she was a grown-up now, and even if she liked playing with new toys, I was no longer her babysitter. I gathered she was excited and approved of my gift.

I prayed I hadn't sent her an IED. I didn't want to relieve Nick only to slap a target on Patra's back.

No one could know Patra had the report yet. She should be good. I texted her a warning to lay low and keep quiet. If I could have found a skull and crossbones in idiot-pics, I would have sent that too.

Then EG and I went to the movies. EG did *not* dress as a Disney princess. But she enjoyed the 3-D glasses and behaved like a normal kid and not a miniature Goth for a few hours, and I was pleased. This was what life was supposed to be about—raising kids to make this world a better place. Even fairy tales could teach them not to judge people by their looks.

No matter how hard I tried to make EG's life normal, my life had never been so. Turning my phone on as we left the theater, I had three dozen messages—all from Nick, increasing in urgency. One from Graham showed a video of masked men lurking in vaguely familiar shrubbery, cutting what appeared to be wires for a security system.

Was this Nadia's house? The killers had come calling already? I freaked.

CHAPTER 6

I FRANTICALLY TEXTED NICK TO VERIFY THAT EVERYONE WAS SAFE. GET HERE NOW was all I received in reply. I thought many foul words, but at least they were alive.

I showed Nick's messages to EG, who shrugged, as if she'd known skullduggery would happen. As long as everyone was still alive, we needed to eat. We ordered pizza we could pick up on the way.

At Nadia's house, my suave, aristocratic brother answered the door wearing a gore-splattered apron and dark circles under his eyes. The front room looked as if vandals had partied all night.

"What happened?" I gestured at the front room.

"They only took the computer as far as we can tell," Guy called from the interior. He was in a tattered t-shirt, paint splattered jeans, and bare feet, looking panicked and harassed.

Remembering the security footage of masked men, I tried not to panic, but my first thought was to move everyone somewhere safe. Graham would go ballistic if I tried to take them home with me. But if Scion's goons knew how to find Nadia's house. . .

I swallowed my first reaction and studied the chaos. In a back room, both kids were screaming and crying. I hoped Nick's apron stains were actually tomato juice and not blood—he likes to pretend he cooks Italian when he's showing off. No one had been harmed, yet. I needed to think.

EG calmly handed Nick the pizzas. I followed her example and carried in the wine and soft drinks. Guy and Nick looked as if they were ready to weep. I intended to take that as gratitude and not desperation from two grown men reduced to tears by babes.

"Explain," I demanded, tamping down my panic.

"We took them to the doctor. When we returned—" Guy made a helpless gesture.

I considered the strewn sofa cushions and scattered toys. It was a little difficult sorting childish chaos from vandals and thieves, but it gave me cold shivers to think of killers flinging the kids' toys around.

Pouring wine, Nick seemed to be making a quick recovery. "I had Sam drive us to the doctor for the kids' checkup. The thieves cut the alarm wires while we were gone. I don't know if they realize Guy is living here, or if they just waited for a car to leave before breaking in. Nadia's alarm system is primitive, and we didn't have time yesterday to do more than add cameras—which show next to nothing."

Yeah, the footage of the thieves cutting wire had been useless. They'd known to conceal their faces, and bulky overcoats hid everything else.

"How is Nadia?" I asked in trepidation.

"Still in a coma," Guy said. He looked even more drawn and frightened than yesterday. "There may be brain damage. The doctors are not hopeful. I have her power of attorney, so I have authorized organ donation should it come to that. Nadia would have wanted it."

Good people die too young. If only it could be Rose or Scion in that bed. . . Neither would have signed up for organ donation. People like that think they'll never die.

I was diverting my agitation with idiocy.

EG was sensibly performing our family ritual of checking lamps, phones, and behind furniture for bugs. Nick told her to start in back, that he'd already checked the front and found nothing. She grimaced but braved the childish roars from the rear.

I took a deep breath to regain my inner peace. "If no one planted bugs, then we're either talking common thieves, or someone after something specific, like the drug report." I fretted over the report I'd sent to Patra, but now that I'd come down off my panic, I realized it was a given that assassins would have researched Nadia's address. Since no one had been killed this time around, I was gonna guess they were merely wiping out Scion's report and any evidence Nadia had compiled.

What would happen when they realized the report was no longer in her computer? Were they smart enough to figure out someone else had it?

The kids needed their familiar surroundings. With Nadia currently out of the picture and the computer gone, I could hope the baddies were satisfied. What was best for the kids?

I'd been making snap judgments about the safety of children all my life. I didn't like it, but someone had to be the adult. "Gauging by the state of affairs around here, professional childcare is in your future."

That was all the reaction I gave them while I sorted out multi-levels of danger and followed EG and escalating roars down the narrow hall to a small bedroom.

Anika had apparently spilled juice on her new monkey and was weeping hysterically. Vincent had somehow managed to escape his wheelchair and was on the floor, throwing an old-fashioned fit.

I plopped his slender frame and heavy cast back into his chair, took Anika's wet monkey away, and pointed at the door.

As I may have mentioned, I'm not a cuddly person, but sometimes kids just need to know someone is in charge and listening. They gibbered their complaints as I wheeled Vincent back to the kitchen. They brightened at the smell of pizza.

Nick sipped his wine and looked dubious. "Professional childcare?"

"Not me. Let me make a few calls." I grabbed a slice of pizza and retreated to the living room with my phone, leaving Guy to entertain the kids. Nick followed me.

I'd met a few people over the last six months. I liked to think I helped some of them. I wasn't too proud to ask for help in return.

After a few calls, I had a waitress I knew with a teen in a wheelchair lined up to teach Guy how to deal with Vincent's limitations. Maggie O'Ryan's schedule revolved around school and work, but now that we'd found her a new home, Maggie didn't live too far away. She thought she could transport Vincent from school to home in the afternoons and was willing to stay until Guy returned from work—if he went to work.

Nadia already had Anika enrolled in daycare, but Guy needed someone to handle household duties like dinner and baths. Nick might learn, but not if he ran for the hills. He really needed order to be happy.

So I called my soft-hearted, good Christian half-sister Juliana, Zander's twin. She worked for a non-profit along with a lot of other poor students, all of whom needed money. She volunteered to come out and bring a friend with her. I had no doubt that they'd develop a rotating schedule for housework and childcare and build a homeless shelter while they were at it. Problems were easily solved when money was no object.

And for once in our lives, we had money. It felt good to use it for a worthwhile cause. Helping others made so much more sense than buying a Jaguar.

I handed the list of people and phone numbers to hovering Nick. "You and Zander and Guy figure out how to reimburse everyone."

"You're good at this," he said with an admiring whistle after perusing the list.

"How do you think we survived childhood? It takes a village and all that." I'd once blamed Magda for dropping all her cuckoos in other people's nests, but I was less angry these days. I was learning that a single mother took help any way it was offered.

"Can Guy work from here for a while?" I asked. "If the villains trashed this place, they've hit his home as well. Their offices may be next. Once they figure out he's not been blown up, we may need to find new digs."

"I'm thinking Alaska," Nick said grimly, listening to childish laughter from the kitchen. "He has no idea of the rabid hornet's nest he's stirred. Have you read his report?"

"Do I need to?" I countered, heading back to the kitchen to mop up whatever mess they were making. I didn't need to be reminded that we were juggling a grenade. "We grew up surrounded by street thugs. Corporate ones just have prettier houses. Mallard says Scion hires ex-IRA old geezers for security at their Irish headquarters. Old doesn't mean less dangerous."

"Worse." Nick opened his phone and punched buttons. "I've been digging through embassy files. Since Scion opened their Russian market, drug overdoses have escalated all across Europe. Every attempt to investigate has been squashed. Scion blames doctors for over prescribing. Guy's report proves Mylaudanix is far more addictive and dangerous than advertised. I just sent you my files."

Swell, more hot potatoes. Maybe even assassins would have difficulty keeping up with them.

"Have you found any reason for the Scion balloons at the Rose rally?" After verifying the kids weren't swimming in soft drink, I checked my inbox and saw Nick's email arrive—which meant Graham could read it too.

Nick was staring at his phone in resignation. "No, but Alaska is looking better." He held up the phone for me to see.

Officialdom had finally put together the puzzle pieces. Guy's car had been found in the bombed-out garage. Then they'd realized that Guy had been at the congressional committee meeting on healthcare and some bright specimen had recognized his connection to Nadia and her hit-and-run case. Rumors were flying. My guess was that Graham's FBI contact had arrived on the scene and helped them put two-and-two together.

"Next, they'll realize Guy's body isn't in the car," I said for him. "The media will be all over it. It will be a race to see who knocks on the door first, reporters, the feds, or the cops. It's either Alaska—or call the authorities."

Nick said some words I hadn't taught him. The kids looked horrified and fascinated, so I was guessing Nadia wasn't a potty-mouth. Guy simply sank onto a counter stool and gulped his wine.

"I vote cops," Nick said in resignation. "I like civilization."

Guy nodded. "I like my job. And the only way to avenge Nadia is to stand up for our report. Maybe people will listen now."

"In this case, the publicity may protect you," I agreed, crossing my fingers and praying I was right. "Once the rumor starts that Guy was targeted for his report, do the thugs dare go after him again? Nick, you should call the embassy. Guy, are you an ex-pat?"

Guy nodded. "French and British passports, US green card."

"The children?" I nodded at the kids, who had returned to scarfing pizza.

"Ukrainian-American," Guy explained. "Nadia was born here. Her parents left the Ukraine half a century ago. She met her husband when visiting her grandparents in the old country. He never got a visa. Viktor is the reason Nadia was working with me. She thought he worked for Scion too, but she learned he's Russian mafia."

"That widens the pool of suspects considerably," I said with a touch of sarcasm. How many grenades could one juggle at a time? With resignation, I added, "I'll have Graham contact the FBI. He'll know who's handling the bombing. Guy, call the police, tell them you just saw the news and that you're alive. Request protection."

"They don't have enough personnel for around-the-clock care," Nick protested, already poking text into his phone.

He was only repeating my own fear, so I couldn't argue. "Graham does," I reminded him, hoping I spoke the truth. I was taking a lot for granted. "That's his job. And car bombings make this very personal for him." And me, which was why I was counting on him.

Even as a little kid, I knew my daddy had been blown up. I'd learned it by hiding in closets, spying on the dangerous adults who occupied my environment. After my father's death, I had a desperate need to know what was going on, but I feared being noticed. Concealing myself was now second nature to me. My office was in the basement, out of sight, for a reason. Graham and I had that much in common. We're both behind-the-scenes players, but we kept our eyes on the hot potatoes and grenades of our world.

While Nick called the police, my first instinct was to take EG and slip away before the authorities arrived. But this was Nick, my best friend and brother in crime. We'd been there for each other too many times to count. He would not want to be seen in public wearing tomato-splattered clothing.

I sent him to take EG home and stop at his place for clean clothes. He looked grateful and relieved. He'd done the same for me in the past. I knew the feeling.

Guy and I got the kids bathed and in clean pajamas before the doorbell started ringing. With no computer, we couldn't check the new security cameras. Before I could peer out a window and decide whether to answer, my phone rang.

"Let Mac in," Graham ordered, then hung up.

I guess that answered that.

I let in a skinny young man with shaggy hair and a soul patch. He was accompanied by an equally young girl built like the storied brick house. She looked considerably more reliable, but she didn't speak as they barged in and took over.

By the time the doorbell rang again, they had a new computer installed in the office and high-power cameras and bugs all over the living room and the outside doors. I wasn't certain which tech was Mac, but the male opened the computer, and we had a clear view of the front step and street.

A black Crown Vic waited on the curb, and a black guy in a black suit stood on the doorstep.

I held up a penny I found on the desk. "Heads, he's FBI, tails, he's local."

The humorless kid simply flipped on the mic. "Identification, please."

Our visitor flashed a badge at the camera. FBI.

"Here's where I play nanny. Nick should be here any minute if you want to stall," I told Guy, before retreating to put the kids to bed.

The two geeks continued wiring the rest of the house and possibly half the universe. I offered them the leftover pizza and drinks, and they consumed the pizza cold and the Coke warm. Their ability to eat anything made me feel old. I didn't protest their taste buds or their greasy fingers, and gave myself points for coolness.

Mostly, I hoped all this equipment would warn Nick and Guy if the bad guys came after them. I'd have to provide them with baseball bats. Neither were the type to allow guns around kids. The realization of how unprotected we all were gave me cold shivers.

Patra called and put Sean on speaker with her. I took the call to the farthest room from where the doorbell was ringing again.

"Can we talk to this Guy Withers?" Sean asked first, in his official reporter voice. "We need more than his word that this report isn't complete fabrication."

"Yeah, and that's the reason Nadia is in a coma, and Guy is under siege." I settled cross-legged on Nadia's bed. The plain-vanilla room didn't contain a chair or any adornment other than pictures of and by her kids. "You fancy journalists will have to find other sources. I'll give Guy your number, but he's likely to be busy with Nadia's offspring and officialdom for a while."

"And you think someone in Scion's organization ordered their deaths?" Patra asked, speaking my fears.

"Given the timing, seems logical. Nadia and Guy are mere cogs inside huge companies, not the usual target for assassins. Their report is the only thing that makes them stand out. You're sitting on a ticking bomb," I warned, to make certain she grasped the extent of her danger. "Mallard hinted that we should look into the ex-IRA car bombers that Scion employs. But Nadia had a Russian mafia husband who also ostensibly worked for Scion. And for all we know, Afghan terrorists thought to stage a protest in a parking garage. The world is our stage." Which made me very nervous indeed.

"The FDA has been ignoring the studies showing Mylaudanix as addictive," Sean said. I could hear him clicking a keyboard, presumably through electronic pages, unruffled by my warning. "Scion has to be buying off a lot of people if this report has any truth."

"Mylaudanix is hugely popular." I leaned back on the pillows and flipped through my own phone, keeping an eye on female Mac as she positioned a camera aimed at the bedroom window. "Patients demand their painkillers. Docs don't have a better alternative. And Scion Pharm supports powerful politicians."

"Drug lords," Patra said in disgust. "I'll hunt for a connection with growers in Afghanistan. Opium flows freely from there through Turkey to Eastern Europe. That will be their supplier."

"Above my paygrade," I told her. "I thought this was a chemical painkiller?"

"Read the report," Sean retorted. "Your guy," he said it in Americanese to rhyme with *cry*, "has done a chemical analysis. The main ingredient is only one molecule different from opium. I'm turning that part over to our science people. They'll find labs to confirm."

"Freedom of the press at its best," I said with satisfaction. "The congressional committee didn't even give the report a hearing."

To my shock, Girl-Mac finally spoke. "My brother was a soldier who took any painkiller he could get so he could keep fighting even when he was hurt. When he got back home, he overdosed on Mylaudanix. He didn't know the pills were stronger than the heroin he'd used in the field."

My jaw probably hung open for a full minute. I snapped it shut. "Was your brother in Afghanistan?"

She nodded curtly, picked up her gear, and moved to the next corner, geek silence fully restored.

"There's your features angle for those who don't read hard news," I told my two reporters, using cynicism to cover my fury. "Soldiers hooked on heroin for their wounds, dying from Big Pharm when they get home."

After I hung up, Girl-Mac returned to take my phone. She downloaded an app and opened it to show me video images of Guy's living room. Nick had returned in full aristocratic regalia. He'd be using his plummy English boarding school accent on the guys in black suits.

"Does it hook to the nursery?" I asked, punching arrows on the app. I found it before she could take the phone away again. The kids were sleeping with their arms curled around fuzzy bunnies. "We all started out innocent like that," I said with regret.

"And then the world corrupts us." Girl-Mac picked up her tools and stomped out.

Tudor finally returned my text, telling me to check my email box. I opened his message, which was merely a link to a secure website and a reminder to destroy the message. My geek brother has hacked major companies and governments. He knows something about cyber-security, but most of the time, he plays too many cyber games and gets paranoid.

The website provided a lot of computerese that I forwarded to Graham. Then I read Tudor's translation: Nadia's laptop couldn't be traced because there was a net around all her communications waiting for fish to drop in.

That almost made sense. The rest of Tudor's message was more succinct: the net had been constructed using known Russian spyware.

I was so in over my head.

CHAPTER 7

"The Russians and the *Irish*?" Graham muttered to himself, adding a few expletives as he explored the link Tudor had sent Ana. Damn, *there* was the origin of the prior night's cyber-attack, the damned report Ana was calling the Hot Potato. What did the Russians really think corralling that report would accomplish? Were they stupid enough to think they could suppress anything as explosive as that drug report?

Not stupid, just ignorant enough to underestimate American ingenuity.

He sent Tudor an urgent warning to stay away from the resource where he'd obtained that information. The geniuses had really embroiled themselves in hot water this time—boiled hot potatoes. Obviously, he'd been working too hard.

He sat back and rubbed his scarred brow. Ana probably thought he'd hidden in this attic because of the scars. He'd rather she kept thinking that, but the truth was much deeper and uglier and would endanger her entire family—one of the reasons he'd tried to keep them out.

But he'd decided months ago that she and her family would find trouble no matter where they went. He was looking at evidence of that now. They were genetically incapable of keeping their noses out of other people's business—chips off the old block. He'd spent his teen years with their grandfather and admired the old man for good reason, but Max had been a stubborn reckless fool upon occasion.

Like Ana. It was better if he kept the lines of communication open so he could watch over her and her family, as Max had intended.

Because it was Max who had opened the gates of hell. Harvey Scion was one of the demons who now roamed free.

Knowing the feds had no way of pinning the car bomb on anyone in particular, Graham read through the initial findings on the bomb that had detonated the gas line.

As he'd feared, evidence indicated it was old-fashioned gun powder connected to a basic timer and an independent electrical circuit—classic and the same type of device used to kill his father and Ana's. This century's bombers used more sophisticated plastic explosives and radio control, but the geezers stuck with what they knew best—timers and commercially available gun powder. This one simply crapped out by hitting a gas line.

With a grimace of reluctance, he opened an old file, one he hadn't added to in a long time. He'd hoped he'd laid the case to rest, that all the participants were long dead, in jail, or otherwise neutralized. The bomb could mean one of the more lethal demons had escaped his net.

~

I LEFT THE KIDS SLEEPING AND NICK AND GUY DEALING WITH THE FBI AND local cops. I knew from sad experience that the men in blue wouldn't give me the information I needed. Nick would have to text me and let me know what little he dragged out of them.

I needed serious down time in which to think.

Once upon a foolish time, my life's goal was to protect my family. They were almost all grown up now, but not because I'd made the world a safer place, for sure. We'd have to live in a hole in the ground in Iowa before we'd be semi-safe, I figured, and that just wasn't happening.

The alternative, I was slowly realizing, was taking the offensive against the bad guys who circled us. I'd learned to defend myself against street thugs and taught all my siblings but the twins to do the same. But our current environment was a different kettle of fish than the bullies we'd previously encountered. Our enemies now were people of power and wealth who were driven by the same thuggish motivation—greed, control, and a privileged expectation that they could take what they wanted.

The cops might eventually track down the murderous criminals who smashed Nadia's car, but they couldn't bop Scion Pharmaceuticals on the nose and take our wallets back.

Maybe I should think about getting involved. Maybe. Somehow.

Once I got home, I checked on EG. She was building a monster—or a princely Beast—out of papier-mâché and had plastered her room with wet newspaper and paste. I introduced her to Mallard's cleaning closet and gave her an hour to clean up before bed.

I continued on my way upstairs. I no longer hid my travels to Graham's lair from my family. We'd all been up there at Christmas. The upper story was no longer a mystery. My family just respected his need for privacy. I didn't. Now that my family owned half the house, he didn't get to make the rules any longer.

His office had once been my grandfather's clubroom. The bar was now Graham's elongated desk. He wheeled up and down its length on a tall, expensive mesh desk chair that accommodated his size. The billiard table was long gone. The windows had been boarded up and covered with wall-to-wall computer monitors, mostly reflecting security cameras Graham had installed all over town. I never asked if they were all installed at the request of clients or not. Some were public security cameras he'd hacked into. Basically, Graham was the King of Snoops.

Tonight, his monitors were even more disorienting than usual. He had files of text flowing across several screens. Two monitors were showing the yard surrounding Nadia's house. I was pretty certain one screen displayed an ambassador's residence down the street. I had no idea what the others were all about.

"Russians?" I asked wearily, querying what he'd found out about Tudor's message.

"Go to bed, Ana," he said without turning around.

"Are you going with me?" I countered.

I didn't need his snort to know the answer to that. I had to stand on his desk naked to get his attention some nights. I could do it. I was too tired and too worried to bother.

"If that's the Russian ambassador's residence you're watching," I studied the lovely French mansard roof his camera was trained on, "you'll see me heading up the steps in the morning if you don't give me more information than that."

"You have no stake in this game," he said, without turning his head. "Go invest your wealth in politically correct corporations."

Some days, I thought he was a mind reader.

"Yeah, there's what, all of two of them?" My energy was building with my anger. I despised being dismissed as useless. "Nick is tied up with a guy the Russian mafia could be bombing. Patra and Sean are working on a document the mafia—or at least Scion—is probably willing to kill to get. And my mother is sending up a hot potato warning to a dangerous man who employs ex-IRA. Tell me again I have no stake in this game."

"Hot potato warning?" he asked in what sounded like amusement.

"One potato, two potato, duck. I don't expect you to understand. She's weird like that."

"Other people say *one potato, two potato, three potato, four*," he said. "It's a counting game, not for combat."

I grimaced. He wasn't ignoring *me*, just my demands. Since he so seldom commented on my personal life, I chose to reward him. "Magda is creative in ways beyond the obvious. When we were little, she told us fairy tales of the runaway Hungarian princess and the evil king—her way of explaining her past, although I gather the story is warped."

"Max opened up the hell gates that got your father killed, but he wasn't evil except in your mother's mind," Graham agreed, catching on quickly. He was still scrolling through text and switching up screens—serious ADD combined with PTSD, a volatile mix.

"But the point *is*," I continued, "that when Magda was home, which wasn't often, she got bored and made up things on a level that little kids can understand. We occasionally lived in war zones, but she couldn't teach toddlers to duck and cover without terrifying them."

It had taken me years, and the help of a few dozen counselors, to sort through these memories.

Graham glanced over his shoulder, his dark eyes revealing his understanding. "One potato, two potato, duck—teaching you to obey the command through games. Clever. How does this apply to Rose?"

"Clever would have been raising us in green fields with cows," I said resentfully. "And if it's Magda behind the balloons, she's warning Rose she's after him. Third time's the charm. But that's just my cynical surmise."

"You don't need to be her," he warned. "She has people looking after her. You're not on their radar. Stay low and stay out of it."

She had people looking after her? Since when? I chose to stay on a more interesting topic—me.

"If you tell me to stay home and take care of the kids, I'll bean you with your chair." I was tired, frustrated, and needed understanding, so I was ready to bop him anyway. I gripped the back of his spare office chair, testing its weight. I'd taken out windows with these things.

He finally swung completely around. I am not immune to his deep-set, dark blue eyes by any means. He had the square jaw and wide cheekbones made for movies, but it was the pain registering in the crinkles around those eyes that did me in. I set the chair down.

"Your twisted genius of a mother isn't in this game because she wants to take out a drug lord," he said wearily. "She's come home to finish what she started decades ago. You really need to stay clear to protect your siblings from the fall-out."

Twisted genius? Well, yeah, that about nailed my mother.

"Tell me what you know and maybe I'll listen," I still said stubbornly.

"I don't know enough," he retorted, equally obstinate. "I was only ten when our fathers died, not old enough to know what went on. I didn't live here then."

"So whatever is happening now dates back to the day our fathers died?" I asked in incredulity. "That's over twenty-five years ago!"

He gave me one of those stony looks that said he was aware of the obvious.

"But you lived with Max all those years. He knew what happened, didn't he? Surely, he told you more than I know." I was tired of dancing around this old sore. I wanted it laid to rest for once and for all.

He hesitated long enough for me to lift the chair again. He shot out a long leg and kicked it from my hands and across the floor. Apparently alleviating some of his tension with that blatant male display of force, he turned back to his keyboard and began typing. I knew better than to mistake Graham for a desk jockey. The man could be a macho ape when he put his mind to it.

"You will be sorry you asked," he growled. "I'm sending you the file. By the time you read through decades of trash, maybe this will all have blown over."

I doubted it. Reading through entire libraries was my specialty. Foreign languages slowed me down, but I doubted that would be a problem here.

"Magda could marry and have another baby before this is all over," I said cynically. "She's the queen of long and drawn-out. And if she's reached her final mark, expect public torture. My mother is beautiful and smart but not an especially nice person."

"Is she into Mata Hari hats?" he asked unexpectedly.

I blinked, then glanced up at his monitors. He was returning a video to its beginning. A banner announcing *West Virginia welcomes Senator Rose home* crossed a stage.

He switched camera views. I caught a glimpse of a slim woman in a huge floppy-brimmed black hat entering the darkened auditorium. Beside her was a very large person in a spy-style trench coat and fedora. My suspicion-ometer revved into overdrive.

Graham paused the video. The fur coat on the floppy-brimmed hat female was certainly Magda's style, but between the coat and the hat, there were no distinguishing characteristics that screamed of my mother. Her back was to the camera as she patted the large person reassuringly and turned whoever it was over to a young man who escorted him up the aisle between chairs.

With her back to the camera, Hat Woman slipped out the door of what appeared to be the kind of auditorium colleges or schools might have. Having spent my formative years in palaces and hovels and the occasional overseas military school, I had little experience of auditoriums beyond EG's current school.

But these were adults in theater-type seating. They were focused on the stage and not the trench-coated giant strolling toward the front as if looking for a seat.

A second camera picked up, and I could see a podium where a silver-haired bureaucrat introduced a too-familiar figure: *Senator Rose.* My gut clenched, and I examined the floor and ceiling for evidence of balloons.

The audience roared and rose from their seats clapping as the politician beamed down on them with his artificially white smile in his artificially bronzed, fake face—not that I'm prejudiced or anything.

Instead of pontificating this time, Rose opened to questions from the floor as if this were a town hall meeting. A tall, model-thin blonde stood at a microphone on the floor below the stage. She called out a name from a card. Apparently, speakers and questions had been prepared before they began.

How. . . *artificial*. I wanted water balloons to pop over Rose's head to see if his face would slide off.

I feared balloons would be the least of his worries as Trench Coat walked up to the microphone. I waited in anticipation as much as dread. A spotlight fell on the fedora. The large person dropped the coat and removed his fedora, revealing he was a she. I would have breathed a sigh of relief at the lack of weapons, except the spectacle was more potent—and entertaining.

Mystery Woman had to be nearly six feet tall and three hundred pounds, and she was wearing a pink bikini with pink—how does one say this politely?—*kitty* ears on her thick brown curls.

The audience sat stunned. Even the security guards couldn't tear their gazes away. Terrorists could have mowed down the entire audience. But this was no terrorist.

"Hello, Senator Rose, do you remember me, Gertrude?" the bikini-clad female asked in a high-pitched, girlish voice that didn't match her appearance. "I worked for your mother when you were just out of college, remember?"

Rose actually looked baffled—and very nervous.

Gertrude didn't give him time to answer. "You threatened to have me fired if I didn't have sex with you that summer, remember? My mother was dying of cancer, and I needed the job. When I got pregnant, you paid for me to have an abortion."

The leader of the anti-abortion cadre, Rose turned red all the way to his artificially bronzed ears and gestured for security to take her away.

But Gertrude was having none of it, and she was big enough to sit on Rose's security. She'd obviously waited a long time for this moment in the sun. She gestured, too, and a tall woman stepped up from a front seat, dropping her floor-length ugly down coat as she did.

"Your daughter, Senator," Gertrude said proudly. "My mother died that winter, so I took your money and her insurance, kept my precious baby, and built my own business."

The daughter was. . . buxom, very generously buxom. And wearing a gold lame bikini and matching kitty ears. I was beginning to imagine what kind of business Gertrude had started.

The senator was staring open-mouthed at his *daughter*, who was probably the spitting image of her mother thirty years ago. I started grinning—

until the spotlight snapped off and black-suited figures spilled off the stage and toward the microphone. Gertrude couldn't fight off an army of goons, and the show was over.

The stunned audience merely murmured as the pair were presumably marched off. There wasn't enough light to tell from the video.

"The film clip was generated at a rally this afternoon. It just appeared on Times Square billboards." Graham pulled up a shot of the notorious lighted screens towering over one of the busiest intersections in the world.

Traffic had stopped as people spilled into the street to admire the towering screen. They stood there slack-jawed in disbelief at nearly naked, mile-high giantesses. In neon technicolor, Rose's non-smiling visage finally revealed his whiteness.

For the first time that day, I giggled and felt better, a lot better. The real Senator Paul Rose revealed in all his stunningly callous stupidity for all the world to see—I loved it.

"If Magda was behind this stunt," Graham intoned in that voice of doom of his, "they're going to kill her, in a lot of unpleasant ways."

CHAPTER 8

MEN HAD BEEN TRYING TO KILL MY MOTHER FOR DECADES, RIGHTFULLY SO, most of the time. But if she was behind the stunt with Gertrude, it was more public than most of her schemes. I was guessing that and the balloons were a public declaration of war. If Graham was right, I wanted to know how Magda knew Rose.

It wasn't as if I was in any position to go after Russians and assassins.

So, instead of going to bed, I sat down in my basement office with Graham's electronic files and my big computer and began organizing by date. Since Magda had spent the last twenty-five years out of the country, I started with the oldest files, the ones from before my father's death.

As Graham had said, he'd only been ten at the time, and these files were from the early 80's, in the era of primitive personal computers. I doubted that my grandfather could have scanned and copied all these papers back then, so someone must have compiled them later.

Graham may have added a few of these documents once he reached a position of power and could dig into official government files. I could see his fine hand in the detailed dossiers of all the members of my grandfather's Top Hat cabal, before and after Max had left it. Given what I knew, I assumed Top Hat was the gates of hell to which Graham referred when he claimed Max had opened them.

I was familiar with a number of the people in the secretive group. Broderick, from the conservative media conglomerate, supporter of the white man's Al Qaeda, was now sitting in jail on corruption and murder charges. Personally, I thought Broderick's corruption of the news was a hanging offense.

The execs at MacroWare who murdered their boss, spied on the public with their software, and made fraudulent government deals were either dead or in jail.

Edu-Pub, the book company that had brazenly changed history in school textbooks was defunct. It had been owned by several of the politicians supported by Top Hat, who were now facing charges of conspiracy and fraud. Too bad there weren't laws against incompetence, stupidity, and evil.

Tony Jeffrey at General Defense, the weapons manufacturer that had been caught selling surplus military weapons to terrorists, was up to his ears in financial and legal trouble. His daughter was in jail for murder.

Goldrich Mortgage and its blackmailing owner was under indictment for fraud, and a few execs were up on murder charges along with the MacroWare guys. A lot of people were now homeless because of these greedmeisters, but at least some justice would be meted. Not that the homeless can live under a roof of justice.

With the loss of major members, the Top Hat political and corporate cabal that my grandfather had helped form was gradually crumbling. I liked to think I was partially responsible, because these were the men who had coldly and calculatedly poisoned Max after he'd left the group—and possibly killed my father.

I was hoping powerful bad guys like these were now too busy with lawyers, jail, and salvaging their ill-gotten gains to seek revenge. Unless they had a profit motive, they generally didn't engage. They'd already stolen Max's measly millions once and lost them—to me. I just didn't think them stupid enough to go after us again.

There were a few names on Graham's old Top Hat list I didn't recognize, and I noted them for further research. Senator Paul Rose's name wasn't mentioned in these early notes. I calculated in the early 80's, he was still in his twenties and banging Gertrude. I couldn't find anyone in Top Hat who might have been Rose's father. A lot of these older guys had handed their legacy over to their sons. Rose had to be a new introduction.

Just out of curiosity, I looked up Rose's father. He'd been a congressman representing West Virginia back in the day, the heir to a coal company. Rose's father had graduated from some Podunk college and didn't look like Top Hat material. How had he and his son got in with them—other than the son graduating from Harvard? And his father didn't even have that going for him.

Magda had been a teenage bride, married and pregnant with me in 1981, so the present day senator was about my father's age at the time. Could he have known Magda?

I read through my grandfather's early memos, mostly handwritten, then scanned into his files later. In the early 50's, the original founders of the cabal were all young men. They apparently thought of themselves as the smiling, wealthy tycoon of the Monopoly game—hence the Top Hat label. Competition had all been a game to them—until at some point it had turned ruthless. Competitive rivalry was only fun when peopled abided by rules. Unchecked, it became anarchy and war.

I skimmed through the group's tirades about regulatory commissions and government interference, winced as they worked to buy the votes on government regulatory committees, then advanced to bribing Congressmen to appoint the officials they wanted.

Money could buy almost anything, including judges, apparently. Men who didn't cater to the cabal's wishes often found themselves in hot water legally and politically. That's what they'd done to EG's senator father. Tex would never win another election after he'd turned on the politicians involved in Edu-Pub.

I skimmed to the time of my father's death. The material became voluminous. I could see why Graham thought I'd be occupied for a while. There was a dossier on Hugh O'Herlihy, Sean's father. Here was another on Dillon Graham, and of course, one on Brody Devlin, my father and Magda's first husband.

I'd spent years reading all the material I could find on my father. Brody was the original fiery Irish charmer who had raised hundreds of thousands of dollars in support of the Irish Catholic fight against oppressive Protestant rule. He apparently had support from many wealthy Irish-Catholic-Americans, including Hugh O'Herlihy and Graham's father, Dillon.

Max, my grandfather, probably wasn't a true church-going type of Catholic, and he certainly wasn't Irish. My grandmother may have been both, for all I knew, only she had died when Magda was young.

But Max was a millionaire businessman with the connections to weapons manufacturers like General Defense that my dad needed to gain more funding and buy weapons. I totally got all that.

The rest was murky and left me to fill in the blanks. Brody stayed here, wooed my grandfather and my mother, got her pregnant, married her, and they had me. Somewhere along the line, from my mother's own admission and things I learned from people who knew her, my mother turned against the weapons deal.

She was very young, idealistic, and a new mother. I would have done the same thing. Of course, I'd been raised by that mother who detested guns, so it was easy for me to understand why she'd oppose what her father and husband wanted.

But there was almost nothing in this file about Magda. Had she found the file and edited herself out? Or had Max deliberately kept out his daughter's involvement? Why would Graham do the same—because I knew he'd added some of this material. Or had my mother really been that invisible?

The file contained police and FBI reports on the bombing that killed three promising young men in a parking garage—not unlike the explosion that had almost killed Nick and Guy. I printed out some of the dense verbiage and took it to bed with me, since it was fairly obvious I would be sleeping alone.

~

I woke on Sunday morning to my phone pinging. I unburied my face from the paper-strewn pillow and saw a string of texts from Nick whining about the kids. Did I really want to know if his babysitting arrangements had fallen through? No sirree. My beloved brother could find his own babysitter. I'd been my mother's doormat for too many years. I noted that the sun was up and then dived back into senselessness.

Continual pinging prevented oblivion.

With a sigh, I pushed out of the pillow and eventually, out of bed.

I had no direction. After reading through the file on my father's death last night, I couldn't focus on giants in pink bikinis or drug lords or Nick's babysitting problems.

So I showered and went on the hunt for protein.

Patra and Sean were already downstairs in the dining room, helping themselves to Mallard's sumptuous Sunday morning brunch. EG was at the table, curled up around her tablet computer. I hoped it was with a good book and not manuals on world domination.

Patra scooped up a bowl of berries and pointed at the stacks of newspapers scattered across the massive mahogany table. My grandfather used to give dinner parties here. The table could sit twelve—*without* the extra leaves.

I don't read newspapers, not even the comics. My life had enough going on that I didn't need someone else's problems to entertain me. I poured tea and deliberately sat at the opposite end of the table from the papers.

Except for the curly hair, Sean O'Herlihy is a young Pierce Brosnan look alike, with Irish high cheekbones and piercing blue eyes. He makes a striking match for Patra with her tall, curvy good looks and shampoo-model chestnut hair. But they're journalists, and apparently chameleon camouflage is their dress order. They wore jeans and baggy sweaters and looked as if they'd had about as much sleep as I'd had.

"Rose's popularity plummeted overnight," Patra reported, carrying her unnaturally healthy yogurt-berry parfait to the table. She shoved the *Times* under my nose.

"People don't care if he supports letting the poor die without health care and letting the rich get richer by cutting their taxes, but they care about giants in pink kitty ears?" I asked with a growl of disgust. "Is there even proof that the story is true?"

"Doesn't need to be," Sean said with annoying good cheer, taking the seat across from me. "The public loves sensationalism. Economics are a huge yawn."

"So if I want to run for office, I should wear kitty ears?" I sucked my tea down boiling, then got up for more.

"Well, no, you should be male, have silver hair, and look good," Patra said with my cynicism. "Like the candidate benefitting most from Rose's embarrassment—Bill Smith."

"*Bill Smith*? You have to be kidding me." I took a strawberry-filled pastry to go with my tea. "Did he have to change his name to get any more white bread? One-syllable names are a selling point?"

"Work better in headlines," Sean acknowledged, scooping up a hunk of omelet.

"Lacks character," I countered. "I mean, how many Bill Smiths are there in the world? They're invisible. It's like being a Bob Jones. So who's backing the white bread man and is he capable of setting up women in kitty ears?"

My reporters fell silent and looked at each other speculatively.

"Oh, c'mon." I sat down again and glared at the pretty lovers. "Surely you had to wonder who staged that event?"

"Well, no, we figured it was Magda who found Kitty Ears," Patra admitted.

"Magda is not into presidential elections." I didn't tell them Magda was probably avenging old wounds and somehow Rose had to be bound up in her vendetta. They already suspected that. But kitty ears? That sounded political. "She's more likely to hire assassins than look for old flames."

Well, that was a lie. She hated violence. But it was enough to send Sean to his phone. Mission accomplished. They would dive down another rabbit hole and leave Magda and her dangerous games alone.

If Magda was involved, I wanted to take her down on my own, leave the kids a few illusions.

"How are you faring with our drug lord?" I asked. Last night, I'd realized I had too many angles for approaching the garage bombing and Nadia's accident. I needed to narrow my focus. Sean and Patra had better resources for looking into Scion Pharmaceutical. I was the one with the Top Hat car bombing file, and it drew me like ants to honey.

"Zander just sent a file about Scion's financial assets," Patra said. "It should be in your box too. We've not had time to dig into them, but it looks as if he has a lot of foreign investments."

My phone buzzed angrily. I sighed and glanced at the screen. Nick again. I put him on speaker out of sheer meanness.

"Anika is screaming for her mommy and Vincent refuses to eat and I swear, there are goons lurking in the shrubbery!" he wailed through the speaker.

"Give the kids to the goons or call Juliana, not me. Don't give them sugar. Do give them kiddy videos. Go watch the giant pink kitty and tell us if you think Bill Smith did it." I hit the *Off* button.

"You are awesome mean," Patra said in admiration.

The phone buzzed again. I handed it to EG, who looked startled, then evil.

I went back for the protein I should have got the first time. I needed energy to face the day, and a sugar high just encouraged meanness. I heard

EG tell Nick that I hadn't had my tea yet. He'd settle down once the initial panic was over.

Nick could take care of himself as well as I could. It was the new responsibility of family that was making him crazy.

"Goons in the shrubbery?" I repeated Nick's fears aloud.

"Not mine," the candelabra retorted.

Sean had only recently been introduced to the house. He studied the ornate silver in fascination. I whacked his hand with a silver fork when he started to check under it.

"Only I get to mess with Graham's head," I told him. "Are there reporters lurking in Guy's shrubbery?"

"We're the only ones working the story as far as I'm aware." Sean didn't look repentant for his intrusiveness. "I'd guess Feds."

"What, the law thinks Guy tried to blow *himself* up? Or they think the mafia is stupid enough to make a second try and blow up the neighborhood, so they're hiding in the bushes, waiting?"

"What if the goons really are bad guys?" Patra asked worriedly.

I was trying hard not to think that. "Stupid villains are the worst," I muttered. "They already broke in once. What more can they want?" I took a bite out of my boiled egg, chewed, then retrieved my phone. Nick was still on it. "Back and front yard?" I asked. "And have you thought about getting a pit bull?"

"For the kids or the goons?" he asked wearily. "Different places, different times, not always in the yard."

"Unless you're still contemplating Alaska, use your brains, Nicholas." I knew he knew how to do this, but love had apparently scrambled his thinking apparatus. "Have Juliana start a doggie daycare in the backyard. Keep Guy inside. Have someone take the kids out, preferably while they're screaming. Hire a guard who can sneak up behind your suspects and isn't too proud to torture info out of them."

"My men don't torture," the candelabra informed me coldly.

"I heard that," Nick said with a grim intonation. "I know torture, and right now, I'm furious enough to try."

"Good. The rest of us are working the other end. You just keep your valuable assets safe. The kids will be in school tomorrow. Gear up." I punched out.

Everyone at the table stared at me. I shrugged. "He just needed a pep talk."

"He won't really torture strangers on the street?" Sean asked with interest.

"Don't ask, don't tell," EG piped up from her end of the table.

My little poppet. I'd look on her with pride and approval, except I'd really been trying to teach her to be *normal*.

"Oh wow," Patra exclaimed, staying out of the conversation by perusing her telephone. "Oh double whammy *wow*."

Sean grabbed her phone, grew wide-eyed, and passed it on to me.

Harvey Scion, Senator Rose's chief campaign strategist, contributor, evil minion, and our number one suspect in Nadia's murder, had been killed in his own home while we slept.

CHAPTER 9

GRAHAM DUG DEEPER INTO POLICE FILES. HE HAD FOOTAGE FROM SECURITY cameras around Harvey Scion's home flashing on half a dozen monitors. The pharmaceutical exec had been shot on his own grounds while surrounded by heavy security. Given how many people were gunning for Scion, he had obviously been right to be paranoid.

Other than wanting to stay one step ahead of Ana and her family, Graham had no particular interest in yet another wart on the face of the earth, but this murder was an Agatha Christie stumper.

Graham stopped on a shot showing Scion stepping out on his patio to sneak a smoke at a few minutes before nine last night, according to the video. Guards patrolled the perimeters in other footage, but the patio was private, surrounded by clipped yew hedges. The landscaping was meticulous with potted evergreens amputated into perfect cones, hedges regimented into linear rectangles, and a single magnolia blocking the view of the mansion on the next street.

If someone wanted to kill Scion on his patio, they'd need a gifted sniper. One might climb the wall, into the magnolia, and wait for the moment Scion stepped outside, but study of earlier videos showed the wily old man followed no routine. A sniper could starve to death waiting for him to emerge at any particular time or place. It was January. If the weather hadn't been unseasonably warm, Scion probably would never have stepped out at all.

That left the security guards as the only people inside the grounds. Scion lived alone. His housekeeping staff had left for the evening. Graham set the video in motion again.

Scion turned abruptly, as if he'd heard a noise in the hedge. Three white balloons tied to a bush bounced in the chilly air. It wasn't easy to see, but they appeared to have the caricature on them that had appeared at Rose's rally.

Magda's work? Or just a fan of the balloons?

Scion didn't seem surprised to see them. He applied the lighted end of his cigarette to one, and it exploded. With an air of smug satisfaction, he did the same to a second.

A spark of gunpowder flared from a corner of dark evergreens near the house. A single soundless shot and Scion crumpled, leaving one balloon bouncing in the wind. That was professional work, upfront and personal. The balloons had been a distraction from the sniper near the door.

The body fell out of sight of the camera. According to the police files, the three security guards on duty had heard and seen nothing unusual. How was that possible?

Graham studied footage from the wall. The uniformed guards checked in with each other on a regular basis, as expected. One stopped to light a cigarette. Another stepped away for a bathroom break. No furtive movement appeared over the walls—but someone had to have climbed over, coming and going.

He switched to the front door camera but the door remained resolutely closed through every frame. No one had entered the house and followed Scion out.

The magnolia was the most likely entrance, but the camera's angle didn't cover the deep shadows. If there was movement, Graham couldn't detect it. How had they brought in helium-filled balloons without being seen? That was an act of pure arrogance. The shooter knew he wouldn't be seen. How?

He switched back to the footage of Scion and his cigarette. Scion checked his phone, shoved it in his back pocket, and took a puff of his smoke. Was he waiting for a call? Checking a message?

Frowning, Graham dug into police files. Who had Scion talked to last?

No report yet. He called his liaison who called a contact who talked to the detective.

There was no record of a phone on the body.

He sent a curt message to his liaison, then scrolled back to the scene again.

Checked phone. Put it in his pocket. Puffed cigarette. Swung around. Crumpled.

The body fell out of view of the camera.

If there was no phone on the body—the killer had crawled across the terrace and snatched it. The camera didn't show the patio surface—*who knew that?*

∼

SUNDAY WAS LAUNDRY AND FAMILY DAY. EVEN THOUGH I'D TAKEN EG TO THE movies yesterday, she expected an outing again today.

I had been developing a plan of action to see if there was any correlation between the current garage bombing and the bomb that had killed my father, when we'd received the news that my number one suspect was dead. Now my head was ready to explode and a kid visit seemed a better alternative to real life.

We coordinated with Juliana and decided on taking Anika and Vincent along with EG to the Museum of Natural History. Maggie O'Ryan, the friend I'd called on to help Guy learn to deal with Vincent, brought over her wheelchair-bound teen son, Michael, to introduce him.

My preferred method of transportation was the Metro, but no way were we attempting to transport four kids and two wheelchairs via an underground. We just weren't that adept. I hated disrupting Sam's Sunday, but when we called, he suggested a van service that would work well.

When EG and I arrived at Nadia's place, Anika was sucking her thumb and listening to Juliana read her a book. Juliana's brown hand guided Anika's white one to the words on the page, and I loved the image. My half-sister is just out of college, taking lessons on how to fund the schools she wants to build back in Africa. She has the patience of ten saints. I pressed my palms together and bowed a namaste. She winked.

I could hear Vincent yelling in the back, and a motherly voice reassuring him—Maggie. Nick and Guy were still looking exhausted but a little more hopeful.

I had intended to talk drug lords and bombing with them, but the sullen teen presence in the front room prevented it. Michael O'Ryan was a pimple-faced fifteen. He'd been injured in an accident that left him wheelchair-bound a few years earlier. His mother did her best to support them on her jobs as a waitress, but it was tough being a teen, even tougher when poor and paralyzed. He had attitude to spare.

"Dude," I said, dropping a stack of comic books in his lap that I'd picked up on our way over. "No one's murdered your mother yet, have they? Why the face?"

"What do you not get about my being a *cripple*?" the kid demanded, although probably less vociferously than he'd been thinking earlier since he was examining the comics. "Why did you drag me into this? I can't help with any of this crap."

Maggie chose that moment to roll out Vincent, who'd apparently just been powdered and puffed. His hair was still wet from his bath and his clothes looked fresh. "I wanna see the dinosaurs!" he cried excitedly.

I pointed at Vincent. "Crippled, like the kid who needs help bathing?"

Michael glowered. "I can take care of myself."

"And you can't show him how to do what you do?" I waited, eyebrow raised. He glowered some more. Maggie wisely kept her mouth shut while bundling Vincent into his coat.

Michael glared. "OK, he's a cripple too, I get it. So, I'm a dork."

"Dweeb," I countered.

"Doofus," he said with a small flash of a grin.

I wrinkled my nose. "Does it have to be another D word? Because the next one is too rude for kids."

He reddened. "All right, I'm that too."

Maggie snorted. "Especially when his pain meds aren't working. You need to talk to Vincent's doctors about the ones he's been given. He's too young for Mylaudanix. I gave him Advil instead. I won't even let Michael take the strong stuff."

I looked to Guy and Nick with alarm. They seemed equally shocked. Guy jumped up and hurried to the back, presumably to check the prescription bottle.

Juliana was helping Anika into her puffy pink coat. "I have heard of this

Mylaudanix. At the school, some of the students sell it to each other like drugs. They say it is harmless because it is a prescribed medication, but I looked it up. It cannot be safe for little children."

Guy came out holding the bottle and looking grim. "This form does not use the trade name, but it's the same chemical. We never thought to look at it. A *doctor* gave him this! We trusted them to know best what the children need."

"That was the doctor at the hospital?" I asked.

Guy and Nick nodded, both of their chiseled features frowning adorably. I took the bottle and turned to Michael. "You're old enough to help look after the kids with your mother and Juliana. We can't let Guy and Nick in public yet. What do you say, do you need me to tag along?"

Nick and Guy didn't look happy, but now that the news was out that they hadn't been blown up, they had to lie low.

At Michael's reluctant *nah*, I pocketed the bottle. "I'll take this over to the hospital, locate the doc, and ask a few questions."

"Don't shove the bottle down his throat," Nick warned. "Just get a new prescription for something less addictive."

As long as she had her promised outing, EG didn't mind my departure. In fact, she was probably already plotting her escape, assuming the others didn't have my eagle eye. But she didn't know Juliana and Maggie well. She was in for a surprise.

I left the men to a few hours of peace and quiet and security camera adjusting. I checked the bushes and the area as I walked down the street, looking for men in black and seeing nothing suspicious. I had to wonder if Scion's death had changed something. If he had been behind the bombing, then maybe the hounds had been called off my brother.

I found the nearest Metro and returned to the hospital where they thought I was Vincent's aunt. I didn't count on anyone recognizing me, but I was prepared for all events.

I sneaked up to ICU to check on Nadia. She still lay there looking like a corpse, her naturally white face even whiter. They'd shaved her gorgeous hair and stuck machinery in her from head to foot. For the sake of the kids, I winged good thoughts to the universe. Then I took the elevator back to the pediatric ward.

It was Sunday. The attending physician wasn't available, but an over-worked, underfed intern remembered the kids. He looked at the prescription bottle and shrugged. "The hospital gets a bigger discount on these than the older painkillers. They're the best ones on the market. The older ones aren't as effective."

"Are the older painkillers addictive?" I asked, all concerned mother and not my usual belligerent self—as long as he was being useful.

He frowned. "If overused, most of them are. Diet soda is addictive. People need to be responsible for taking medication as prescribed."

My short fuse smoldered. "The patient is six years old! He's barely responsible for pulling up his pants. Have you ever tried to hide candy from babies? And think about it—when you're exhausted and have a patient complaining every five minutes about pain, have you been tempted to give them a pill a little early? Especially if it's a crying kid?"

"We have morphine. . ." His voice trailed off as he realized the hospital drug of choice was also addictive—and he'd probably given it more often than recommended just to get a little peace. "I'll write a prescription for acetaminophen. It won't help the pain as much."

"He doesn't seem to be hyper-sensitive to pain," I said with a shrug. "Mostly, he's annoyed at confinement and wanting his mother. Knocking him out might give us tranquility, but teaching him to medicate himself isn't wise."

"How many kids do you have?" he asked grumpily, scribbling the new script.

I didn't have to explain I'd raised half a dozen siblings on Band-Aids and Neosporin. I just took the script and trotted down to the pharmacy to poke my nose around more. That the hospital got a cut on Mylaudanix didn't surprise me. My guess was that they didn't pass that discount on to the consumer. I wasn't sure how to verify that.

I held up the prescription bottle and asked the pharmacy clerk what it would cost to refill the prescription. She quoted an obscene amount. I pulled out the insurance card Guy had given me and asked for how much they charged the insurance company. Apparently familiar with this tactic, she began a long spiel about how they had quantity discounts with the insurance companies they couldn't give to consumers.

I showed all my teeth. "I just need the numbers, please. We're adding up our deductibles."

Armed with the cost that a dozen Mylaudanix would bring on the open market, I presented the heavy duty acetaminophen prescription. It cost a fraction of the price of the new drug.

My dangerous curiosity carried me to two more pharmacies, one a large discount chain and the other a small independent. I repeated my spiel. As suspected, the big box store got a more substantial discount from the insurance company than the small store. My cost was the same—exorbitant.

Remembering what Juliana had said about students selling these pills to each other, I took the Metro to a different part of town. I'd lived in an area of Atlanta that had drug dealers on every corner. We learned to leave each other alone. But I'd picked up enough of the scene to calculate the information was worth the risk.

I chose to accost the hoodlum nearest the Metro. He wore ratty Rastafarian braids, a three-day scruff, and carried concealed. I was wearing my expensive leather coat, so I couldn't pull off my usual I'm-one-of-you routines. So I went with rich white stupid student. "Dude, I've got a dozen of these. Josh said you'd pay me top dollar."

I pulled the name Josh out of a hat because it was one of the most popular names for twenty-somethings. Everyone knew a Josh.

"Who are you?" he asked, sniffing and looking down his skinny nose at me.

I'm not very prepossessing, so he didn't perceive me as physically dangerous, although I am. But I didn't have *narc* written all over me and probably looked safe. He was suspicious, just not enough.

I shrugged. "Nobody. And you won't see me again. I just need some quick cash and my kid brother doesn't need these anymore."

I'd ripped off the label but figured the pills were recognizable. He opened the bottle and checked them out. "These are everywhere, dudess, I can't give you nothing."

"Fine. Then I'll take them over to the school." I snatched back the bottle. I wanted street prices, not attitude.

He held up his hand. We negotiated. I figured I got half the street price by the time we were done. The street price was cheaper than heroin. I didn't feel guilty selling drugs to a drug dealer.

I handed the cash to the first homeless person I encountered. It was like investing in the lottery. They might take the money, get a room for the night, a hot bath, and some food. Or they could take the cash back to the dealer for their painkiller of choice.

I'd philosophize on how society was killing itself with guns and drugs, but I understood why and changing human nature wasn't happening on my watch.

On the way home, I decided to finish reading Graham's bombing file, then draw up a plan of action. Except now I had to decide if I needed to know more about Harvey Scion.

Magda wouldn't get even with him for attempting to harm Nick and his boyfriend, would she?

Of course, she would.

CHAPTER 10

GRAHAM GROUND HIS MOLARS AT THE TIME IT WAS TAKING TO LOCATE SCION'S phone. His contacts had uncovered half a dozen phone numbers listed in Scion's name. Apparently the drug exec liked to have different phones for different businesses—which meant he probably used unlisted burner phones as well. He had no good way of tracing that last call if it was made from a burner.

Rather than invest any more time in haystacks, Graham set his people to connecting with the cell tower nearest Scion's abode. Oddly, the cell tower didn't belong to a publicly owned entity, so the usual gateways weren't useful. The crafty old bastard had really surrounded himself with security.

While he waited, Graham looked into the odd cell tower company. It was owned by a privately-held corporation and licensed under the name of Rustel. Had it been established just for Scion and his minions? That took mammoth amounts of money, but Top Hat had the funds to spare.

With a little research, he found more Rustel towers in and around DC, but if they were anywhere else, they were under a different company name. Interesting—a cell phone service just for Washington insiders. That degree of privacy screamed criminal activity on a high level.

He set his top hacker onto finding Rustel's database. A small company like that wouldn't normally expect to be a target and might skimp on security. Graham had a feeling that wasn't the case here.

One of his monitors showed Ana entering the front door. At least she hadn't gone to the Russian ambassador as threatened. She'd probably remembered it was Sunday, and there wouldn't be anyone useful available.

She wore her long braid outside her leather coat today, which meant she hadn't expected to run into trouble. He was learning her warrior mode signals. He'd thought she was going to the museum with the kids, but she headed straight for the basement and her office.

She opened the big computer that connected with his, so she wasn't hiding anything. He could probably bug her private laptop, but then she would cut his throat. He respected that.

When she began a search for her mother in the files he'd given her, Graham rolled his eyes. The little witch was as suspicious as he was. He called up an image of an expensive bouquet of roses, inserted another image of the latest tablet computer, and added a link inside the screen.

He'd wooed his late wife with the promise of wealth and power. Ana was far more complicated. She liked information. And it pleased him when she dived into his image gift with zeal. He hadn't felt pleasure in a long, long time, and he was still prickly about it, but he smiled when she found the link and jumped on it.

The woman was too clever for her own good and understood him far too well. Dangerous, but he went back to work with a smile on his face.

Ana would never ask her mother where she'd been the night of Scion's death, but Graham had no such compunctions. The list of phone numbers he'd just sent her ought to keep her busy a while longer.

I BLINKED IN SURPRISE AT THE ROSE PHOTO. GRAHAM WASN'T IN THE HABIT OF sending me bouquets or even pictures of them. I appreciated the high-end technology he'd included more, so I figured he was just trying to catch my attention and throw me off-guard at the same time. Which is when I realized the tablet screen had a link embedded.

Clicking the link, I opened a list of phone numbers, dates, and times. Frowning, I studied the document, realizing it was a list of calls from a particular number. I ran a search on the number and it came up unlisted.

The area code was local. I pulled out my phone and opened my contact list to see if Graham had been spying on my family—the only local numbers I knew.

And there it was—a number I never called—Magda. Why was Graham spying on Magda?

Well, yeah, there were probably ten thousand reasons to keep tabs on her, but generally he left my family to me. He and Magda didn't exactly see eye-to-eye, although they were both in the snoop business.

I was both appalled and fascinated by the list of numbers. I didn't really want to know who my mother was calling or what she did for a living. She'd set herself up as journalist, party planner, hausfrau to diplomats, employee in embassies, and a host of other roles that gave her access to important people and information. I didn't know what disguise she hid behind currently, even though she'd returned to this continent for the first time in decades.

But I couldn't keep looking at her in suspicion if I might have the opportunity to discover her innocence.

Who was I kidding? Magda hadn't been innocent as an infant in her cradle.

Reluctantly, I tried searching the last number she'd called on the afternoon of Scion's death—one with a West Virginia area code. Rose had come from a West Virginia family, I remembered.

Apparently so did Gertrude and her daughter. A reverse number search found Magda's last call went to a company called G Whillikers. A quick search found a website for G Whillikers Bar and Dance Hall outside Huntington, West Virginia. Gertie's smiling face beamed from the website's sidebar. She really was quite lovely despite the kitty ears.

Would a bar owner use a cell phone for her business? Possibly. So Miss Kitty could have been anywhere—like leaving a Rose rally—when Magda called her. I checked Rose's schedule of appearances and verified that the time of the call was half way after the rally started, about the time Gertie would have been released from questioning by Rose's goons and heaved out. It was thoughtful of my mother to check to make sure they hadn't cut Gertie's throat.

So, Mama Magda was involved in helping to bring Rose down. I could appreciate that, except I was reasonably certain it had more do with her personal vendetta against Brody's killers than out of righteous distaste for his politics, although I'm sure she considered that a side benefit.

Rose had been just out of college when my father got himself blown off the map. From all indications, Rose didn't have enough clout, brains, or connections at the time to be one of the conspirators.

But he could be the *son* of a conspirator and carrying on his old man's traditions. Or Magda could be playing a long game. Did I really want to add researching Rose to my list of tasks?

I checked again but the coroner's report only said Scion appeared to have been shot around nine. The call was made about six hours before that. Was Graham telling me my mother had most likely been the woman in the big hat in West Virginia and that she would only be on her way back to DC at the time of the murder?

I was pretty sure she hadn't shot Scion—Magda hated guns. Still, I sent out a query asking if it was possible to tell which cell tower had bounced this call. Even if it was possible, the result still wouldn't be proof positive. I'd learned deviousness from Magda, after all, but I liked to close as many loopholes as I could.

I decided to set Rose's history aside until I'd worked through the rest of Magda's calls. I marked off the half dozen to Gertie and picked a non-US number next. I recognized the Brit international code and checked Tudor's number—bingo. She'd been using our cyber genius for her evil plots. It wasn't as if she'd called to ask if he was eating right.

It was late evening in the UK, prime Tudor time. I didn't trust phones. We'd developed an intricate encrypted instant messaging system for delicate messages—although Tudor tended to use it to ask if MIT would let him bring his own server and other anxious teen-related stuff. He might be brilliant, but he was young.

DOES MAGDA HAVE YOU TRACKING RUSSIANS? I typed a wild guess to stir his interest.

YUP was his laconic reply.

Eye-rolling and beating the computer to death would not shake info out of the kid. SPILL OR YOUR ALLOWANCE VANISHES INTO CYBORG'S CAVE.

THOUGHT YOU KNEW, he replied. SCION ONCE WORKED FOR IRA. HAS RUSSIAN CONNECTIONS. BEHIND NICK'S BOMB?

PROOF? I asked, although his question left it open.

NOT YET. I'M HACKING A FEW ACCOUNTS.

NO YOU ARE NOT, I typed. YOU DO HOMEWORK. LET MAGDA HIRE HER OWN GOONS.

He sent me a fire-breathing dragon icon, with GOON printed under it.

I returned a cyborg reminder and let him be. I'd given him an excuse to tell Magda *no* if her requests made him uncomfortable, but he was of an age to make his own decisions. He might be immature, but he was smarter than I was and equally cynical.

I used to relish sitting here in my basement, manipulating events, but I was anxious about my family and impatient to be *doing* instead of digging. Only all I had was crime scenes and unrelated information. I left crime scenes to the professionals. And info required research before I could plan any action.

And Graham was burying me in info for a reason. Huh. There was an action I could handle.

I sent the list of Magda's phone calls to another virtual assistant I knew. It was hard giving up control, but Nick's safety was more important than my curiosity.

As if he'd read my mind, Nick called.

"The dog caught a perp."

"What dog?" I was already on my feet and ready for action.

"Guy has a friend with a boxer. I can't decide what to do with him."

"The boxer, the friend, or the perp?" I set the phone on speaker, donned my leather coat and tucked my waist-length braid under it. I wasn't giving thugs a chance to jerk me around by the hair. I probably ought to grow up and cut it, but I'd be lost without the lovely disguises long black hair creates. And I loved what it did for Graham.

So, I distracted my terror for Nick and his friend with vanity. That was better than my head exploding. I thought we were done with this assassin nonsense. Scion was dead, wasn't he?

"I don't think this creep is part of the crew who stole the computer," Nick said. "Are you coming over? I'll let you decide before I show my hand."

"On my way, unless you just got word the kids are returning and this is your way of getting even."

"Serve you right." He hung up.

Nick was my best friend, but he's also my brother. We fight unfairly, especially when we're anxious.

I hit the train to Nadia's place with a minute to spare, but even getting there within half an hour had our nervous lovers pacing the floor.

I studied the trussed and sullen trespasser tied to a kitchen chair. Youngish, scruffy, overlong mouse-colored hair, lanky, tattoo on his hand and cheek—and probably elsewhere but he was covered in denim and fake leather.

This was not a well-paid goon. Wannabe gang member, maybe, but doubtful—no attitude. I didn't see him as experienced enough to pull off a hit-and-run much less a bombing. I relaxed an iota.

"Name, rank, and serial number?" I asked, setting water on for tea.

Nick was taking out mugs and teapot. No teabags for our lordly Brit.

The kid glared silently.

"He only knows curses, and he ran out of them a while back." Guy got down another mug for himself.

"In Russian?" I guessed.

Guy and Nick both glared at me in tandem. I preened and took a seat to let them serve me.

"Tattoo." I pointed at his ring finger circled in ink with another circle where a real ring might have a stone. "Russian criminals used symbolism to indicate status way back pre-Khrushchev. Call it retro, but the symbols are coming back. What does yours mean?" I asked the kid.

"Loyalty," he said fiercely.

"So, how is Viktor faring these days?" I sniffed the tea Nick gave me—a *Russian* Caravan, nice. So Nick was thinking the same as me. His brains weren't entirely addled yet. I added more water and some honey.

I'd run some quick research on Nadia's ex, the kids' father. Word of her condition hadn't yet made international news, but she worked for Scion, and presumably, so did he, in some manner. He could have heard about her through the grapevine. Nadia's house, Nadia's Russian husband, non-professional villain. . . My guess that the kid was related to Viktor wasn't too much of a stretch.

The lad looked fierce. I sipped my tea. He sent my cup a longing look. I smiled.

"Viktor works hard," our spy said gruffly.

"I'd pour you some tea, but I can see you're a bit tied up. Maybe if you tell these good gentlemen what they want, we can all laugh, set you free, and have a nice tea party."

I could think of several things Nadia's ex might want, and none of them were laughing matters. But I liked to add a bit of positivity to my life upon occasion. I've heard it's healthy—like a chocolate and glass of wine a day.

Guy sipped his tea and studied the boy as if he were vermin. Nick merely performed his elegant, blond James Bond lounging act, leaning against the kitchen counter instead of a bar.

"He wants his children," the boy finally decided.

"Well, if you just mean to lie, we'll call the cops and see if Viktor comes to bail you out," Nick said. His cold glare beat my sympathetic ploy by a kilometer. We pretty much invented good cop, bad cop on our own since we seldom saw TV growing up. Or maybe we learned it from the people around us.

"Children cost money," I reminded him. "Nadia has none. If Viktor thought eliminating her would win the lottery, he's stupider than I thought."

The boy's eyes widened. "He would never harm the mother of his children! She was hit in accident."

"I'd tell Viktor to ask his boss about that *accident*, but his boss just got killed." Nick was relentless when he got all nasty like that.

"Boris is dead?" the kid asked, genuinely puzzled.

"*Scion* is dead." Guy looked like he was enjoying the cloak and dagger routine a little too much. "Looks like your lot may be out of jobs soon."

I doubted if Guy was *good* at this, but he deserved a chance to play.

The boy's English had only a slight accent, like Guy's, only more eastern Europe than Guy's French. I'd like to know more about the little thug, but first, we needed to know how to make Viktor leave his kids alone. Our visitor still looked as if he didn't understand.

"Doesn't Viktor still work for Scion Pharmaceutical?" I asked, all concern.

"Nyet," he said, using Russian dismissively. "He works for Boris. He is salesman in Ukraine. He is worried about his children."

"And who are you to find out for him?" I finally asked out of exasperation.

"His nephew. I live here. I look to see if children okay," he said proudly. "It is what family does."

"Viktor's family is mafia," Guy said in disgust. "What do they really want?"

The boy finally looked uncomfortable. "You will let me go if I tell you? Viktor will not like it."

"Viktor is over there. The cops are here. You're better off talking to us," Nick said harshly.

Nick is a pussycat. He hates the bad guy routine, but at six feet, he can pull it off easier than my five-two, even though I'm the mean one.

"Nadia has something that belongs to him." The boy was back to sullen.

"What?" Guy demanded. "The house is small, with nothing valuable in it. The children are all he's ever given her."

"The babushka dolls." He slumped in his seat and eyed the tea more openly. "They are family heirlooms."

Nick apparently knew where they were. He set down his mug and left the room, returning with a set of the ubiquitous nesting dolls. These were larger than usual and a particularly garish Chinese yellow and red. They were very definitely not heirlooms.

Nick dropped the heavy set on the table in front of Guy. I watched the boy. He was as interested as Guy in opening the lot.

The interior dolls all looked the same—definitely cheap manufacturing and nothing valuable. Guy shook each figure and Nick examined them for hollow bottoms. Hand-carved dolls often had good hiding places, but not these manufactured ones.

The last doll wasn't as tiny as most sets—and it wasn't empty. Guy unfolded the papers twisted into it. From what I could see, they were written in Cyrillic and came accompanied by a grainy photo printed on regular paper.

Guy scanned the lot and snickered. "This is how Nadia kept Viktor away from her and the children. You can have the dolls, but I think we'll keep the papers, although we'll find a more secure place for them."

The boy slumped even more. Nick and I waited impatiently.

Guy threw the papers on the table. "Copies of Viktor's arrest warrants for murder in three countries—enough to have him thrown out on his ass if he dares come near the children."

I picked up the blurry pixilated photo. It showed a big dark-haired brute in an open collar shirt and gold chains pointing a Russian Makarov pistol at a bloody victim on the ground. Even if it had been staged, it was enough to identify Viktor to authorities. Nadia was a brilliant woman. I hoped I had a chance to meet her.

"Salesman, indeed." I threw the papers back to Guy. "Banks aren't open today. Better send a dozen copies to people you trust."

He tucked the papers in his shirt pocket and glared at our thug. "Tell Viktor he will never see his children again."

He stalked off to the new computer. I poured another mug of tea and nodded at Nick to untie his prisoner. Now *my* interrogation could begin.

"Well, we can eliminate Viktor as Nadia's would-be assassin," I said conversationally as the boy shook circulation into his arms.

"He is not in that business no more," the boy said indignantly. Then he looked sly. "But I bet he can say who is."

CHAPTER 11

WE POURED A SHOT OF VODKA INTO THE BOY'S SECOND MUG OF TEA. WE'D learned his name was Dima, son of Viktor's brother, who had moved to New Jersey when Dima was little. The father purportedly ran a candy store in Hoboken.

Viktor had offered Dima a lot of cash to obtain the dolls. Dima liked gaming and wanted to start a video store.

Nick put a fat contribution toward his goal on the table. "A list of people who might want to harm Nadia is valuable," he suggested.

The numbers made Dima's eyes cross. Nick was a gambler, but he was also good with money. He wouldn't be investing this much in a future criminal if he didn't love Guy a lot.

"Call Viktor," he continued. "Tell him Nadia has already sent the papers to the government, and he'll never get a visa. I work for an embassy and will personally see to that. But if he wants to set up his own drugstore in the Ukraine, we'll help. All he needs to do is give us a list of people who may have tried to kill Nadia and to blow up Guy."

Without a trace of conscience—or family loyalty—the boy hastily punched a number into his pricey new phone.

The front door opened and the noise of excited kids spilled in.

Nick steered Dima out the back door, leaving me with the little woman's job. I wanted to stab him with the fancy cutlery in the chopping block, but that would not aid my need for information.

"We saw dinosaurs!" Vincent cried excitedly, wheeling his chair into the kitchen like a pro. "Mike made the guard yell."

"Didn't fall for the poor cripple routine, did he?" I asked the smirking teenager.

"She almost did, until I cuffed him upside his scruffy head and made him apologize," Juliana said cheerfully, pulling her wool cap off her dark curls.

My South African twin siblings were a mocha mix of my mother and their late diplomat father. Their hair kinked wildly in DC's perpetual damp. Zander shaved his short but Juliana was letting hers grow out in a wild mane that framed her beautiful dark eyes and broad features. Despite her gentle nature, she could go all African goddess tough when she chose.

"You're good with kids. You'd make a great teacher." Short, round, with a black Irish temper, Maggie was rosy-cheeked and happier than I'd seen her last. She worked hard and deserved an occasional outing.

"I will make a better builder of schools," Juliana declared. "Maybe we will start with a school for teachers. "

Until Zander worked out how to invest and divvy up our grandfather's millions, we all lived on dreams. Juliana's was the least selfish one I'd heard so far—which was why Zander would do his best to tie up her investments so she'd always have enough to live on.

I looked for Anika and EG and found them in the front room gleefully gluing inappropriate costumes on paper dolls from the gift store. Sacajawea appeared to be wearing Daniel Boone's coonskin hat, and Lewis and Clark had on skirts. Made sense to me.

Guy emerged from Nadia's office to hug the kids. They beamed and showed him their new toys. He started pulling nutritional food out of the refrigerator as if he knew what he was doing. That was promising. Nick couldn't cook much beyond pasta and peanut butter.

I left the group fixing dinner and joined Nick out in the freezing backyard. The day's warmth had left with the sun.

Nick showed me his notebook with scribbles of names, numbers, and the occasional address, presumably garnered from Dima's call to his uncle. Like his nephew, Viktor would probably sell his own mother for cash. I stared at the list in abstract horror—Nadia's husband knew this many assassins?

"When do we get paid?" the kid asked anxiously.

"You can have your check now." Nick tucked it into the boy's shirt pocket. "Your uncle's list has to check out before we release funds to him."

"He must have euros," Dima insisted, as if he were negotiating.

"Wouldn't have it any other way," Nick said blithely. "We'll take care of his kids and find who hit Nadia, and he'll have his drugstore in no time."

Well, I was pretty sure Nick had made up the drugstore and Viktor had less legal plans, but if the line was tapped, it sounded good.

Still shaken that we'd been right about assassins, I used my phone to take a picture of the list and shoot a copy off to Graham. He might not help, depending on his level of interest in the Scion case.

Since finding the villain who tried to blow up Nick was my priority, I meant to dig into the hit man list immediately.

∿

GRAHAM WHISTLED AS ANA'S LIST OF EUROPE'S MOST NOTORIOUS KILLERS appeared on the screen.

He sent the names to a contact in the CIA to ask if they were aware of any of them in the US lately—or at least not active elsewhere. They couldn't have entered the US unless under an alias.

He dug into files and turned up the most recent photos of the assassins. He loaded them into the latest reincarnation of facial recognition software his experts were testing—one that promised to work with any image resolution. Then he ran the security tapes the feds had gathered from around the parking garage before and after the explosion. The detonation had been crude, using old-fashioned techniques like a timer and Tovex, favorites of old terrorists like the IRA because they were easy to obtain. Graham doubted any of the younger killers would use them.

While he had parking garage images running, he called up an older file, one from the 80's with the suspects in the death of his father and Ana's. The similarities of the two bombs were worrisome. He needed to verify these people were all dead or in prison where they were supposed to be—but if he asked Ana to start digging, he was afraid she'd go rogue on him if she realized what she was looking at. He never underestimated Ana's intelligence—or penchant for taking matters into her own hands.

On another monitor, he watched her return with two of her sisters and wondered what it would feel like to be a normal family who got together over dinner.

He'd never known that kind of life. Why start now?

But watching Ana laugh at her kid sister as if she hadn't a care in the world had him wondering if it might be possible for *her* to have that kind of normalcy someday—if he got out of her life.

His computer pinged a match, and he returned to studying his monitors. He paused the street scene outside the of the garage—a limo driver leaning on the outside of his car, smoking, presumably waiting for his employer. Graham zoomed in on the driver's face and matched it against the one the software had found from Ana's list.

Anatole Bernard? The limo guy looked seventy. The assassin's image from Interpol was old and grainy, hidden in shadow, with only the hard edges of nose and jaw to judge by. The date of the photo was unknown.

Graham ran the limo footage back and forth but there was no better shot. The driver climbed out—back to the camera—lit a cigarette, waited, and after a few minutes, checked his phone. It simply looked as if he'd parked to wait for a summons from his employer. The camera caught the brief glimpse of his face just before he dropped his cigarette, climbed back in the limo, and drove off—with no evidence of the use of a detonation device.

The garage blew a minute later. Definitely a timer and the reason Nick and Guy were still alive.

Graham zoomed up the good image. The hand holding the cigarette was missing a finger and appeared knotted with arthritis. The driver was tall but hunched as if his back hurt. His face was lined with wrinkles from years of smoking.

Carefully copying the one shot of the driver's face, Graham transferred it to another program and turned back the hands of time. A beak of a nose emerged, thicker eyebrows, a single line on either side of a softer mouth— he ran the image through facial recognition again, using his own old file photos as his database.

This time, when the computer binged, Graham swore viciously and hit the intercom for Mallard.

～

MALLARD WAS SETTING DINNER ON THE TABLE WHEN THE CANDELABRA bellowed his name.

Unused to talking tableware, Juliana eyed the silver skeptically. I'd persuaded her to come home with us and eat a decent meal, but I kept stupidly forgetting our ghost in the attic.

I knew better than to tell Mallard to ignore the despot. He treated Graham as if he were still the president's right hand man, but I was tired of being ignored. I was part of the team now. They couldn't keep snubbing me.

Ordering my sisters to stay put, I put down my starched linen napkin and marched up the stairs in Mallard's wake. Since my siblings didn't have my anger issues and were hungry after their outing, they happily obeyed. Mallard's bouillabaisse was delicious.

Mallard tried to discourage me, but I was itching for action and Graham usually provided, one way or another. I didn't have kickboxing or love-making in mind this time. I marched into his office prepared to take him down. "Just because you don't eat like normal humans doesn't mean you're entitled to—"

I shut up when I saw the monitors.

Mallard used a Gaelic word I was pretty certain he didn't normally use.

I sat down, cross-legged, on the floor and just stared at Graham's damning windows on the world.

One screen showed two faces—one lined and weary, the other younger and meaner but obviously identical, like father and son. Judging by the hair styles and clothes though, I'd guess the younger photo was taken decades ago. The more recent one—I found on the next screen, in an image of a limo driver outside the parking garage that had almost taken Nick's life.

But those weren't the images that had Mallard cursing and me sitting down.

Below them were familiar images of my father, along with photos I recognized of my grandfather, Sean and Graham's fathers—all taken with the hard-eyed, cigarette smoking thug who might be the limo driver.

"Tony Byrne," Mallard finally said in disbelief. "He was supposed to have died in Dublin gaol after he helped import those boatloads of Libyan weapons in the 80s."

"He now goes by Anatole Barnard and has a French passport. He knew we were gunning for him." Graham spoke in a flat dead voice I didn't like.

"Are you saying he's the one who killed our fathers?" I couldn't believe I was looking at my distant past, alive, right here in the present. History is supposed to stay dead.

"*One* of the suspects," Mallard corrected. "He was our explosives expert. He was supposed to choose the weapons we needed."

I'd known Mallard had been a general in the IRA back in the day, but to hear the stiff and proper butler speak so casually of engaging in illegal weapons and terrorism. . .

He looked down at me apologetically. "Your father and his friends saw no alternative to the years of violence except continuing to fight. I was just filled with hate for the deaths of my family. I was older. I should have stopped them."

I couldn't tear my gaze from the monitor. Our fathers weren't laughing. They looked as weary and jaded as the older man called Tony.

And my mother had persuaded these hardened fighters to back out of a weapons deal?

"So this Tony Byrne murdered our fathers and went ahead with the GenDef arms deal that kept the fighting going longer?" I was trying to process my fury and sorrow and disgust into logic. It wasn't working. There was the man who had quite possibly turned my mother into a monster and ruined my future as pampered princess.

Not a rational reaction, I knew, but processing fury and hurt at that level wasn't my finest moment.

"GenDef already had the weapons money Brody raised. Brody wanted it back," Mallard said matter-of-factly. "Everyone was appalled except your mother, and maybe Hugh and Dillon. Brody had grown pretty thick with his American friends and may have had other plans that involved them. We'll never know."

I'd love to believe that they would have used the gun funds to promote peace, or at least support widows and orphans. Monsters had prevented us from ever knowing who our fathers really were. *That's* what guns did—stole the future.

"Tony and his cohorts took the weapons they needed from the GenDef deal and sold the rest to terrorists in Iran. They used the profits to continue fighting—and buying more of GenDef's guns." Graham ran through the security footage from the parking garage but the limo drove away without revealing more.

"Max approved?" I asked cautiously. No one had ever told me about my grandfather. I'd only been four or five when I saw him last, and my memories were those of a bewildered child—not reality.

"I can't say," Graham said curtly. "Max played a close hand. I just know at some point after that, his old Top Hat cronies started vanishing from the public eye."

"Blackmail," Mallard said succinctly. "That was Max's style. He hired me to help, then kept me on since I couldn't go back."

I had always assumed Mallard had been Max's spy and bodyguard. Looked like I wasn't far wrong.

"By the time I was of an age to understand what had happened to my father," Graham continued, "Max had arranged for almost everyone who may have been involved in the arms deal to be dead or in jail, including Tony. I helped Max nail a few strays. I thought the case was laid to rest."

"For all intents and purposes, it is," I pointed out. "Scion is a totally different matter."

"Harvey Scion was once one of my men," Mallard said, looking older than I'd ever seen him. "He was a sharp shooter with a way of making a profit from anything. I've seen him sell the same gun three times, after the buyers died. But he was young then. He got out of gun fighting long before your father came along."

Hence, Harvey Scion had never been on Max's or Magda's hit list. Only men like Mallard would know about his past as a street terrorist.

Mallard continued, "Harvey preferred selling drugs to guns and made his fortune."

"Not legally, I'm guessing," I said. "And he obviously stayed in touch with old acquaintances."

We all stared at the image of Tony, ex-bomber. Could a wealthy Scion have helped him escape jail?

"No identifying marks, no proof." Graham played more video footage showing the black plastic cover over the limo's license plate.

"And Scion is dead, so we can't interrogate him. Could Tony have killed Scion?" I knew that was too simple, but I was ready for simplicity.

"Find Tony, and we'll find out." Graham glanced at our stoic butler. "Talk to your buddies?"

Mallard nodded. He met with an old goats club down at the local Irish pub. IRA buddies? I hated to think those loud drunks had once been young, deadly terrorists.

"We don't know the limo is Scion's," I contradicted my earlier suggestion.

"Find Tony and we'll know," Graham repeated. "But whoever took out Scion had modern weapons and apparently the ability to wipe camera footage. We're still working on that."

Doctoring sophisticated cameras didn't sound like the act of a 70-year old explosives expert still using old-fashioned timers.

"It makes no sense," I said, climbing off the floor. "Yeah, I understand Scion hiring someone to kill Guy and Nadia to prevent their testifying about their report. But who would want Scion dead? Someone who hates incompetence?"

Both Mallard and Graham turned to stare at me.

"What?" I asked in bewilderment. "He failed to stop Guy. Nadia is still alive. There may be some chance she'll recover. Maybe Scion gave the wrong advice on how to handle the report. I know they say you can't fix stupid, but haven't you ever wanted to *kill* stupid?"

Mallard sniffed and aimed for the door, the vision of ruffled dignity. "Your dinner is going cold."

Graham winked and returned to calling up a new set of images on his screens. The wink tingled parts of me that didn't need to be tingled with family waiting downstairs. Unsatisfied, I followed Mallard out.

But later that night, after EG had gone to bed and Juliana back to school, I started making lists of people who would want Scion dead.

There were a lot of them. A man who made his fortune in drugs and then turned around to use his wealth as a blunt instrument to manipulate politics would never earn a Mr. Rogers award.

After the balloon caricature debacle and the failure to kill Guy and Nadia—or making the attempt in the first place—even Paul Rose might be willing to terminate his pal.

Any patient who got hooked on his drugs—or their families—might want to kill him.

My bet was that Scion took a lot of dirty secrets to the grave with him. The big problem here was whether any of them would affect me or mine if I dug them up.

CHAPTER 12

AFTER I SAW EG OFF TO SCHOOL MONDAY MORNING, AND FIELDED HALF A dozen calls from an anxious Nick about the kids, I returned to my list making.

I was fully cognizant that labeling Rose a killer of Scion because he'd been stupid was irrational, but I'd spent these last six months trying to nail the Teflon senator for other horrific crimes, without success. We'd turned in his minions by the dozens, but no evidence indicated Rose did anything except take their checks and advertising support. If the voting public didn't mind a president who got elected with dirty money, who was I to care?

I was willing to pin the rap on him out of sheer frustration, except Rose had utterly no incentive for killing his moneymaker that I could see.

Apparently my spider in the attic had been busy while I slept. In my mailbox this morning was a heavily annotated version of the list of assassins Viktor had provided. Graham had done his best to determine where they all were these past few days.

Keep in mind—these were international criminals wanted in half a dozen countries, and *Graham knew where they were*. I hoped he had used his powers of good and turned their locations over to law enforcement. *How* he had found them sounded too 007, so I concentrated on the part important to me—which one could have been in the US when Nadia was hit, the garage exploded, and Scion died?

None, according to this list—except for three names that were completely untraceable in recent years. Chances were good that they were flying under the radar and had been for years. Or had died anonymously and been buried in unmarked graves.

Graham had provided photos of the three, a variety of their passports and aliases, and last known locations. As with the list of Magda's phone calls, he was trying to keep me at my desk and out of trouble.

I'm an introvert by nature. I honestly preferred my basement hideaway under most circumstances. This wasn't a normal situation. My family in was danger, and I couldn't sit still and do nothing.

I sent him a message recommending that he run his facial recognition program on this charming trio of assassins and match it against Rose's security detail—just to keep *him* occupied.

Then I went upstairs and dressed to talk to Scion's household employees. Tony Byrne, aka Anatole Bernard, was in the country and at the scene of the bombing. I didn't see any reason to hunt further.

Since he didn't appear to be on Scion's payroll, the cops wouldn't know of his existence. Old Tony might be hiding in plain sight. At the very least, I hoped to verify he was Scion's chauffeur. Or Rose's. I grinned evilly.

∼

HARVEY SCION'S ESTATE WAS IN A WEALTHY AREA OF BETHESDA WITH MONSTER brick mansions on intensely landscaped lots. I gathered the dense foliage prevented the neighbors from looking in each other's third story bathrooms. On my grandfather's mansion-strewn street, we used drapery and shutters. Neither solution allowed sunlight to touch the dragon hoards.

Yellow police tape still blocked the gates to Scion's drive. I'd arrived by taxi, which left me to explore on foot—not always a great idea in a densely populated area. Oh well.

We'd passed an area of restaurants and boutiques on the main road. Starbucks might be open, but coffee drinkers weren't a talkative lot in the morning. I hoped there might be a breakfast café, but my best bet would be a sports bar. It was too early in the day for a good turn-out at a bar, though.

So I wandered around to the street behind Scion's place, checking for openings, stray workers, whatever I could find. At this hour on Monday morning, the street was empty. I found a nanny with a stroller on the way to the park. I stopped her and indicated the high wall around Scion's place. "My friend Tony works there, but they have police tape all over. What happened?"

She'd looked nervous when I first approached, but everyone loves a good gossip. She struggled with her English. "Burglars. They shot the owner. The house, it is empty now."

"So everyone is out of a job?" I asked in horror. "Tony's too old to find a new one."

She looked sympathetic. "His housekeeper is friend with ours. Maybe she know." She pointed at a more accessible house across the street. "Her name is Ursula. Tell her Marie said to ask."

"Thanks!" I trotted off, taking the drive to the delivery door in hopes of not disturbing anyone but the servants.

A woman with erect carriage and graying hair pulled tight in a bun answered my knock. Dress her in silk and pearls and she could be any society matron, but she wore Wal-Mart cotton and an apron and held a dust cloth.

"Ursula?" I asked. At her withering glare, I continued, "Marie said you might know if Mr. Scion's employees were let go. I'm concerned for a friend of mine, Tony? He's too old to be looking for a job."

The woman's glare disappeared. "It's a tragedy. I don't know what this world is coming to. The lawyers gave them all notice that they'll only receive one week's pay and a reference. With the economy as it is. . . I am sorry for your friend."

I wasn't sure if the tragedy was the loss of jobs or Scion's death but rather suspected the former. Neither verified Tony's existence—or the location of anyone who might know him. Dang.

"You wouldn't happen to know how to reach Mr. Scion's housekeeper? I always know people looking for housekeepers. But limo drivers— there's not much call for them." I added just the right note of pathos.

"I have her cell number. Just a minute." Not in the least security conscious, she left the door open. In these days, with the division between rich and poor reaching French revolution explosive, that was a mistake.

She came back with a piece of paper and a number. "I hope you can help her. She's a real nice lady, even if she doesn't speak much English."

"I thank you." I returned the favor by gifting her with a touch of paranoia. "Look, I work for security people. They advise keeping a locked door between you and strangers, even if they look harmless. After what happened across the street, you can never be too cautious. I'd hate to see a nice lady hurt."

Her eyebrows shot up, and she suddenly looked nervous. My good deed done, I waved good-bye and jogged off.

I only got voice mail on the housekeeper's number. After her harrowing few days of police interrogation, I could understand that. I left a message and headed down the street to check for a bar or café.

I'd already run through publicly available lists of Scion employees and found no Tony, Byrne, Anatole, or Bernard. I'd have assumed I was wrong about the connection between the limo and Scion, except I knew way too much about how wealthy households operated. With his alias, Tony probably didn't have a social security number and might even be an illegal. He could easily be taking cash under the table from Scion, or be working for room and board, neither of which would show up on tax records, unless Scion was honest. The financial records Zander had been sending me had already established that wasn't likely.

I trudged along a busy street until I found a high-end bar with huge TVs and wine cases, but it had just opened. It didn't look like the kind of place an old Irish terrorist might frequent, but Bethesda isn't a place that caters to Tony's sort. Yet, I surmised he lived nearby if he drove for Scion.

The bartender was waxing down his counter while two old guys who looked out of place took the heads off their beers next to a shiny new giant television blaring a soccer game.

I hesitated in the doorway to study the old men, just long enough for them to look up, check me out, and dismiss me. What can I say? I dress for success.

But my pulse rate accelerated. My basement theories were easily researched and deleted. Real life wasn't so simple. The lankier old guy looked dangerously similar to Tony/Anatole. Could it really be this easy? I couldn't run a real-life man through facial software.

Could I have found my father's killer when no one else could? I fingered my phone with the camera.

He reached in his shirt pocket with a four-fingered hand to pull out cigarettes, and my knees grew weak. Only the bartender reminding him to take it outside returned me to the moment. The city had banned smoking in bars just a couple of years ago.

Now what did I do? At the very least, I had an ex-IRA bomber, possibly an escaped convict, in my sights, but even I knew better than to fling accusations. I needed a delete button for real life.

I sat down, ordered Irish coffee—I hate both coffee and whisky—and unlocked my cell phone. Punching in Graham's number, I improvised to his voice mail. It would have been nice to have a little advice, but that wasn't happening. Instead, I discreetly snapped a few photos while I talked to a machine.

"I can't make it, his driver quit again," I said in annoyance. "He won't take a taxi. He expects me to haul him all over creation and back. If you can't magic up a licensed driver, it will be next week until I can escape. Cousin Viktor has a list. Talk to him."

I hoped that last was clue enough to Graham that I hadn't gone barmy. I tucked the phone back in my leather jacket and sipped the awful coffee.

The bartender looked like a fresh-faced college kid, eager to earn tips. He'd been listening when he delivered the coffee, but I couldn't tell if the old goats had overheard. Once I put my phone away, Joe College came back, still polishing a glass.

"I couldn't help overhearing—are you looking for a driver?"

Ding, ding, trap sprung.

I sipped the bitter brew and eyed him skeptically. "My uncle. They took away his license on account of he's a senile old drunk. Why, you offering?"

His smile wobbled a little as he considered senile old drunks. "I have a friend who works for Uber. He could use a steady job."

"Bill, leave the lady alone," the lumpy old fart who wasn't Tony said loudly. He glanced at me apologetically, "My boy is eager to help, but his friends are druggies. You don't want your uncle near them."

I saluted him with my cup. "I'm not entirely certain my uncle cares if they're druggies, but he eats the young ones alive. His last driver had enough experience to handle him, but he got married and moved away."

Old Fart punched Old Tony's bicep. "My friend here has experience. Tony, talk to the lady."

Tony looked at me balefully, jotted a number on a bar napkin, and gestured for Bill to carry it to me. "Have your uncle call," he said sourly.

A real charmer was Old Tony. Interrogating him would take waterboarding. I didn't want to scare him off. I'd leave it to the experts.

I took the napkin and folded it up, wondering if the number was real or a show for his friend. "Thanks, I'll pass it on. Have you worked for tyrants before?"

That earned me a narrow-eyed glare. "I work for who pays me."

"His last employer died," Old Fart said cheerfully. "Tony's solid, I can vouch for him."

Like I trusted him any more than Tony just because he smiled. I saluted them with my cup. "Thanks. I'm tired of being his unpaid flunky."

I checked the time on my phone, squeezed in a few more photos, and left a ten on the table. "This was the most helpful coffee I've had in a while."

I walked out as if I didn't feel eyes piecing my back.

Then I hid around the corner and waited. I wasn't about to lose my suspect or miss the interrogation when Graham's forces arrived, because—despite his attempts to ignore me—Graham would have been on that voice mail like triggers on guns.

~

GRAHAM STARED IN DISBELIEF AT THE IMAGE AND PHONE NUMBER ANA SENT him. He hadn't translated her voice mail, but the image was clear—*Tony Byrne*, in person.

She'd removed the GPS from her phone so he couldn't track her, but she'd sent the name and address of the bar—*show off*. If Scion had paid Tony off the books, the cops didn't even know he existed. And the cops most certainly didn't realize Anatole Bernard was the man who may have killed three young men twenty-five years ago.

He could wring Ana's neck for endangering herself, but she was too damned good to yell at.

He'd simply have to take Tony down himself, because his other contacts told him the circus had come to town, and Ana would go into full lion-tamer mode shortly.

CHAPTER 13

I LEANED AGAINST AN OUTSIDE WALL OUT OF SIGHT OF THE BAR CUSTOMERS, but able to watch people coming and going. I read my email while making certain Tony didn't leave before Graham's men arrived. I was placing a lot of confidence in my spy's invisible powers for the forces of good. Besides, Tony had most likely been the one to blast Graham's childhood apart as well, just as he had mine. Graham's motives weren't necessarily all honorable.

A couple of men in baggy khaki blazers concealing revolvers arrived. Here we went. I kept my phone on *camera* and slipped in behind them, taking an empty booth.

Old Tony the Bomber was still sitting at the bar, just the way I'd left him. Looked like he was on a fresh beer. The kid bartender was flirting with a waitress at the far end of the bar. He looked up to greet the new customers but didn't notice me. Old Fart was nowhere in sight.

The newcomers started toward Tony. Nursing his beer, he checked the mirror over the bar and stiffened. Old terrorists and murderers lived on the edge and recognized trouble when it arrived. He slid off the stool and ran for the hallway with the restrooms—and probably the kitchen exit.

Joe College blocked the two guys in khaki from following. While they manhandled the kid, I ran out the front and around to the alley where I'd been watching the door. No way was I letting the old coot who may have killed my father get away.

I was debating how I would bring him down when I hit the employee parking lot in back. Outlined against the big blue Dumpster was a familiar silhouette that shouldn't have been there—*Graham.*

Graham never left the house if he could avoid it. This vendetta was serious.

I gaped as he stopped Tony with a single blow to the jaw. The old bomber spun, kept his balance, and futilely attempted to stagger down the alley. One had to give the old coot credit for trying.

Rubbing his bruised knuckles, Graham jogged past him, swung, and applied a side kick to the groin. I knew the power of Graham's kickboxing blows. Even I groaned as Tony bent over, defeated.

If this was the man who'd killed our fathers, I wanted to do more than kick him in the groin, but that was a darn good start. I patted myself on the back for resisting kicking the back of his knees and bringing him down completely. The man was ancient, after all.

The guys in khaki finally arrived, but Graham had Tony by the collar, shaking him. They stood back.

I had never seen Graham getting his hands dirty. I think I was a little stunned because I did the same as his men, stood back and let him do the work.

"Tony Byrne?" he asked. "Alias Anatole Bernard?" He nodded at one of the khaki guys, who rummaged through Tony's pockets for a wallet. He flipped it open and nodded.

Tony just snarled.

"You can answer our questions or we can hand you to the cops and call Interpol," Graham said in a smooth voice that I knew held a bucket load of fury. It felt really strange watching cool composed Graham vent all the rage I would have blasted on the old bomber.

Tony grunted and shook his head, possibly to shake off the effects of the earlier blow that had to have rattled what remained of his brains.

"Whadaya wanta know?" he finally spit out.

"You planted the bomb in the parking garage Friday?"

Tony shrugged.

"We have footage of you standing outside Scion's limo one minute before the bomb exploded. Me or the cops?" Graham shook him again.

Graham was lying, just as I would have. He didn't know it was Scion's limo. Tony didn't know that he didn't know.

The old guy seemed to crumple inside himself, pretty much proving our theory. I couldn't feel sorry for a cold-blooded assassin.

"Nobody got killed, did they?" Tony asked. "Scion fired me, called me an incompetent old Mick. You want to blame anyone, it's him."

Except Scion was conveniently dead and couldn't be interrogated. Had Tony got his revenge?

The guys in khaki stood ready, hands in position to grab their guns. Shooting Tony wouldn't give us what we needed.

I'd never been part of a physical shakedown. I was clenching my teeth to keep them from chattering. Graham looked furious enough to kill, and I really hated guns.

"Looks like someone decided to take Scion out, too. Any ideas who?"

I wanted to shake Graham. Who cared about slimebutt? I wanted to know about our fathers.

Tony shrugged again. "He hired new security. Ask them. I ain't a gun man anymore. New guns are too slick."

I couldn't see the skinny old man climbing the wall either. He was so crippled with arthritis that he could barely stand straight.

"Did you know Brody Devlin back in the eighties?" Graham finally asked.

Tony squinted at him in surprise. "Yeah, him and a lot of other buddies."

"Was that your bomb that took out those buddies?" Graham asked, his face a mask of dispassion.

Tony's face crumpled. "That bloody kid snitched on them. I had no choice. We *needed* those guns."

My eyes widened in horror. *He was admitting to killing my father?* Could I pound him into the pavement? I fingered the brass knuckles in my pocket and waited for Graham to release him. One punch. Just let me have one punch—

That's when I noticed Tony's face was drooping.

"Graham, he's having a stroke," I shouted as Tony slumped.

The khaki guys jumped in to help lower the old man to the ground. One cleared Tony's throat and applied CPR, but it was obviously too late.

Could a stroke kill in a minute?

Graham looked fierce and furious, not in the least regretful. He glared at me, probably for my presence, not my interference.

He hadn't been involved in palace intrigues the way I had. In horror, I watched foam appear on Tony's lips.

"Someone needs to check the beer Tony left behind," I warned in what I hoped was a steady voice.

One of the khaki guys got up and headed inside, through the kitchen.

Graham grabbed my arm and steered me out of the alley. "We don't need to be here. Go home."

"Where are you going?" I demanded, yanking my arm away.

"The circus is waiting for you at home." He turned and walked away, talking into his phone as he went.

I'd spit on the man, but he was right. I had other obligations, and he wasn't one of them.

~

WRESTLING WITH THE KNOWLEDGE I'D JUST GAINED, I APPROACHED THE mansion I now called home. I didn't know how Graham would handle the information about the decades-old car bomb or the more recent one—especially with a dead body on his hands. The deaths of our fathers was old news to anyone but us. Reporting either bomb wouldn't accomplish much. And with Tony and Scion both dead, did it matter to us who committed the crimes? As long as Nick was safe, why should I care?

We hadn't had a chance to ask about Nadia, but I doubted that Scion would have given any employee that much insight into his dirty dealing. Tony may have owed Scion for his room and board or whatever, but I could hope the old guy had limits when it came to killing mothers. He certainly hadn't had time.

Turning the corner onto our street, I spotted an official-looking black sedan parked conspicuously in the no-parking zone in front of our house.

Oh, man, had Graham actually called the cops?

I reversed direction, returned to the circle, took a seat at a coffee shop, and pulled out my phone. The text message binged before I could sign in.

TELL ELIZABETH I'M FINE.

Magda never used our nicknames, although she occasionally called me

Ana when she *wasn't* angry, just to designate the difference. Wishing I'd drunk more of the whiskey, I waited for the rest of the text to scroll in.

I'M SURE FREDDY WILL IRON OUT THE CONFUSION. I'LL BE IN TOUCH.

I blinked, waited, and received no more. Confusion? Magda lived for chaos. A little confusion never deterred her.

Freddy? Who was Freddy?

Remembering Magda had lived in DC for the first twenty-plus years of her life and knew everyone from that time period, I had to assume Freddy was an old acquaintance.

Thinking of the car outside the house, I pinged Graham. He sent me a snarling lion instead of words. For that, I almost flung the phone across the shop. I could go watch a movie. I was a millionaire now. I didn't have to deal with Graham's testiness any longer.

But just because I preferred words to pictures didn't mean I got to bail when family called. And Graham was now my family too.

For years, he'd lived under the radar, no one even knowing he was still alive. Provided the world acknowledged his existence at all, they thought he was Thomas Alexander, owner of a security company. He did his best to keep out prying eyes—which was why he'd just left the scene to his hirelings. I was still amazed that he'd been there at all—but Tony had been a personal demon. I understood.

Since my family had moved in, Graham's private shield had developed holes. He really didn't like it when we brought in the authorities, so if that was a cop sitting at our door, chances were good he hadn't called them.

I traipsed back to the house, using the alley and the kitchen door. Mallard glared at me as I entered.

"Where have you been?" he demanded. "We cannot let officialdom interfere with our work."

"Officialdom?" I opened the refrigerator and grabbed some juice. "Local? Federal? And aren't they on our side?"

"Captain Frederick Bottom, homicide," he said as if he had a nasty taste in his mouth. "*Homicide!*"

"Ah, Freddy," I said knowingly. "I'll tell him Magda sends her regards but her dance card is full right now."

I escaped before Mallard could respond. Had he left the cop cooling his heels in his car, or in our cave of a parlor? Did I care?

Once upon a time I'd hidden in closets and basements and avoided all eyes, especially those of authority. With Magda for a mother, it had been the simplest form of self-preservation. It's a lot easier to avoid questions than to remember lies.

But I was gradually climbing out of my hiding holes and trying to teach my siblings to be law-abiding citizens. The times, they were a-changing, and all that. Greater freedom came with greater responsibility.

I hadn't changed enough to tell the cops about Tony—unless Graham already had. I was guessing from the snarling lion that he hadn't.

Wearing my black leather jacket over my usual shapeless denim dress, I debated taking the hidden stairs up to my room to change, but I wanted to meet Magda's old beau on my terms. So I strolled into Mallard's Victorian parlor looking like me and not a wealthy snot.

Since I hadn't entered the front door they'd been watching, the two men prowling the parlor appeared startled at my entrance. The one with captain's bars—I was learning the insignia—was probably in his early fifties, a little older than Magda. The detective with him was older, wore plain clothes, a paunch, and a cynical expression. I could hardly blame him.

I wasn't a genial hostess. Mallard had presumably offered them refreshments—there were coffee cups on the table. I nodded a curt greeting, said, "Gentlemen," and remained standing. Old habits die hard.

"Miss Devlin?" the captain asked, producing a business card and handing it over. "I'm Captain Bottom. We'd like to speak with your mother."

Gloves right off, fine. I tucked his card into my pocket. "Concerning what?"

"That's between her and us," the detective said, *not* handing me his card. "Just answer the question."

He was *nervous.* I almost smiled and preened like a cat. "No question was asked," I corrected. "As far as I'm concerned, you don't need my permission to speak to my mother."

The captain intervened. "This is the only address we have for her."

"You're kidding, right? Magda hasn't lived here in twenty-five years. She and my grandfather weren't on speaking terms."

"But you know where she is," the paunchy detective said belligerently. "All women talk to their mothers."

I gave him my patient sphinx smile. "Not if their mothers are dragons." I'd decided not to pass on my mother's message to *Freddy.* I didn't want my phone confiscated. "I saw my mother at Christmas when she indicated she was returning overseas." Truth, on my part, anyway.

"Do you have her current address?" the captain asked with the diplomacy that must have moved him up in the ranks.

"As I said, one doesn't disturb dragons. She could be anywhere." I pulled out the leather photo case she'd given us at Christmas and produced a note on which she'd scribbled her phone number. "This is the number she gave then. But I think it would be common courtesy to tell me why you're asking."

"We have an image of her speaking with a suspect in a murder case," the captain said, taking the paper I held.

Swell, what suspect? What murder? Did I dare ask? Why bother? I'd just look up the file later.

"And if you know my mother at all, you'll understand that's all she does —talk and charm." And find things out, pass them on, and let things happen, but they didn't need details.

"Dragons aren't charming," the detective said with a snarl.

"Dragons protect their treasure and breathe fire," I said solemnly. "Don't threaten them, and they can be anything you want them to be."

The captain almost looked amused—but then, he apparently knew Magda. "You'll let us know if she calls?"

"Probably not," I said honestly. "My business is to protect my younger siblings, and if that includes protecting their mother, I will."

The captain did smile then, and poked his unfriendly companion. "She just told you that she's a chip off the old block. Don't threaten her, and you might eventually get cooperation instead of scorched."

"Thank you for understanding, Captain." And I meant it. Most people didn't appreciate my enigmatic remarks. I'd have to respect this one. "I will gladly help where I can, but if you're not inclined to share, then you can expect the same."

He saluted me with his cap and strode for the door. I bared my teeth at the detective, who returned his most intimidating glare.

I could have told him I'd stared down rabid camels worse than him. Camels had no rules. Law enforcement was hog-tied by them. I almost felt sorry for the old dear as he stomped out. Almost.

As soon as they were gone, I ran up the stairs to tackle the snarling lion returned to his den.

CHAPTER 14

WHY WAS MY MOTHER A MURDER SUSPECT?

Hitting the third floor, I saw Graham's office door open. As I suspected, he had returned. His mode of transportation is faster than Metro, and I'd been delayed—by *cops in the parlor.* He sat there on his wheeled throne as always, not appearing in the least ruffled by my appearance, the death of our fathers' killer in his hands, or whatever had brought Captain Freddy into our safe house.

There'd been a time when Graham had roared like a wounded lion over our ability to attract the law. Was he ill or just coming to expect our talent for trouble?

"What murder? What suspect?" I demanded of our resident spy, too furious to ferret out the info on my own.

Knowing me too well, Graham punched a key and brought up a police file on one screen, a bad security camera photo on another.

I studied the image. It was hard to disguise my mother's almond-shaped eyes; they were as distinctive as mine. We didn't need eyeliner to elongate, or mascara to lengthen lashes, although Magda used cosmetics to enhance her high cheekbones and come-hither look. I was pretty sure most of her blond came from a bottle these days, but her sleek coiffure gave her an unmistakable Sophia Loren quality that bypassed me.

So, that was Magda sitting at what appeared to be an artificially battered, polished trestle table. I had no idea why people paid big bucks for a glorified picnic table, but I'd seen the architectural magazines Nick waved in my face. I'd heard about the country kitchen style. I guessed it proved they were rich enough to have space no one would ever use.

The man with her was less visible, as if he knew where the camera was placed. He looked older than Magda because he was going bald and his jaw was starting to sag, but it was impossible to tell more than that.

"Who is he?"

"Michael Moriarity," Graham answered without hesitation. "Possible heir to some portion of Scion's wealth. If there is a will, it isn't public yet, but Scion had no offspring. His sister, brother, and their families are next of kin. Michael is his nephew, on his sister's side."

"Did Scion not designate an heir-apparent, someone to take over his shares of the stock or place on the board?" Don't ask me how I knew this stuff. My research was often boring but informative.

"He evidently thought he'd live forever. Or he was paranoid and afraid a successor would kill him. Take your choice."

"With his background, I vote both. Whose kitchen is that?"

"That's the odd part. They found this footage on one of Scion's private security cameras, one not on his network, but that's not his kitchen." Graham called up an image of a gleaming stainless steel kitchen with black granite counters—and no trestle table. At least the table in the shot had a homey look. Scion's kitchen looked like a factory.

"Someone hacks his security, replaces footage, and the cops don't realize someone is framing them?" I asked in incredulity. "Captain Freddy didn't seem to be a stupid man."

"Captain Freddy?" he asked, gifting me with a glance from those sexy, deep-set eyes. "No, Bottom isn't stupid. The bulldog terrier isn't either, but he's used to intimidating gangsters and lacks finesse. That's why they sent Bottom. If your mother would simply tell them the time and place of this meeting, life would be easier."

"Magda is apparently busy bringing down Rose's campaign if I'm to judge by her phone calls from this past week. She may have been responsible for the Scion balloons as well as Miss Kitty."

"There were some of those balloons at the murder scene."

I winced but had to defend my mother. "If Magda meant to murder someone, she wouldn't leave arrogant messages. The balloons were planted just like this tape," I said dismissively. "Besides, if that was her in the Mata Hari hat, she didn't have a lot of time to race down the mountains from West Virginia to DC. If there's no real footage of her in the kitchen, they have nothing."

"Driving time, six hours," he said with a shrug. "Close, providing the coroner's time of death was accurate. The security guards didn't find Scion until a midnight shift change. Rigor mortis had just begun to set in. The cops have nothing else. Persuade Magda to talk."

At any other time, I'd have rolled on the floor in hysterical laughter at the thought of me persuading Magda to so much as peel an apple. But someone framing my mother was too creepy for laughter.

"Bottom will have to earn his reputation. I gave him her number. That's all I've got." Well, that, and my research abilities.

I turned to leave, but Graham stopped me by changing the screen and using a dire tone of warning, "Ana."

With trepidation, I looked up again. There was Old Tony the Bomber, sitting in the bar, just the way I'd left him well over an hour ago, before the confrontation with Graham. He was nursing a nearly empty mug—so it was a while after I'd left. The kid bartender was flirting with a waitress at the far end of the bar.

Old Fart was on the phone, looking concerned. He glared at the phone, stuck it in his pocket, and stomped out of sight.

"What am I looking at?" I asked. "Are we waiting for your men to show up and blow it?"

"Keep watching."

Old Fart returned with a fresh mug of beer, setting it down in front of Tony. For the first time that day, the old man brightened. He'd only taken a few sips before the guys in khaki showed up, Tony's hand jerked, and he spilled his beer.

I was a little slow. "I saw that part. They chase him out the door."

Graham zoomed in on the mug. "Thanks to the diligent bartender, the beer was gone and the mug washed before we could examine it, but the medical personnel we called think it wasn't a stroke."

Horrified into stupid, I stared as Graham replayed the scene of Old Fart glaring at his phone. "Then it really was poison? Does that mean Old Fart *knew your men were coming?*"

"The old guy wasn't there by the time we arrived. He was warned. Looks like my sources may have been hacked," Graham replied angrily. "We're dealing with professionals."

The same professionals who were setting my mother up for a murder rap? Had Tony known something about Scion's death?

~

ANA WAS TOO WELL-VERSED IN ESPIONAGE TECHNIQUES FOR HER OWN GOOD, Graham concluded after she stomped out in a fury. He'd like to blame Magda for Ana's upbringing, but reality was that her whole family had Machiavellian intelligence and too much curiosity. He supposed it was better that Ana apply her assets for the forces of good than waste her time and millions going to spas and buying jewelry.

But he'd been the one who'd given her the drug report, then dragged her into Tony's case. He'd let her see him lose his temper. He'd been holding back his fury over his father's murder for over two decades. He should have mellowed by now, but how did one forgive a murder that disrupted entire lives and kept a country at war for years longer?

It had felt good plowing his fist into the old goat's jaw. Graham flexed his bruised knuckles and still couldn't feel bad about it. He wouldn't have killed the man, no matter how much he deserved it. He hadn't anticipated someone killing Tony for him.

He could hope that the scene had been worth it so that Ana had the closure of knowing who had murdered her father and tried to blow up Nick. Maybe she'd let well enough alone now. He'd rest easier if she would go downstairs and read the comics instead of. . .

Staring at the monitor that connected with her computer, he frowned. What was she doing now? She'd opened a file called Old Fart and started digging into the bar's ownership. Damn, she had a devious mind. And unfortunately, he liked the way it worked. She had no personal interest in Tony's death, but she was doing exactly what he meant to do. She was like having an extra arm—and brain.

He had already ordered his IT people to start cleansing his servers after the Russian cyber attack. How had anyone hacked his communication with Ana or his men? He ordered IT to set up completely new IP addresses and encryption.

While others performed technical tasks, Graham clenched his molars and began systematically digging through his resources looking for an on-line mole. He had the IP path of the Russian hackers but didn't have the resources to physically knock on Russian doors once he found their nest. It didn't matter. He had other means of blasting them to hell once he found them.

⁓

GRAHAM AND TUDOR COULD HANDLE THE HACKED COMPUTER PROBLEM better than I could. I had a hard time imagining any common criminal with the capability to worm inside Graham's impregnable computer fortress, but if we were dealing with Russians hackers as Tudor had indicated. . . They apparently had nothing better to do but poke around inside US computers, admiring how the other half of the world lived, if the paranoids could be believed. Not my line of work.

I was simply irate that Old Fart had denied me the satisfaction of seeing Tony twist in the wind. I wasn't any too happy about Magda being involved in Scion's death either, but she was a big girl. As long as she didn't drag us in, I'd stay off her case.

The time and date stamp on Graham's video of his men entering the bar was barely half an hour after I'd gone outside. He worked fast.

There had been no one else in the bar besides Old Fart and Joe College. If Tony had been poisoned, they had to have done it, and since Fart had handed him the beer, it had to be him. Why?

The bar wasn't part of a chain. I traced the ownership to an LLC. *Amateurs.* It's hard to hide corporate ownership behind an LLC. Two people by the name of Ivan and Piotr Popov had filed the papers.

The names sounded vaguely familiar. I ran a search through my computer and found them in one of Graham's files about the cell tower Scion had used—the Rustel Corporation had major stockholders by the same name.

I'm very good at jumping to obvious conclusions, but I wanted more evidence before deciding Scion was funding his Russian connections in legit US businesses. It didn't make sense.

I dug out what I could on Ivan and Piotr. Old Fart hadn't had any accent that I'd noticed, although the Popovs could have been born here for all I knew. Old Fart had acted like an owner—maybe he was just management?

He'd called the bartender "my boy" and "Bill" but I didn't have anything else on either of them. I couldn't find pictures of Ivan and Piotr. Frustrated, I dug back through newspaper files, looking for grand opening stories. The bar had looked fairly new.

Yup, there we were, Old Fart proudly cutting ribbons. The caption called him general manager, Robert Estes. Beside him stood the owner, a portly old gent in a horrible plaid golf blazer, "Peter" Popov.

What the heck did I do with all these puzzle pieces?

Scion Pharmaceuticals had Eastern European connections. They hired mafia thugs like Viktor, and apparently, old IRA terrorists like Tony. Scion himself had been in the terrorism business many long moons ago.

Senator Rose had done Scion's dirty work by suppressing Guy's report, which put Rose in the pockets of terrorists as far as I was concerned. In return, Scion had been funding the PAC supporting Rose's campaign for president. Theoretically, that didn't give him the right to micro-manage Rose's platform and staff, but the media called him Rose's campaign strategist. That was a pretty close relationship.

Who was stepping into Scion's campaign job now? Too soon to tell, probably. Wouldn't it be lovely to be a flea in Rose's ear?

I pulled out my Top Hat spreadsheet from previous cases. Where did Scion fit into the wealthy cadre of corporate bullies? He'd come from an Irish slum, much like my father. Unlike Brody, he hadn't gone fundraising or mingled in my grandfather's elite circles. He just bought and sold drugs and guns like any low-level gangster.

I'd been able to trace Max's involvement with the original founders of Top Hat back to the fifties. By the mid-eighties, they'd been bringing in offspring and the newly rich. At that point, my father died, Magda fled, and Max's involvement became less clear.

Rose's father had been one of the newer members who came in after Max started fading out, if thirty years ago qualified as new.

Most of the members served on each other's boards, owned considerable amounts of each other's stock, attended the same country clubs, and funded the same conservative charities. No Planned Parenthood or ACLU donors in this bunch. They'd mostly attended the same Ivy League schools. Top Hat was a good old boys' club to beat all old boys' clubs.

A thug like Scion simply didn't fit the picture. How the heck did he get to run Rose's campaign?

The phone jarred me from my fugue state. Patra never called if she could text, so this had to be important. "They've offered you a Pulitzer prize for non-reporting," I said just to wake myself up.

"If we don't receive a Pulitzer for this Scion article, it will be because World War III has broken out," she said with excitement. "Do we get to make speeches so I can thank you for the story of a lifetime?"

"Keep me out of it," I said in genuine alarm. "I don't want people knowing my name. And Nick is the one who provided the report. He likes a little glory. What have you found?"

"I'm sending the full research to your box. But we've confirmed the addictive properties of Mylaudanix and the correlation with opium. Guy and Nadia already had the numbers on cost, which is nominal with the Middle Eastern opium connection we've verified, and sales price, which is astronomical. We've had third parties corroborate them."

"Pharmaceutical companies claim they need that profit to continue research and fund less profitable but valuable drugs," I said, quoting repeated PR articles on the subject.

"They could pay every man, woman, and child on the planet to do research with this kind of profit. What they're funding is a huge promotional campaign, pushing the drug in Third World countries as well as here. I had Zander send us his findings on Scion's investments. The promo doesn't even begin to touch the profits. Outside of advertising, the money is *not* going into Scion Pharmaceutical for research. The profits are pouring into buying weapon factories across Europe, mineral companies in Africa, oil in the Mideast—he could have started his own war."

"And into Rose's presidential campaign to buy his own government," I added, shuddering.

"So who is heir to this vast network of war machines?" Patra asked, understanding.

Reluctantly, because Patra deserved to be included, I told her about Magda and Moriarity.

She must have passed the name on to Sean. I could hear him shouting in the background.

"Tell me Moriarity isn't the new guy running Rose's campaign," I said, trying to translate Sean's shouts.

"The opposite," Patra said gleefully. "His mother is in Bill Smith's PAC.

Moriarity is a lawyer for the ACLU. The Scion family did not get together for happy holidays."

"Oh wow. Then Top Hat is gunning for *Moriarity* as well as Magda."

"And us, shortly," Patra said cheerfully. "Our first article is on the editor's desk. We're starting with Guy's report."

I'd taught myself not to swear so my younger siblings wouldn't learn to behave like uncivilized ignoramuses. But I ran through a mental list of profanity as I thought about a beautiful, intelligent young couple like Sean and Patra in the crosshairs of a bunch of ruthless greedmeisters and the Russian mafia—as our fathers had been.

"Could you take a vacation to South Africa, visit Zander?" I asked with a sigh.

"That's what Magda does when a country gets too hot," Patra reminded me. "Send her."

The phone clicked off.

Out of sheer masochism, I Googled Harvey Scion's family. Scion had grown up in war-torn Dublin. His parents had taken their younger two children to the US when teenage Harvey brought bombers to their door. Harvey Scion had stayed behind with his gang of hooligans. Well, I was reading between the lines a lot here.

In the ensuing years, Scion had made a profit off war and drugs, while his family had lived in peace in New York. In a normal world, Scion should have been a union sympathizer and supporter of the poor like his family, except he'd decided being rich was more fun. Admittedly, he had been good at it.

I had the nasty feeling that Scion had not left his fortune in the hands of his liberal, peace-loving family.

I dug through police files. Surely they'd had the sense to ask about a will since they considered Moriarity as a suspect. But all I found was the name of Scion's law firm and their refusal to cooperate. There was no record of a will filed in probate yet. I was not the level of hacker that Graham and Tudor were. I sent a request to both of them asking if they could get into the law firm's computers.

I received crickets in return.

Nick texted me a link that I clicked on out of frustration.

A mob of women wearing varicolored kitty ears marched in front of Rose's DC campaign office carrying protest signs. That made me smile. It was good to know that someone besides myself had paid attention to Gertie. I hoped Rose was frothing at the mouth—*like Tony*. I winced.

Focus, Ana. Who killed Tony the bomber, and who was framing my mother? I didn't really care who killed Scion. He deserved to die. But I didn't want my family dragged down a dirty pipeline, and I was still furious at being denied the chance to question my father's killer—and the man who tried to kill Nick.

With Scion and his IRA bomber dead, could I assume Nick and Guy were safe? Or would someone else in the company want to squash that report?

I wasn't entirely certain Patra and Sean could look after themselves any better than Nadia's kids, but killing them wouldn't stop the articles. If I was really lucky, I could let my family look after themselves and concentrate on who killed Tony and Scion and framed Magda and Moriarity.

Huh. I needed to question Robert Estes, alias Old Fart.

~

GRAHAM WATCHED WITH INTEREST AS ANA DUG OUT THE LIFE HISTORY OF Robert Estes and the Popov brothers. He'd already located the Popov's Russian passports, so he knew they weren't citizens—the reason Scion probably had his name on their business dealings. The question would be— why was he involved with the Russians? And the answer probably involved drugs and bribery, since Scion wasn't known for his big-hearted generosity.

Graham's IT people had confirmed the Rustel cell network's involvement in the hacking of his server. He saw no reason to push a hothead like Ana over the edge by filling her in on these little details. This one was personal. He wanted to handle the hackers himself.

He punched the intercom in Mallards' lair. "I'm taking down a few cell towers and their owners. Want to come?"

Mallard all but growled back. "You only go out when the job is obviously illegal. Isn't it time to grow out of that?"

"Can't send someone else to do what I wouldn't do myself," Graham retorted. "These guys are probably infiltrating the Defense Department by now."

"Then call the Defense Department."

"And wait while they dicker over costs and who does what and my security gets wiped out? I don't think so." Graham released the intercom.

He'd spent years looking for the man who'd killed his father—until Tony had been declared dead in prison. He was furious to know the bastard had been alive and well all these years. He couldn't kill Tony again, but he sure as hell could go after the bastards who'd taken away his chance to do so.

CHAPTER 15

I'D LEARNED ROBERT ESTES, THE BAR MANAGER, LIVED IN A LOWER MIDDLE class neighborhood way over in Hyattsville, an ugly commute to Bethesda every day. Apparently working for the Russian mafia didn't pay well. Of course, that was assuming the Popovs were mafia. Was I turning into a bigot or was my survival instinct speaking?

I couldn't find any correlation between all the threads I was gathering, which was making me crazy. I just didn't like that the mysterious Popovs were involved in the cell tower company that hid Scion's phone calls. That they also owned the bar where Tony may have been poisoned—after Graham's servers had been hacked—spoke volumes.

And yeah, I know I jump to conclusions, but that's how I survived to talk about them. I didn't have to collect evidence for a jury.

I wanted to go to Hyattsville, but it was getting close to time for EG to come home. I couldn't count on Mallard as babysitter, and Graham would pop a gasket if I asked.

So I called Nick to see how he was faring. He had apparently felt safe enough at the embassy to go to work.

"Guy is working from the house this week," Nick said. "He thinks he can handle picking up the kids from daycare. Maggie has done wonders, but we can't keep imposing on her."

I liked that Nick was slipping into "we," as if he really was part of a couple. I'm not a romantic, by any means, but Nick has an outgoing personality, and he needs people in his life.

"I need to run over to Hyattsville. What if I bring EG over with some carry-out so no one has to cook? Fair trade?"

Nick considered the downside of a nine-year-old evil genius added to their menagerie. "For how long?" he asked with reasonable suspicion.

"I'm just on a scouting mission. Mostly travel time. And EG can learn to babysit under adult supervision. Promise her a video with dinosaurs, and she'll probably have them in bed right after supper."

"You wield your weapons well, grasshopper," Nick said with resignation. "I'll tell Guy."

Deciding EG really did need to get out of her tower more, I didn't feel guilty in the least catching her at the door and turning her back into the cold winter gray.

"What's your favorite carry-out?" I asked, distracting her as we aimed for the Metro.

"We never have carry-out, so I don't know," she said with suspicion. "Are we going to Nick's again?"

"We are, bearing gifts of food." I glanced up as we passed the Russian ambassador's house. I felt like eyes glared down from the narrow windows.

"Kids like macaroni and cheese," EG said in disgust.

She distracted me from my ominous premonition. I had Graham and his hackers on my mind instead of little kids. *I* needed to get out more.

"Nick likes gourmet. You like chocolate. I have a plan."

We sauntered up and down the streets around Dupont and stocked up on everything from Vietnamese to falafel, throwing in a side of burgers and mac-and-cheese, with truffle oil, of course. And chocolate torte for a sugar high.

Smelling like a diner, we took the Metro up to Guy's place. I left them happily digging into the gourmet spread and returned to the nasty cold damp and the Metro.

I didn't know why I kept doing this. I could have stayed there and enjoyed the warmth and the food and the company.

But Old Fart, alias Robert Estes, had presumably killed the man who could have answered a lot of important questions, and not just about my father, although that opportunity nagged at me. Tony had been one of my dad's *pals*. He could have told me things...

Water under the bridge many long years ago. I quit crying at night when I was a toddler.

Tony's death robbed us of valuable information. He might have been able to tell us who had been involved in Nadia's accident or more about Scion, like what hold did he have over Senator Rose? If Estes had to take him out, Tony obviously had known *something*. Estes obviously wasn't just a bar manager, so I'd better play safe.

I'd made notes in my phone of the direction to the Estes house. I doubted I'd find taxis in Hyattsville, but I called up Uber as the train pulled in. The driver was young and smiley, and probably ambitious, so I'd have to bribe him to hang around once we were out in ticky-tacky box land.

When we arrived, the Estes address looked oddly abandoned. I asked the driver to wait down the block, gave him a nice tip and promised another. I never knew what I was going to do when I checked out a suspect. I was wearing my leather coat and long denim dress, so I didn't look particularly out of place here.

I decided to simply walk up to the front door and pretend I was a magazine salesperson if anyone actually answered. They might conclude I was a knock-knock thief, but they couldn't call the cops if I stole nothing. Studying the house's unlighted windows, the misaligned and drooping blinds, and the dirt patch of a yard, I didn't think there was much chance of finding anyone home.

I knocked. The door sagged open on one hinge. I peered through the crack. Worn orange furniture from the seventies had been knocked askew or left upside down with the lining ripped out. A pole lamp leaned rakishly against an ancient end table. A battered wood floor plank had been pulled out and thrown under the dirty picture window with the bent blinds.

Either Old Fart had made a hasty exit, or someone had done it for him. Not being stupid, I didn't enter a possible crime scene. I snapped photos and emailed them to Graham. If there was a body inside, his security people could find it.

Just as a precaution, I stopped at the house next door, where I saw a lace curtain discreetly inched back, as if someone was watching me. In this neighborhood, that was an excellent idea. I pushed the bell and heard it working—always a promising sign.

The door inched open on a chain lock, another sign of intelligence. I smiled at the bird-like, gray-haired woman peering through the crack. "I'm sorry to disturb you, ma'am, but I was told to deliver a letter to the address next door, but it doesn't seem to be occupied, and I'm afraid I'm in the wrong place. Do you know if Robert Estes lives there?"

"Are you a bill collector?" she asked with suspicion.

I shook my head vehemently. "Good heavens, no. I shouldn't think bill collectors would be bothering Mr. Estes. I'm one of his employees."

She narrowed her eyes but couldn't find a way around answering what might actually be a legitimate question. "He lives there as far as I know. He's hardly ever home, leaves early and back late. Come to think of it, he never has visitors either, but there were a couple of men over there a few hours ago. He doesn't usually get back to near midnight though."

I was blamed lucky to have arrived late and not when they were tearing the place apart! Who would be after Estes? Someone who hadn't wanted Tony killed? Or who had ordered him killed and now wanted to eliminate witnesses?

Eager to depart for fear the house was watched, I glanced at my phone screen. "Oh dear, I can't wait until midnight. Thank you so much! At least I know I went to the right place." I punched my Uber app as I hurried away.

With any luck, the two men who ripped apart Old Fart's house hadn't found the bar manager at home. But if Robert Estes had poisoned Tony's beer, he might be on his way to Mexico.

I'd hate to think that every person I suspected became a dead body.

~

UNDER COVER OF EARLY WINTER GLOOM, GRAHAM PULLED ON HIS GLOVES AND yanked a hood over his hair. His men had taken out the security cameras. The cell tower had no illumination other than the blinking warning lights on top. He climbed the hill containing half a dozen legitimate towers and met his engineer, similarly clad in black.

"They're definitely bouncing signals off a Russian satellite," the engineer reported. "The hackers are here in DC though, tapping into the Rustel network with private servers."

"Have we located the servers?" Graham watched from a short distance as other black clad men worked around the base of the Rustel tower.

"The signals have been funneled through servers all around the world, impossible to trace. They're taking no chances. We probably ought to notify the CIA."

"We will, after we take the tower down. Your men have figured out how to do it without harming the other towers?" Graham watched a figure climbing the metal scaffolding.

"We think so. There should be enough pieces left for the feds to find any illegal equipment."

Several figures worked around the middle of the tower. One lone figure settled on a platform and set to work.

"No way he can leave the package and come down with the others?" Graham asked, eyeing the layout dubiously.

"Top has to be pulled this way or we could disrupt coverage across half the eastern seaboard if it fell into any of those other towers. Can't take that chance."

The lower figures scrambled down almost in synchronization, waiting with Graham and his engineer until the man on top blinked his flashlight. As one, the engineer and his men dashed down the hill toward their chosen shelter.

Graham ran *toward* the tower. He'd specifically chosen this job for himself. He hadn't the expertise of the man on top, but he knew how to see he came down safely.

Flipping off his light, the man on the tower shoved off his seat. Attached to a bungee cord, he plummeted straight toward Graham. Calculating his arc, Graham braced himself, caught the heavy blow, and unclipped the cord, stopping the swing.

A loud pop sparked on the top segment. Graham and the man beside him pulled on the bungee cord as they ran for cover in a concrete equipment bunker down the hill. The top of the tower began falling toward them.

Graham hit the ground and released the cord just as three more pops shattered the silence. A moment later, pieces of metal debris rained across the frozen ground.

"Damned good job," Graham said, peering over the bunker to be certain the legitimate towers remained unharmed. "Let's notify the feds now— through the Russian's network."

The tower bomber snickered. "Want us to take out a few more?"

"They'll be expecting that. Let's not risk good men. All the feds need is a little information and then they'll do it for us, the legal way." Graham got up and jogged down the hill to join the others.

"Check your bank accounts. Your paychecks should already be there," he told the waiting crew.

"The military never paid this fast," the engineer said in satisfaction. "Call us anytime."

Graham saluted, lifted his motorcycle from the shrubbery, and rode off. He favored BMWs to Harleys, less conspicuous.

Only when he'd parked the cycle in the over-sized garage on the street behind the mansion did he turn on his phone.

He cursed at Ana's images of the ransacked house. They guaranteed that another witness had gone off the radar, maybe permanently. This was the reason he seldom left the attic—he could monitor more operations from his chair than from the field.

He sent another crew out to check the Estes house.

~

UNDERSTANDING THAT NICK NOW HAD FAMILY OF HIS OWN TO CONSIDER, I hopped a couple of trains and arrived well before EG's bedtime. They had the kids blessedly in bed, and EG was happily glued to a video of Jurassic Park, filmed well before she was born—good choice, dinosaurs and horror all rolled into one.

"I like babysitting," she said through a mouthful of popcorn.

"And she decided macaroni with truffle oil isn't too bad," Nick added, with only a slight grumpiness.

"Ate your share, did she?" I tugged EG's hair. "We leave on the dot of nine. Speed it up."

I gestured with my head at the kitchen. "I haven't eaten. Anything left over?"

They got the message and followed me out of EG's hearing. Guy generously opened the fridge while Nick waited expectantly.

"Your parking garage bomber is dead," I said flatly. "He implicated Scion, who is also dead. Guy's report will hit the paper by the end of the week. I'm going to say you should be safe now. Have you checked on Nadia lately?"

"A team of people from work are taking turns stopping by," Guy reported, inserting a container in the microwave. "If it's okay for me to leave here now, I'll do the same. Her condition hasn't changed, but her brain is still alive. The doctor said we could talk to her, keep her stimulated, but he's not making any promises. She sustained severe damage to a lot of vital parts, any of which could fail at any moment."

"She's not in ICU anymore?" I asked, already fretting about security.

"They've done all they can. They can't keep her there. She's hooked up to monitors and the nurses keep a watch. Why?" Guy handed me warmed over falafel in pita bread, heaped with goodies.

I noodled around with my concerns as I chewed. ""Because Nadia kept secrets," I decided. "Why did she help you with this project?"

"Because I asked?" he said, doubt creeping into his voice.

"Nadia has an ex selling Mylaudanix in Eastern Europe, so she investigates his profits?" I ate falafel and let him stew over that a while.

"We met online in a discussion of Mylaudanix. I mentioned wanting to do a report on the chemical composition and asked for information." He hesitated, then said, "She volunteered to run the numbers."

"I think she had an agenda, which means she could very well have more information than we know. I haven't really looked into the contents of her computer because they're meaningless to me. You might want to take a closer look." I was starved and bit off another hunk, letting Guy ponder while I munched.

Knowing me well, Nick stepped in. "What set you down this path?"

I finished chewing and sipped the wine he'd poured for me. I wasn't fond of wine but this one worked oddly well with fried beans. "The bomber who killed my father and tried to kill you died today, probably of unnatural causes, may the devil eat his rotten heart. He claimed he was hired by Scion to bomb Guy. He may have died because he knew too much about whoever ordered the bombing, or failure was not an option. Who knows how the mind of evil works? All I know is that the man who may have poisoned him has disappeared. Scion is dead. *So there has to be someone out there besides Scion running the show.*"

Guy whistled. Nick asked, "Russians?"

"Can't say. How long was Nadia in the Ukraine?"

"She wouldn't work with the Russians," Guy said in alarm. "She was raised here. She has security clearance. You can't—"

I held up my hand and put the wine glass down. "That's not what I was thinking. I'm thinking she saw something over there that set her down this path. How dangerous would that something be?"

"Nadia's laptop," Nick muttered, catching on. "They took Nadia's laptop. If there was anything dangerous in it that mad Russians want. . ." He already had his phone out, punching numbers.

"Until he solves his hacking problem, I'll have to wait to tell Graham in person. I don't know if he has enough men for twenty-four hour security around Nadia on top of everything else that's popping." I checked my watch. "Sorry to pass on the bad news, but I've got to get EG home."

"You really think the guy who bombed our car was the same one who took out your father?" Nick asked in concern before I left.

"Same type bomb and he as much as admitted it. Scion was former IRA, a was my father, and they knew the bomber back in the day. It makes sense."

"You didn't have a chance to ask questions?" Nick knew what that meant to me.

I shrugged. Nothing would ever fill the hole my father's death had left. I at least now knew why and who. "He was old and unreliable. At least we know more."

"Is there any chance the hackers know we have the contents of Nadia's computer?" Guy asked worriedly.

Graham's heavily secured computers had been relentlessly hacked until someone had broken through his security. Graham's computers were connected to mine. And the contents of Nadia's computer had been in both of them. Guy's enemies could now be focused on my home.

Oh double filthy crap.

I stormed out with EG under a black cloud of fear and fury.

CHAPTER 16

ONCE WE WERE BACK AT THE MANSION, I SENT EG OFF TO BED, THEN RACED upstairs. Graham met me at his office door and hauled me back to the bedroom.

I was becoming really addicted to these interludes of Graham's sexual prowess, but I had to wonder what had set him off this time. Adrenaline and frustration were our usual triggers. I wasn't arguing. I needed this too.

After we got ourselves hot and sweaty, we took a long shower where we worked off more steam. Collapsing into bed, I summoned the effort to plant my elbows on his hardened chest. "What did you do now?"

"The hackers were using Rustel's towers," was all he gave me in explanation.

I fell back on the rumpled sheets to ponder all the implications left unsaid. "Are the Popovs really Russian then?"

"Da," he answered grumpily, turning his back on me.

I punched his shoulder blade and he grunted. "Then you'd better have a pharmaceutical expert take a look at Nadia's files, because the Russians now have access to them." I hadn't had time to dig through Nadia's less than meticulous files. I had a feeling she had deliberately concealed the contents with the hodge-podge.

"They have the files in the laptop," he said less grumpily, following my train of thought.

"If there's anything dangerous in there, they may still want to take out Nadia."

"And us." He growled, turned over, and planted his arms over me. "I hate it when you do that."

Since he leaned over and kissed me thoroughly, I considered that a mixed message.

~

TUESDAY MORNING, I DECIDED IF NADIA'S COMPUTER HAD PUT HER AND MY entire family in danger, I had to keep going after Scion's Russian connections, even if Scion was dead.

Of course, opening my phone at the breakfast table to a text from Patra provided different distraction. ROSE IMPLICATED IN SCION'S DEATH read the headline. In smaller headlines: Heir Provides Evidence of Blackmail.

My eyes bugged out. I didn't believe screaming media headlines often, but this one deserved a happy dance. I so seldom got to read good news.

The headline at least explained what Magda was doing with Moriarity—looking for dirt. The big question was—what did any of this have to do with my father's death? Or guns. The men behind those two obsessions were all Magda fixated on. She might trade information or tasks to obtain what she wanted, but after she'd blown up GenDef's weapon stores last month — GenDef had sold weapons to my dad and Tony—I'd finally accepted that it was all about vengeance.

I scanned the article, then read again for details while EG slurped cereal at the end of the table.

The only real implication was the blackmail. There was utterly no other evidence that the senator had killed his campaign fat cow. So this was the usual media smear campaign. I wasn't complaining. Rose needed to be smeared. But I really liked a few facts with my hysteria.

From what I could gather from this article—I really wanted a red pen to edit all the indefinite pronouns—Rose had borrowed money from Scion to pay off Gertrude all those many years ago.

After EG finished eating and left to get ready for school, I called Patra. She actually answered. "Fun stuff, huh?" she answered with glee, knowing I'd just read the article.

"Let me run this theory past you. Tell me where my logic fails." Patra politely waited, so I rearranged my thoughts and did a quick timeline. "Scion was more Mallard's age than my father's, right? So when my father was buying guns and Rose was boffing Gertrude. . . Scion was already making his fortune in drugs and war."

"Sounds about right," Patra agreed. "According to the article," she stopped, apparently to skim through it. "At the time, *Scion was a salesman attempting to make contacts with Paul Rose's wealthy inner circle.*"

"Way to gloss over details, people," I complained. "I translate that as Scion needed Rose's wealthy father or Top Hat or both for nefarious purposes. Paying off Gertrude put Rose Junior right in Scion's pocket."

"But why would Scion need Rose's father and Top Hat? Scion already had wads of cash, and he wasn't exactly good old boy material," Patra argued, playing my devil's advocate.

"Because Rose's father had something Scion wanted besides money. Scion had just bought the guns my father had tried to refuse. Rose's father had. . . coal mines? For storing *weapons*," I cried in excitement.

"Your mind leaps like a grasshopper," Patra grumbled. "And you might just be right."

I saw EG off to school and ran down to my computer, where I looked up Rose's father. In the 1980s, his coal mines were still booming, but one had recently been shut down for health and safety violations—therefore there were no workers inside. They had a train right there to offload and upload goods, with tracks that connected to shipyards all up and down the east coast.

Rose Senior had a hole in his budget and Scion had a way to fill it.

After a quarter of a century, I doubted we could find anyone to testify that trains ran to an empty coal mine or that they stored boxes of ammunition and weapons, but *my* curiosity was satisfied on that point.

If Rose had been directly involved in storing and transporting illegal weapons, Scion had a hold over him, not a huge one, but it was probably the start of Rose's relationship with the dirt bag. Over the next quarter of a century of Rose's political career, I'm sure there had been opportunity for more dirt to accumulate.

And really, unless another member of Top Hat was turning snitch, only Magda and Moriarity could possibly have revealed any of this. Magda would most certainly have followed the weapon trail from the moment of my father's death. Moriarity might have had access to the family papers to confirm some portion of it.

Oh, jolly fun. I could almost appreciate my mother's insane perseverance —now that I didn't have to live with it.

I toyed with Tony's odd comment about the "bloody kid" snitching on my father. Rose would have been a kid to him at that point. Graham knew more than I did about that period. I emailed him: *If Rose was looking for someone to help him pay off Gertrude—would he have known my father?*

I got a laconic: *Yup*, in reply. I glared but didn't disturb him more.

Fine, if Rose knew my father, he might have heard that Brody was looking for a way to end the weapon deal. If Rose had snitched that news to Scion so he could make nice with the powerful men in Top Hat, they'd have easily concluded my father and his friends were expendable.

And my mother knew that. Magda would have known about Rose and Tony, just as she'd known about Gertrude.

I didn't have time to yell at my mother or gloat over the pieces of Rose's platform toppling. I had other plans. My brain processes a lot while I'm sleeping, and I had a whole new to-do list to start my day.

Someone with technical know-how had knocked off Scion. I wanted to find that person. I had the gut feeling he could split open this rock hanging over our heads and spill gold. I needed to know who Scion had called the night he died, if he'd been expecting company.

It had belatedly occurred to me that I might have Tony's phone number, if he hadn't made up the one on the napkin. Tony's phone might contain Scion's private numbers. I checked police files, and they didn't find a phone on Tony's body.

I dug through Graham's neatly categorized videos and found the one dated for yesterday and labeled with the name of the bar. I ran it again. There was Tony at the bar, empty glass in front of him—shortly after I'd left and he'd given me his number. He pulled a phone from his pocket and glanced at it, then set it on the bar—waiting for my fake uncle to call? It was still there when the men in khaki arrived and Tony ran, *leaving the phone on the bar.*

Graham hadn't copied the rest of the tape, but my bet was that Bill the Bartender had flung the phone in a lost and found after he washed the mug. He struck me as that kind of neatnik.

The coroner's report on Tony hadn't been filed yet, so the cops weren't actively suspecting murder. Tony was a smoker and obviously not in the best of shape. They'd have better things to do than investigate a possible heart attack. So they hadn't seen this video or looked for the phone.

With Tony's record, the cops had no reason not to believe whatever lies Graham's security crew had told. Authorities still didn't know Tony had worked for Scion. Naughty Graham. But naughty Graham was providing the security protecting Nadia, so I couldn't quibble.

Since it was too early for the bar to be open so I could look for Tony's phone, I called the other number I'd collected that day, the one for Scion's housekeeper. I hoped she spoke a language I might stumble around in a bit. The person who answered sounded young and spoke fine English.

"Hi, my name is Linda Lane." That was my alias of choice today. "Ursula gave me this number for Maria. She said she might be available for house-keeping?"

"In what part of the city?" the young voice asked crisply.

All I had was Nadia's place, now Guy and Nick's. Heaven only knew, they needed help. Since they now had security out the wazoo, we could spy on her if she decided to spy on them. Keep your friends close and your enemies closer and all that. "Upper Northwest," I said. "Not far from the Metro."

"How many rooms?"

I wanted to be the one doing the interrogating. Dang. "It's not a large house. Three small bedrooms and a family room, plus the usual. Are you Maria?"

"No, I am her daughter. I help her. Her English is not so good. Will that be a problem?"

The name sounded Spanish, but the daughter had the slightest hint of accent that didn't. I threw a wild guess anyway. "If she speaks Spanish or French, I'll be fine."

"Russian," the daughter said crisply. "But I can translate."

Oh my my. We were really going to have to spy on this one. I kept that thought to myself. "Good to know. Are you interested? I can meet you at the house today."

We made an arrangement to meet at Nadia's place in an hour. It was north of here, so I could travel on to Bethesda after. I called Nick and warned him of what I was up to.

"Espionage and housekeeping in one blow, nice multitasking," he said with cynicism. "We'll be certain not to bring any secrets home. Any clue as to who blew up one of Rustel's cell towers last night? There are rumors flying all over the office, and I'll get a gold star if I can produce a credible theory."

Cell tower? I remembered Graham's adrenaline overload last night, connected it to his fury with the hackers, and opened door number two. "Let us assume the Russian stockholders used Rustel for nefarious purposes, and they hacked the wrong server."

Nick and I had learned to speak in riddles back in the day when anything we said was overheard. We could figure his office was tapped. He knew I was talking about Graham and my theory was credible. The Brits didn't need to know that, although they'd probably hired Nick for just this reason.

"Rustel—Russian telephone?" Nick connected the dots quickly. "I like it. The feds are reportedly crawling all over the other towers this morning, so something is up. Rustel's office has been cleaned out. Mission accomplished."

If taking out the hackers was the mission, yup, but I wish I could have dug into Rustel's records first. There was the little matter of Scion's missing phone to start with.

Graham had demolished a cell tower? Wow. He worked fast. Pity he couldn't take out the hackers while he was at it. Hackers got nasty when thwarted. If anyone could handle them, it would be Graham.

Unless I wanted to dig further into my father's files or Magda's phone calls, I didn't have a lot of other leads. I wasn't optimistic about cell tower demolishment stopping anyone who would try to murder a mother and chemist and anyone in their vicinity.

Since the weather had turned colder, I'd dressed in leggings under a black wool ankle-length skirt that concealed my furry boots. For fun, I donned my leather spotted furry hat that only needed ear muffs to look Russian. I still wore my leather coat over my sweater, though. I didn't want to play wealthy sophisticate by wearing my matching faux leopard coat.

I took the Metro to Nadia's place. Guy was still working there, but Nick had warned him I was coming. Gauging by the level of disarray in the front room, I was at least accomplishing a good deed by bringing in a house-keeper. We'd just have to watch out for wire taps.

Maria and her daughter Lillian arrived on schedule. Maria was short and chunky and wrapped up like a babushka doll, but Lillian was in her early twenties, polished and svelte. While Maria exclaimed over the chaos in mixed English and Russian, Lillian and I followed her around.

"Ursula said all Mr. Scion's employees received good references from his lawyers," I said while Lillian jotted notes. "As you can see, my brother needs all the help he can get. Would you have the contacts for Scion's gardeners and handymen?"

"Maria has all that in the little phone he gave her," Lillian said absently, examining a drapery falling off a rod. "She kept his house running. She is very good. Perhaps we cost too much for a place like this? There are children, yes?"

"The children are the reason my brother needs help. He and Guy can't afford what Mr. Scion paid, I'm sure, but the house is much smaller. They don't have room for live-in help, but someone who can occasionally cook would be good." I was improvising madly, hoping to find out more about the phone. It all came back to the wretched phones.

She nodded and jotted more notes. "Mr. Scion had his own cook. We could call her. But if Mama comes three days a week, she could prepare a hot meal those days."

Guy popped out of his office. "That would be ideal," he said in relief. "I could go into the office those days and work here the other two."

I left them discussing arrangements and followed Maria into the master, where she was studying the toiletries strewn over the vanity and shaking her head. Nadia may have lived simply, but Guy and Nick were spoiled single men with money to spare.

Out of sight of Lillian, I took out my phone and gestured at Maria's. "We should exchange phone numbers," I enunciated as clearly as I could.

She nodded and carelessly handed over her treasure trove. There were only half a dozen contacts in it. I sent them all to my phone and left Nick's number in hers. Without a search warrant, the police couldn't do this. I had a purpose in life as a cockroach.

I left Maria compulsively sorting men's hair products from hygiene products and putting them into drawers. That would teach the slobs to buy baskets and sort things out themselves. Bathrooms had shelves for a reason.

"I have another appointment," I told Guy and Lillian, who were happily ticking off check boxes on a list. "Make sure you exchange phone numbers."

Guy gave me a thumbs up. Lillian offered an absent nod of dismissal.

That kind of focus would take the kid far someday. I let myself out and trotted back to the Metro, my good deed done. I'd look up the phone numbers I'd just stolen when I got home, but right now, the only number I needed was Tony's. Had Scion given him a handy-dandy private phone too? I knocked wood and sent wishes to the heavens.

Joe College wasn't behind the bar when I arrived in Bethesda. The waitress from the other day was there, chatting up early lunch customers. I took a table near the corridor I knew led to the kitchen and office, ordered tea, and pulled out my phone. Holding my breath, I punched in the contact I'd labeled with Tony the Bomber's number.

I nearly toppled in surprise when I actually heard it ring. I hadn't really expected this to work, so I wasn't prepared. The waitress looked up to see what was ringing. I got up and jogged toward the restroom corridor calling, "I found it! I thought I'd left it here."

A customer called for a refill and the waitress shrugged. With no other wait staff available, she couldn't do much more.

The office door wasn't locked. The room looked as if a hurricane had struck it, but my interest was in the stack of phones I discovered in the desk drawer. I grabbed the ringing one, switched it off, and stuck it in my pocket. I really wanted to take the rest but couldn't justify it.

I knew I walked a fine line between seeking justice and criminal behavior when I pulled stunts like this.

I worried that the phones would disappear before the police decided Tony's death justified a search warrant. Estes apparently hadn't considered them important enough to take when he'd fled.

I returned to my tea and waited until the waitress came over to ask if I wanted more.

"The half sandwich and cup of soup sounds good. I'd like to thank Mr. Estes for saving my phone for me. When will he be in?"

"He lost an old friend yesterday, said he was taking some time to help the family. Bill should be in at noon. He can pass on the message. You want beef or tuna?"

"Tuna and chowder, please. I'll leave a note, thanks. Do a lot of people lose their phones here?"

"Yeah, but everyone has those tracking apps now. You oughta see if yours has it." She trotted off to wait on a new customer.

Should I wait for Bill the Bartender?

I opened Tony's phone and studied his contact list. I couldn't expect labels like *Scion's private cell* or *Hired Assassin*. I grimaced at contacts called *Chink* and *Spic*. A real charmer had been Tony, unless Scion had labeled the contacts. Huh.

Ruskie leapt out at me. Russian? The Popovs maybe?

That decided it. I was taking this new treasure trove to my dragon's lair to tear apart and find the gold I needed to nail Nadia's would-be killers.

I hurriedly ate my mediocre lunch and left for home. I wanted to be somewhere safe when I started calling assassins.

CHAPTER 17

GRAHAM LEANED BACK IN HIS CHAIR AND STUDIED THE VIDEO LINK OF ONE OF his men interrogating a visibly shaken and tired Robert Estes. The bar manager wasn't a very good fugitive. If the police had been looking for him, they would have had him before he reached Virginia.

"Estes claims that Tony always said he was never going back to prison, that he carried a poison capsule on him at all times," Jack, one of his security employees, said into the speaker.

"So why did Estes run then?" On his other monitors, Graham caught a glimpse of Ana entering the bar Estes managed. Not seeing anyone dangerous in the vicinity, he scanned his other monitors and clicked his keyboard to change scenes. He loved watching Ana at work too much. Better that he spend his time on more useful prospects.

"Popovs," Jack said. "He's terrified of them. He figured the cops would be ransacking the place and the owners would blame him. Apparently people the Popovs don't like disappear. He told the bartender to run too, but the kid has classes and refused. He's hiding with friends somewhere."

Popovs made people disappear? Nadia hadn't precisely disappeared, but close enough. Graham glowered at his monitor and switched back to watching Ana work Popov's bar. "And Estes knows nothing about Tony's work for Scion?" Graham asked.

"He thought Tony worked for the Popovs as well as Scion. Said Tony complained the Russians stank of sausage, and Scion's aftershave polluted the limo. Estes is one of those guys who takes everyone at face value. Not a deep thinker. He just figured Tony cared more for his car than his employers."

"Does he know the connection between Scion and the Popovs?"

His operative shrugged. "All he knows is that the bar makes loan payments to a company he *thinks* Scion owns, just like a mortgage payment. After the employees and bills are paid, the Popovs skim off the rest. They complain if Estes hires too much help, so our boy has been holding back on them, giving them the same amount every week and tucking cash away to improve the place. I figure that's the main reason he's antsy. He says they usually come in on Mondays to skim off their share, but he was gone before their usual arrival time yesterday. We haven't checked the bar's security video yet."

"I'll do that, thanks." Graham opened the bar camera cloud account again. The manager's house had been trashed by the time Ana had arrived in early evening. That meant the disgruntled Popovs could have left the bar empty handed in early afternoon and hunted down the manager at home. They could have tossed the place hunting for their money or clues to the manager's location. "So Estes has no addresses, no phone numbers, no means of reaching the Popovs if needed?"

"Just Tony. I think he saw Tony as a friendly safety wall between him and the Russians."

"Charming friends he keeps. Which brings up another matter—did Tony have any friends? Where did he live?"

"He was staying at Scion's place, but he's been living in his car since the cops moved in. The only friends of Tony's that Estes would recognize are from the bar. We can probably locate the car and search it."

"Yeah, that would be good. Offer Estes a safe house until this is settled. Station someone at the bar to watch for anyone who might be the Popovs." Saying that gave him a cold chill. Was that what Ana was doing? "Follow. Don't interfere," he told his operative.

"Will do." Jack signed off.

Keeping one eye on Ana playing with her phone, Graham scanned the bar's Monday security footage.

There was no camera in the corridor covering the office door. The camera over the register showed only employees. The camera over the front entrance displayed an increasingly steady stream of customers as the day wore on. Graham had the one facial image of Piotr Popov that Ana had found to run through the software, but it found no matches.

He had better luck with the camera over the kitchen exit. He didn't find a match with the photo of Piotr, but a portly older man wearing a badly fitted suit came in the kitchen door . Most of the kitchen staff was young and wore aprons and hats to cover their hair. The businessman stood out. He entered the corridor where there were no cameras, then came back not long later, looking unhappy.

Graham captured the image and saved it to his files, then checked the parking lot camera. The unhappy suit climbed into a black limo that looked a lot like the one Tony had been standing by at the parking garage.

Graham caught an image of a partial plate and sent it for tracing. Then he returned to see what Ana was doing in real time.

She was walking out of the bar wearing a smug expression and looking at a phone that wasn't hers.

He suffered a little frisson of fear every time she looked like that. At the same time, his pulse raced. He blamed it on anticipation, but he didn't define for what.

He left notes in her cloud account, along with the photo of not-Piotr.

∾

I HURRIED HOME WITH MY TREASURE TROVE AND AN AGENDA. IDEAS WERE perking.

Whoever had killed Scion had cut out the security footage in his kitchen security camera. That was an indication that someone had been in the house when Scion went outside. Mr. X then replaced evidence of his intrusion with the film of my mother and Moriarity talking. I'm sure he thought he was clever, but the replacement simply verified that someone had been there and erased the evidence. That was the work of someone who wanted to brag, not a professional.

I was going to guess the Popovs or Rose were the most likely suspects for hiring an arrogant assassin. People of that age weren't likely to have the tech know-how to replace video footage, but with their level of experience and wealth, they could have hired anyone. I just didn't quite grasp their motives for blowing Scion away after all these years. Surely his wealth and influence balanced out any blackmail schemes?

I studied my two newly acquired lists of phone contacts. I didn't expect to find murderous employees in Tony's or the housekeeper's phones. What I wanted was *Scion's* number.

I gave the lists to one of Graham's contacts who had more resources than I had, and occupied my wait time by hunting through the contents of Nadia's computer. I systematically worked my way through, file by file, removing the uninteresting ones to a portable drive until I'd reached files with more obscure information. Anything that looked remotely chemical, I sent to Guy for translation. Anything that looked financial, I sent to Zander.

As far as I was concerned, the road to hell was paved with data. It was too late to send Scion down it, but I hoped to find his partners in crime and push them down my information highway.

The phone person sent me a list of names to match the numbers in Tony and Maria's phones. Maria's were mostly innocuous—plumbers, handymen, etc. One number came back as belonging to Rustel.

Tony's phone was a little more mysterious. The one labeled *Mick* matched the Rustel number in Maria's. Was that his designation for Scion? Did old comrades call each other Mick? Yuck.

The other numbers, including the *Ruskie* one, traced back to Rustel, too. Dang.

So, if the feds were now digging into Rustel. . . could they identify these numbers? I pondered that for all of half a second and the answer was no, not with prepaid phones, not unless Rustel kept records of who they sold the phones to. I sent an inquiry to Graham, but I didn't hold much hope. The point of prepaid phones was to hide ownership—which was probably also the point of Rustel.

So my next step was to see if these numbers went to phones with GPS. I had taken the GPS out of my burner because way too many applications log into it, and I don't trust the setting that says "turn off GPS."

I'd learned most people don't even know the setting is there.

Tracking calls required access to cell tower records and got complicated, as I'd discovered with Magda's numbers. Tracking *phones*. . . If they had GPS, there were a multitude of ways, including social media. I couldn't imagine Scion using Facebook, but I also couldn't imagine him knowing how to turn off his GPS function.

I dove down the rabbit hole of spy sites used to keep track of the phones of rebellious kids and cheating spouses. It was amazing how many ways one can track someone's phone. Since I'd not implanted any devices, I had to choose the hard way.

Using a website I found, I gave them the Rustel/Mick number that I suspected belonged to Scion. I used Tony's phone to text a message to it. If anyone answered. . .

They did! *Someone had the phone.* The website had just located it in the vicinity of Scion's home when I heard EG returning. Childcare interfered with serious sleuthing.

Most of the time, I didn't mind, but I really wanted to find what could be Scion's missing phone. If there was another killer out there, I wanted Nadia and my family safe. The only way I knew was to find the X factor who had killed Scion and possibly sent Estes running. I had no evidence that Scion was shot by the same person who tried to kill Nadia with a car, but I knew there had to be a connection. None of this made any sense otherwise.

Until I found the killer, we were all sitting on an explosive minefield that could go off now or the minute Patra's story broke.

I headed for the stairs. EG didn't need me to bring her milk and cookies, but kids needed someone they could talk to. Magda wasn't that someone. And since I was here and Nick and Patra weren't, the responsibility came down on me.

Now that we were no longer living in a war zone, I accepted the child-care responsibility I'd rejected when I'd escaped my mother's net. As long as no more kids were getting blown up on my watch, I could handle normal childhood dramas.

EG came in carrying an enormous stuffed dinosaur I was pretty sure she hadn't left with that morning.

"You're planning on making it anatomically correct?" I suggested as I met her before she escaped to her room.

"Dinosaurs do not have fur," she said in indignation. "Teachers are encouraging ignorance to even suggest that they are cuddly."

"So you stole the cuddly dinosaur and will replace it with what?" I knew my sister well.

"I found a model for a Velociraptor online. I just need sixty-nine dollars plus shipping. It has real-looking claws and teeth." Beneath her currently blue bangs she looked fierce and determined. "We have money now. It should be used to promote education and eradicate ignorance."

She wasn't quite ten but she's talked like this since she uttered her first word, I swear. Well, maybe she focused on things like bad milk at the time, but she's scary smart. I wanted to encourage her better qualities, like eradicating ignorance. But expecting money to fall off trees. . . I'd scraped by all my life. It's character building.

"Sixty-nine dollars will cost you ten hours of babysitting. Or maybe Mallard can find something for you to do. In the meantime, why don't you use cardboard to glue scales on that thing?"

I hadn't told her no, so she pondered my suggestions. "When do I start getting an allowance?"

She was negotiating. I was proud. "When you start contributing to society or family. None of us receives an allowance yet. We need a family meeting first, and giving back is the first part of the discussion."

She frowned but accepted the verdict. "Okay, where can I find cardboard? And when does Nick need a babysitter?"

I directed her to Mallard's recycle bin and promised to call Nick to schedule babysitting time. Since that mostly meant he'd be babysitting EG while she learned to deal with the kids, I needed him on the same page.

After I explained what I'd promised, dutiful Nick agreed to a trade-off. "Bring her over here and we'll look after her until seven. Then you come in for a few hours, put the kids to bed, and let us go out for an adult meal. Fair?"

"Very much so, thank you!" I almost crowed. That would give me time to hunt down the phone I hoped belonged to an evil drug lord.

EG happily packed up her dinosaur, cardboard, and paste, and we tootled up to Nadia's place. Guy had just brought home the little ones from daycare, and they gleefully tackled EG. Well, Anika did. Vincent merely dumped his day's griefs on her. EG pulled a book out of her backpack, Guy provided cookies, and they were all happy.

I ran back out and hopped the next train to Bethesda. It was rush hour and nasty crowded, so I called Sam and asked if he'd have time to pick me up in time to get me back to Nick's by seven. He agreed, which gave me a little more time to explore.

I hated relying on paid drivers for myself, but for others. . . I'd learn how to play spoiled rich girl.

The GPS locator I'd used had provided an address partially between Scion's mansion and the Popov bar, two streets away. I'd think the killer flung the phone into the bushes but someone had to answer it to make the locator work. Or, more likely, was the locator slightly off? For all I knew, the number belonged to Popov or Bill the bartender or anyone, but I was placing my bet that Scion's menials would have a number to reach him, and that this was it.

I really hoped the phone wasn't in the late drug lord's mansion. Until now, breaking and entering hadn't been on my list of insane acts. Generally, I drew the line at criminal action. Besides, if the phone was in the mansion, then it wouldn't lead me to a killer. I would just let Graham know about it so he could have the police locate it. A phone only menials called probably wasn't important.

I wanted it to be the phone he'd had in his hand when he was killed, the one that had disappeared.

I found the address indicated in the locator on the street between the mansion and the bar. I'd found a charger for Tony's phone, so it was fully operational as I tentatively called the Rustel contact labeled *Mick* in his list, then listened. This was a normally quiet neighborhood of high-end mansions, but it had a fair amount of traffic at this hour. The address indicated was an empty lot, though. I tried the number several times while walking up and down the street. I heard nothing that might be a phone ring. Would I hear it if it rang behind thick hedges and iron gates?

How many times had that phone rung after Scion died? Maybe it had given one last gasp and now the battery was dead? Tony's still had some juice when I found it, but that meant nothing. I trotted toward Scion's mansion, stopping to call occasionally. Nothing. I wasn't certain if I'd hear it ring inside the house, but maybe in the yard. . . I walked around and tried it again. Nada.

Dang. I'd told Sam to meet me at the bar. I took a back street over there, occasionally hitting redial and listening. I'd had so much hope for this number. . . Back to research.

I really didn't think a wimp like Estes would be a killer, so I held out little hope for the bar. I couldn't see old guys like the Popovs sneaking into the mansion, shooting Scion, stealing his phone, replacing the video in the camera, then tossing the evidence into the lost and found in an unprotected drawer. They didn't strike me as that smart or that stupid.

But when I walked into the bar's parking lot and hit redial, I heard the phone ringing through the open kitchen door. A male voice cursed, and the ringing stopped. I looked down at my phone. The call had been disconnected.

That proved nothing, but I shivered. Did I dare walk in now and see who was holding a phone? The place was loud and noisy and all the sweet young things probably had a phone in hand.

I was torn. I really wanted to look inside, but I knew how dangerous it was to show my face after making that number ring. It would be safer to send one of Graham's security guys over.

I was relieved to see Sam trotting out from the bar, making the decision for me. He headed for a discreet black Lincoln and not the enormous limo. I caught up with him, still clutching the phone and seriously worried.

"Sorry, bathroom break," he apologized, holding the door for me. "I thought I was early."

"You are. I just reached a dead end." I climbed into the still warm car but continued to shiver. "You didn't happen to notice anyone with a ringing phone, did you?"

Sam has Asian eyes, dark coloring, and kinky hair. He cast me a look of disbelief through those narrow eyes and started the car. Oh well, I had to try.

If Scion's phone was in the bar, did that mean the *killer* was in there now? We knew Tony was a killer. I hadn't thought him capable of the Scion murder, but maybe two killers had frequented the bar?

Who was the second?

CHAPTER 18

Nick and Guy were ecstatic to see me. As long as Sam was there, they commandeered the car for the evening. I waved at the security camera over their door, knowing Graham had access to the camera files even if he didn't happen to be watching at that moment. He never joined us for dinner, so I felt no guilt in leaving him alone.

The kids had already eaten. I warmed up leftovers from the refrigerator for myself. It appeared to me that Mallard had been sending over casseroles. I couldn't imagine Nick preparing curried potato tart with cilantro, although I suppose Guy might have. It probably got boring for Mallard to cook only for Graham, or even just EG and me.

For Christmas, I'd bought Mallard a share of his favorite Irish pub, using our family funds since he catered to all of us. I hoped he spent his spare time teaching their kitchen help how to cook. The last time I'd eaten there, it had been pretty disgusting.

We sat at the kitchen table and finished coloring and gluing cardboard scales on the furry dinosaur and laughing. Vincent and Anika plastered more glue on themselves than the dinosaur, so EG and I scrubbed them down and wriggled them into jammies. I was kind of getting into this normal family life thing—until they asked if they'd ever see their mommy again, which slayed me.

I needed to be looking for a killer, not babysitting needy kids. But

Graham had security on Nadia at the hospital, and I was here doing family time. I had to quit worrying about Nick and Patra. They were adults now. I tried to tell myself the killer might not know that we had Nadia's data and that they were safe.

And maybe birds don't fly, but I just wanted normal for a little while. Until six months ago, I'd been a hermit. I wasn't ready for full scale, insanely difficult detective work outside my computers. I'd scared myself a bit by hearing what was presumably a murdered man's phone at the bar.

I'd texted Graham with the information about the phone's location, so I hoped his men were looking into it. My best guess was that Tony had somehow come across Scion's phone and thrown it in the drawer with all the others—after scrubbing off his prints, of course. That wouldn't help us find a killer.

Sam returned with Guy and Nick and took me and EG home. It was dark and cold and no time to be on the streets, so I didn't argue with the arrangement. He watched until we entered the house.

Inside, I sent EG up to bed. Then I trudged up to find Graham at his desk, as always.

Looking weary, he actually stood up, took me in his massive arms, and kissed me. He never did that without my teasing, so I totally appreciated the moment. I melted into him. It had been a long day, but I'd take this reward for my efforts any time.

"Jack didn't find the phone in the drawer," he murmured, lifting me and carrying me off to bed. "Someone in that bar is carrying it or has hidden it and may be Scion's killer. We're tracking it now."

"You're still hiding Estes?" I asked, tensing.

"No, he decided he wanted to return to work." He laid me down on the lovely comfy mattress. "Don't go near him again."

I liked it when he wasn't mad at me for a change. Nibbling his ear, I allowed myself to be undressed as if I were helpless. It was a shocking change from my first thirty years of life. Well, last twenty-five maybe. I was probably a cuddly toddler.

If the phone wasn't in the drawer. . . Besides Estes, who else would have access? Maybe one of the Popovs had picked it up? That would mean they could be sitting in the bar right now. . .

Let them sit. I had better things to do.

~

WEDNESDAY MORNING I WAS ACTUALLY FEELING BRAVE ENOUGH TO OPEN ONE of the newspapers that regularly appeared on the breakfast table. Magda hadn't sent me any more mysterious messages and the good captain hadn't bothered me again, so I was hoping the police had found better targets.

And boy howdy, had they! I stared in disbelief, then nearly cackled as I read the headline story.

As heirs-apparent, Michael Moriarity and Scion's other nieces and nephews had been given access to the CEO's office at Scion Pharmaceutical. The police still wouldn't let them into Scion's house, but someone had to run the company while the board of directors waffled. Stockholders demanded leadership and all that, and Scion's block of voting stock held the majority.

Besides, they were all hoping to uncover a will—and they had, or at least a draft.

The Moriaritys had shown reporters a document file they had located in Scion's office. The letterhead was from a different lawyer's office than Scion normally used—one in Ireland where the drug company was based and Scion still had citizenship. The file included an unsigned draft of a will, hand-annotated by Scion, leaving *Senator Paul Rose* his stock in the drug company. It divided up the remainder of his holdings between various names I recognized from the Top Hat organization—cutting off his family entirely.

Not a cent to charity, naturally. Scion had essentially handed his war machine to Top Hat and his drugs to Rose, and the newspaper was having a fabulous time hinting all around the fact that Rose had motive for murder beyond blackmail.

Well, so did a dozen other people, but Rose bashing made me happy. Witch hunts are fun for all but the accused.

I checked online to see if anyone had reached the lawyer's office for confirmation, but I saw nothing. If I had any authority, I'd be on their doorstep, looking for signed documents. Maybe Moriarity was on his way over there now. Did Ireland have probate courts?

Rose wasn't saying a word, but apparently more Scion-caricature balloons were popping up at his campaign offices around the country. There were several nice shots online. The balloons were now accompanied by spongy hypodermics similar to the foam hands waved at sporting events. If Magda was behind that, she was a creative marketing genius. If the cops knew her at all, they ought to be parked on her doorstep—not that they knew where that doorstep was any more than I did. Her network must be as well organized as Graham's.

I returned to the newspaper and found Sean and Patra's byline on a lovely front page story about Scion Pharmaceutical—the one Rose was presumably inheriting. I grinned even broader. They ripped the company into tatters, making it look as if our presidential candidate would be pushing addictive drugs to Russians as well as our brave American veterans.

I whistled at the thoroughness of their investigation. They had statistics, confirmation, drug deaths, opium correlation—the works. If the FDA didn't come down on Mylaudanix after this, then they'd been bought and paid for by Scion, and a congressional investigation was needed.

The article might not arouse Rose supporters who wouldn't necessarily make the connection—or who consider killing people a necessary part of doing business—but everyone else. . . *yeah, mama.* Scion Pharmaceuticals was in for some major headaches—suitable for a company pushing addictive painkillers like aspirin. Opiates for the masses, indeed.

Another front page headline warned everyone to stock up in preparation for the snow moving in. DC shut down if a snowflake fell, but I'd lived in real blizzards. Here, I just dressed warmer in case the prediction was anywhere close to right. If it was anything like Georgia, where I'd been living, it usually wasn't. The news just liked excitement.

After seeing EG off to school, I tucked the paper under my arm and set out under gray skies to visit Nadia in the hospital. The police weren't any closer to the hit-and-run driver, but Scion was dead, and now the information he wanted to conceal was out in public for all to see. I was hoping that meant Nadia was no longer a threat to the killers.

Graham had been unable to locate the three assassins on Viktor's list who had disappeared off the radar. If he couldn't find them, I had to assume they were dead—which put us back to zero.

My sources hadn't found any names associated with the numbers from Tony's phone—indicating they may have been discarded burner numbers. I could start calling them to see who answered, but that sounded risky if we were talking angry Russians and killers. Graham had the list. I'd let him do what he does. I was tired of death. I wanted to see if the kids' mother had any chance of living to be their mother again.

I'd taken photos of the kids playing with the dinosaur last night and printed them out. I stopped at the gift shop and picked up a card to put them in. I assumed aides or visitors could tape the pictures up somewhere if she ever showed any sign of coming around.

I inquired at the nurses' station and was asked for ID and to sign in. Nice but probably not going to prevent any mad killers. They directed me to a door with a burly guard sitting outside, reading his tablet computer. I showed him my ID, and he checked it against a roster. Amazingly, I must have been on it, so this was one of Graham's men.

There were times when I wondered just how much money Graham had that he could spare employees around the clock on mercy missions, but we had just barely settled the matter of sharing the mansion. I wasn't touching any more sensitive subjects that weren't any of my business. I figured he was being paid—or had been promised payment—by someone who had as much interest in protecting Nadia as I did.

The room was small but private. She lay motionless against the white covers, her head bald and bandaged. Tubes and wires were everywhere. It was early, so none of the visitors who had set up a reading schedule were here yet.

I set the newspaper containing the Scion article, plus the card with the photos, on a nightstand, really hoping someday she'd see them and appreciate what she had contributed to the world. I wasn't much on hand holding, but I told her about how well the kids were doing, and that Guy was a fabulous guardian. She might have twitched a little, or it could have been my imagination. Her eyes seemed to be moving behind her lids, so she wasn't dead. Her brilliant mind was in that cracked skull somewhere.

She'd tried to help the world. She'd raised really good kids. She deserved to live.

At times like this, I wished I believed in an all-powerful presence and prayer. The best I could summon was hoping all humans were connected by an essence that responded to hope—which was what prayer was. So I sent warm rays of hope from my essence to hers, patted her pale hand, and departed.

It felt strange to just visit the hospital without threatening anyone. It felt stranger to not be directly involved in tracking down the person who had tried to kill Nadia. But Russians and international assassins were pretty much out of my league. All I had was untraceable phone numbers.

And Nadia's computer and Scion's will—nice boring safe occupations I could work on in my quiet basement without endangering my family. Just because I was feeling restless and wanted action didn't mean I should go looking for smoking guns, right?

As I stepped into the wintry wind outside the hospital, I thought I saw Bill the Bartender and a female friend crossing the parking lot. Not in a hurry to return to my basement, I turned around to follow. The kids were probably just visiting one of the druggie friends the bar manager had complained about.

Bill got in an elevator and the doors closed before I could catch up. His girlfriend lingered in the line at the water fountain.

The phone in my pocket rang. I froze, realizing I'd left Tony's phone in there. Did I answer it?

I pulled it out of my inside jacket pocket. The number showing on caller ID was the one I thought might be Scion's—*the one I thought the killer had taken.*

Shaken, I let the call go to voice mail and hurried back upstairs to Nadia's room. I had no reason to believe the killer was in the hospital, but I'm overly cautious and maybe a tad superstitious. Thankfully, no one unusual lingered in Nadia's vicinity.

I'd used Tony's phone to call that number all over the area around Scion's mansion. *Whoever had Scion's phone would have Tony's number in his missed call list.*

Not trusting that the phone couldn't be tracked, I left it with the security guard in front of Nadia's room, explaining the situation. I had no intention of tackling a technical sniper who could have taken out a man like Scion.

The guard promised to notify Graham and keep a sharp eye out—just in case the killer was in the building and could track a burner.

Shivering, I took the Metro home. I wiped away my fear by philoso-phizing on how I could use my wealth to level the playing field so all kids had the same opportunities. By the time I reached my stop, I had decided we'd have to kill most of their parents. Money simply couldn't solve every-thing. So much for that charitable foundation.

I spent the morning whittling the contents of Nadia's computer to nuggets that might be worth chasing. Zander had sent a complicated chart of Scion's holdings and their relation to other Top Hat members and their businesses. I wondered if the members of Top Hat realized their money was building better guns for terrorists when they bought Scion stock.

Buried deep inside Nadia's files, I found what looked like might be bank account numbers. I was pretty certain Nadia didn't possess a fountain of wealth. I could trace the banks by their routing numbers, but breaking into accounts required special software, time, and a lot of computer power. I set those aside in a folder I shared with Graham and Zander and marked to follow up later.

While I was there, I searched Graham's file to see if any of his operatives were looking into the lawyers Scion had hired, in this country and Ireland. If they were, Graham wasn't putting the information where I could lay my hands on it.

He'd once hired me because of my international contacts. I grinned as I recalled one in Ireland who would be perfect for this job. I sent her a note promising a bonus if she could lay her hands on Scion's file. I didn't much care if they were digital or literal hands.

She gleefully responded that she was getting married and could use the cash and she'd get back to me by my evening—which meant she'd be working through *her* evening. Cool.

Nick called, frantic because they'd just realized tomorrow was Vincent's birthday. He and Guy were both at work, and they couldn't ask Maggie to go shopping for them. The new housekeeper had no car.

I was bored enough to agree. I could have taken a job researching obscure Greek texts for a university professor who had paid me well in the past, but I'd been cutting down on my virtual assistant business and spending more time on family. I'd have to decide at some point what I wanted to do with the rest of my life, but not today. Today, I was kind of liking the idea of planning a party.

It was gray and spitting snow. Good, that meant the stores would be practically empty. I'd researched and found the perfect toy store over in Arlington, so I dressed in the fancy faux-leopard fur coat Nick had made me buy. I shouldn't need my arsenal while shopping in pricey stores. With my fur boots and hat, I almost looked like the other wealthy young women perusing the fancy shops where I intended to go. Sam was busy on Graham's errands, but the Metro wouldn't stop for a splatter of flakes. I got a few stares down there, but it wasn't as if I'd ever cared about being out of place.

I was not a fan of shopping, but I recognized the necessity when it came to kids. The store I'd researched was pretty high-end. It didn't contain the massive water guns and drum sets and all the things my little kid heart would have desired. I'd never make a good shopping assistant, which was why I went to a place that directed me to the age-appropriate toys.

I found a clerk who showed me wooden trains and games that didn't involve batteries. I bought books and brain games—and a small wooden pistol that shot rubber bands that Vincent could conceal in his wheelchair. Really, kids need to be kids. And I bought Anika a pretty pink party dress so she wouldn't feel left out.

I picked up a boxed birthday cake at a bakery and something called party favors at the drugstore. I had no idea what they were but figured we'd all find out. And bubbles. I loved bubbles.

By the time I was ready to leave the drugstore, my arms full of shopping bags, I wished for magic Sam to drive me. In my frugal mind, Arlington was much too far from home for a taxi, but EG would be out of school soon. But I hadn't booked Sam in advance, and it might take him hours to get here.

I really needed to get my driver's license. This was ridiculous. Out the drugstore window, I could see that it was snowing harder, dang it. Even finding a taxi would soon be impossible. I set my packages down, pulled cash and my phone from my purse, picked the whole mess up again, and strode into the biting wind.

Cursing Nick, I was hitting up the Uber app when I saw a taxi with its light off stopped at a light. I walked out in front of it. The taxi driver stuck his fist through the window and shouted at me to move. I waved a few twenties. He glared and quit shouting.

I hurriedly opened his back door and began loading the seat with packages. "How much to take me to Adams-Morgan?"

"A hundred," he said grumpily. "And I want the first fifty now."

"You got it." I gave him the address and the money in my hand.

Just as I was gathering up the huge fur coat to climb in, a hard arm slid around my waist, and I was jerked back to the sidewalk. My phone went flying.

"I need to talk to you, lady," a rough voice growled in a distinctly Russian accent.

He crushed my pretty phone into a zillion pieces with his fancy shoe.

CHAPTER 19

GRAHAM WAS READING THROUGH SCION'S DC LEGAL FILES WHEN HIS *JAWS* ringtone for Ana's family chimed. Ana was the only one of the family who dared called him, and her calls generally justified suspenseful music. He grabbed the phone.

He noted the Caller ID with surprise. Nick? Nick barely spoke to him— probably because Graham seldom spoke to Nick. Fair trade.

With a sinking sensation that this couldn't be good, Graham answered.

"Where's Ana?" Nick asked. A thread of fear laced his usually affable voice.

Graham switched on his household monitors but his alarms told him when someone came and went. "Not here," he said curtly. "Why?"

"A taxi just arrived bearing bags of toys and a cake but no Ana. The driver said she promised him another fifty for delivering in this snowstorm. He said some big old guy prevented her from getting in."

Graham started calling up images of men involved in recent cases. The only "big old guy" he could recall lately was one of the Popovs.

"Did he say she went willingly?" Graham did his best to keep emotion out of his voice, but his pulse had escalated to stroke territory, and his grip on his computer trackball caused the ball to bounce out. "She usually has a dozen tricks at her disposal."

Which was when he remembered she hadn't left wearing her arsenal. She'd been dressed for shopping—for toys apparently.

"He said he didn't get a good look. The weather is wicked, the door slammed, she didn't get in, so he took off with her money. Not a jolly gent is our driver. I've got his name and license but couldn't hold him."

"Give me the name and license. Where did he pick her up?" Graham ground his teeth, retrieved another trackball, and began tapping Nick's information into his keyboard.

"Arlington. I've got her packages here, so I know the stores where she went." Nick didn't sound any happier than Graham felt.

Who would grab Ana—and *why*? Without knowing the why, he had nothing. The old need to put his fist through the wall rose. This was the reason he didn't get involved. He stifled his fury until he could reach a suitable punching bag.

"I can't imagine how anyone could have followed her. It's nearly impossible on the Metro, and she didn't take the car. Even I can't track her phone. Maybe it was random?" Graham said that to reassure Nick but opened up his monitor on Nadia's hospital room as he spoke. That and Scion were the only cases she was looking into right now.

He could hear Nick rummaging in shopping bags. "She used our charge card. Not mine, the family one."

Graham's gut knotted as he recognized the danger. "Does she keep track of charges using the computer?"

"We're talking Ana here. Do mice eat cheese? Why?" Nick demanded.

"Russians hacked my servers a few days back. I blew up their tower, changed servers, and riddled them with malware, but they're experts at grabbing credit card information. If they retrieved anything from the debris, that would be it."

Nick uttered a string of expletives in several languages. "If they could see the card online, they could see the charges as the stores registered them. Looking at the times on the receipts, she was shopping for several hours. But why would anyone care about Ana? She doesn't have anything anyone needs."

Graham watched the monitor showing Nadia's hospital room. A shapely young nurse was flirting with his security guard, pointing down the hall as if she needed something done.

"Nadia," he said curtly. "Ana has Nadia's computer information. The

Russian hackers may know it. Get over to the hospital now and grab anyone who enters that room."

He hung up before Nick could question or protest. Graham hit the intercom. "Mallard, keep the kid here and occupied when she gets in. I'm going out."

He shut off Mallard's splutter and called the security guard at the hospital. "The Russians are on the move. Hold that nurse until I arrive."

Shoving three phones and two computer tablets into the pockets of his coat, he raced for the exit that would take him to the garage. He couldn't call for a helicopter in this weather. The Phaeton was much too noticeable. Sam was delivering documents to the Justice Department. The motorcycle would have to do.

THE FAT RUSSIAN AVOIDED MY BOOT CRUSHING HIS INSTEP, DODGED MY ELBOW to his jugular, and gave me no chance to yank his privates. He heaved me into a waiting limo—probably the same one Tony had used when he tried to blow up Nick.

I'm not large. I *am* capable of flinging a man to the ground if I catch him by surprise, but nothing I tried with this big oaf worked. Wrapped up as I was in all this crappy fur, I was harmless as a bunny rabbit. I vowed never to go out without my leather jacket again.

I took off my gloves, prepared to gouge out his eyes as he climbed in, but he took the front passenger seat, abandoning me in the empty back. The doors locked automatically as the limo started.

He'd crushed my phone! I'd left the burner in my leather coat. I ran through a mental list of international curses as I took in my situation. The door was locked. The window between me and the front seat was closed. Apparently Fat Russian wasn't a professional hitman because he'd left me my purse—or he was an overconfident asshat. I rummaged for possible weapons. In the front, the driver and his burly passenger murmured in Russian. The car pulled away from the curb.

I could hear bits and pieces of words from behind the glass separating us as I located my Swiss Army knife and flipped open the screwdriver. *Nadia* was the word I understood best. It was hard to grasp complete sentences based on the few words I recognized.

I am not a genius like my siblings. I'm just experienced in survival techniques. No one was pointing a gun at my head yet, so I figured I might as well try taking a car apart while they were underestimating me. I'd never owned a car and never had a chance to work on one, but screws are screws and machines are machines, and I could discombobulate both.

The trick was to do it without the driver noticing.

I huddled in my huge coat against the door, presumably looking out the window, and occasionally pounding the glass at the traffic stuck on the outer loop of the beltway. The front seat rightfully ignored me. No way was anyone in the other cars paying a bit of attention to my frantic pounding.

But underneath the coat, I jimmied at the door handle. I couldn't find screws, so I just figured on ripping the wretched thing out. What I'd do after that, I couldn't say. I just liked creating opportunities.

Just for fun, I took an old envelope from my purse and used magic marker to write HELP on it. It's an old kid trick and probably no one would bother to actually call the cops, but I stuck it in a corner of the window where the driver couldn't see it in his rearview. The snow didn't strike me as that bad, but obviously the entire city had decided to go home early.

I had no idea how these jerks had found me or why, but I knew how to prioritize. I'd shoot first and ask questions later.

The wretched limo was built too well. We probably spent an hour of our endless drive stuck in traffic, and I'd barely pried one corner loose before we pulled off into a residential area of monster mansions. It was still afternoon, but the clouds made it dark and the wind-whipped snow kept me from seeing much. I didn't think we'd gone far enough to reach Bethesda, but then, I'd never gone there from Arlington before.

The car stopped at a wrought iron gate, where the driver punched in a security code.

I tried the door handle. It didn't give. I was still struggling with it when the car halted inside a massive garage with no other cars inside. The door handle didn't budge even after I heard the door unlock and the driver came to drag me out. I'd jammed the lock on my side, and he had to go around and haul me, kicking and screaming, from the other side.

Pity I hadn't had time to jam both locks. I went for his eyes. He punched me, and I saw black.

~

GRAHAM CLICKED OFF HIS WIRELESS HEADSET AS HIS CYCLE RUMBLED INTO THE parking garage at the hospital, out of the snowy wind. His calls hadn't produced any sign of Ana yet, but he'd put the wheels in motion. Police and his men were studying security cameras from the area where she'd made purchases. He was hoping for a license plate and swallowing bile with fear. Meanwhile, on the basis of only an educated hunch, he had others scouring the city for the Popovs.

Needing action so he didn't erupt, he'd taken on a job he knew he could handle.

Driving up the garage ramp, he aimed for the skywalk. He knew this damned hospital too well. It hadn't changed much in the ten years since he'd been incarcerated in the hellhole. He found a parking space half in a crosswalk. The other half was occupied by a MINI Cooper. Anger, fear, and rules didn't work well together.

Dashing through the gerbil run, he hit the corridor inside running, dodging wheelchairs and startled interns.

Ten years ago, he had known terror well beyond the human capacity to handle. He'd given up on therapy for the PTSD after a year and put his energy into seeing that he need never suffer that horror of helplessness ever again—but here he was.

Ana wasn't his wife, but in ways, she was even closer. His wife had been a business partner. He'd almost lost his life trying to save her, and it had crippled him beyond measure. Ana—Ana with her taunts and rebellion and hidden sexiness had managed to get under his skin and become a visceral part of his gut. If anything happened to her, it would be like ripping out his liver. Or his heart, if one had to be sentimental. He wasn't, but he wasn't about to let some damned Russian destroy her. Or him. This time, he had a fighting chance.

And yeah, he knew he had issues. Watching his wife blow up with the Pentagon had scarred him more than the fire he'd run into to save her. Life was a bitch. You either stood up and fought or laid down and died. He wasn't ready to die yet, so if they were involved, the Popovs were damned well going down, preferably in flames.

He ran up the stairs rather than wait on the insanely slow elevators. He didn't expect Nick or any of his friends to be here yet, but he did expect the security guard to have apprehended the nurse.

He checked his messages as he ran, noting the ones with all the addresses his agents could find for the Popovs. Finding Ana by address would be searching for a needle in a snowstorm. They owned half the suburbs.

Graham reached Nadia's room. The security guard paced with a grim expression, his hand on a weapon he wasn't supposed to have.

"Security is holding her," he told Graham. "One floor down. How did you know she was fake?"

"Nurses on duty don't have time to flirt," Graham said, checking inside Nadia's room to make certain all her monitors were clicking along. He didn't mention gut fear had caused him to check the camera in the first place.

Reassured that Nadia still slept, he stalked downstairs to the security office. The fake nurse was huddled in a chair, hugging herself. Security pointed at a hypodermic and a vial on their desk.

"Mylaudanix," the guard said curtly. "The nurses say it would have put Ms. Kaminsky into a sleep from which she would never return. No one would have thought to check her blood since they're expecting her to die anyway."

"Why?" Graham demanded of the shivering female. He rummaged through the purse sitting on the desk and found her identification. *Michelle Lee* sounded even more fake than his alias.

"I owe them," she said with a pout. "You heard. She is to die anyway. It saves time and money this way. It was a good deed. She should not suffer."

Graham didn't excel at accents but he'd guess eastern European from context. "Who do you owe and why?"

"Our Uncle Popovs. They gave me and my brother jobs in the old country, and when it was no longer safe to stay, they brought us here. We are good at what we do, but we do not have security clearance here. We cannot get good jobs. They send small jobs our way so we can eat while we try to obtain green cards. I did nothing. This is America, land of the free. You must let me go," she insisted.

"What do you do?" Graham asked, already suspecting the answer.

"We are computer engineers," she said proudly. "We can write beautiful video games *and* fix your computer."

And write a virus that can hack any computer they accessed. They'd never have been brought over here otherwise.

"Did you fix the malware I sent you?" he asked maliciously.

She shot him a narrow-eyed look. "I run the computers at the phone company, but it closed down. I know nothing of malware."

He didn't have time to argue with her. "Your uncles are killers. The comatose patient they sent you to kill has evidence proving it." Graham made that up. They had no evidence against the Popovs anywhere. Yet. "She is the mother of two small children, and the doctors say she will wake any minute. You would have taken her from them. Attempted murder is a crime. You will be deported."

She looked genuinely horrified. She had dyed her hair blond, but her eyebrows were thick and dark and expressive. "That is not possible. Uncle Ivan is a good man. He just does not want Nadia to suffer."

So it was Ivan who had sent her here. Graham texted the man he'd left in charge of hunting Popovs.

"He probably hired the driver who nearly killed her and her kids," Graham said roughly. "Where can I find him? He's about to hurt another young woman."

She shook her head vehemently. "You have wrong man. Our uncles would not hurt mosquito. They are businessmen who do much good at home. They provide jobs that put food on the table."

"Fine, then maybe I have the wrong men. Put me in touch with them and let's find out. Give me your phone." Graham held out his hand since there had been no phone in her purse.

She shook her head. Trembling, she pulled a phone from her coat pocket and punched in a contact herself. "Uncle Ivan, I am in trouble."

Graham snatched the phone from her hand and put it on speaker while he texted one of his operatives to start triangulating the call.

"You cannot do this one thing for me?" the male voice on the other end demanded angrily.

"They caught me," she said, nearly weeping. "Please tell them we meant no harm."

"Tell who?" he asked harshly. "Who is there?"

"Ivan Popov?" Graham asked, setting the phone on the desk so the guard could hear.

"Who asks?"

"Thomas Alexander," Graham lied. "Security for the hospital. We found Miss Lee with a vial of painkiller and a needle."

"I know nothing of this," the voice on the other end said with a verbal shrug. "I am a busy man. I do not have time for this."

He hung up, and the culprit wept openly.

The call was probably too brief to have been successfully tracked. Graham fought another urge to ram his fist through a wall, since he couldn't punch a woman. He took the phone and sent the number to his team in hopes they could find another way of reaching it. He handed her phone to the guard and asked him to copy the numbers and text him with them. Whether the guard respected Graham's expertise or simply followed orders well, he did as requested.

"Uncle Ivan has quite possibly kidnapped or killed another young woman who knows too much," Graham said harshly. "I mean to stop him, and if I have to do that by calling the cops to pick you up, I will. You can talk to me, or you can talk to them."

She kept shaking her head and wringing her hands and watching the guard copy all her contact numbers. "I know nothing. What can I say? I am computer engineer."

"Where does Ivan live?"

She gestured helplessly. "How do I know? He calls me when he has a job."

"You claim to be a computer expert and you haven't tried to track him down?"

A brief flash of guilt crossed her face before she reached for her purse and a tissue. "Why would I do that?"

Graham perched on the edge of the desk, hiding his impatience. "Oh, let me guess. Maybe to blackmail him after he had you hack heavily guarded servers, and he didn't pay you what it was worth. Or after someone destroyed your computers with malware and you were out of a job. Or when you needed money to escape after your credit card theft was discovered. Shall I count the ways?"

She pouted again and tried to look innocent. All Graham could think of was how Ana would have come after him with a big stick and left him pounded into a pulp if he'd annoyed her like this. Maybe he was perverse for knowing where he stood with her instead of falling for womanly wiles, but he'd take a good pounding any day to this pout.

"We are not hackers," she said indignantly. "We are not thieves. We are hard workers and do not blackmail the hand that feeds us."

"I've lost patience," Graham told the guard. "While she lies, a woman is being held captive by Ivan or one of his fellows. Call the police. Let me know when she's ready to talk." He stood up.

"No, no," she cried. "We cannot go to police. They will send us home. They will kill us back there. You cannot do that. I did nothing!"

Graham shrugged. "I'll let the law determine that. Good day, Miss Lee."

"Wait, wait," she cried as the guard sitting at the desk picked up his phone. "Ivan does not use computers. We cannot hack him. We know his phone numbers, that is all. He owns the phone company. They keep no records on his phones. There is nothing."

From what Graham had learned, that was probably closer to the truth. "But you hacked his phone, didn't you?" He knew the mindset. After all, he did the same. One took every precaution available.

She bit her full bottom lip and looked at her lap. "It is what we do," she whispered. "It is necessary, to stay safe."

"You implanted a GPS device and know where he spends his time," Graham said for her.

"We met once or twice," she admitted. "It was easy. He does not understand these things. We never meant to use it!"

"Give me the addresses," Graham said curtly. Fortunately, she wasn't using one of Rustel's cheap burners. The old styles didn't have internet connectivity. But a hacker would have the latest tech. He flipped through her cell, locating icons for cloud servers. He added one of his un-networked email addresses to her contact list and handed the phone back to her.

He watched his email on his burner phone and saw the files drop into his box. Opening them, he scowled. Ivan had to sleep in a different bed every damned night.

"Which one does he spend the most time at?" he demanded.

"The one in Chevy Chase," she said. "We have looked. It is a fortress."

CHAPTER 20

I WOKE UP IN A BEDROOM DESIGNED BY A MOVIE DIRECTOR WHO OWNED A feather factory. Stacks of feather pillows padded with quilted shams, comforters three feet deep—I swear, even the ghastly velvet curtains had to have been stuffed. The red and gold motif was probably meant to be opulent.

My furry boots had probably left snow and mud on the obscenely thick brown and red comforter, but it was impossible to tell in the near dark. Huddling in my faux fur coat, I sat up a little woozily and studied my surroundings.

Had I time and patience, I would have found a sharp object and covered the shag carpet in feathers and batting out of sheer meanness. But after a thorough search, I realized they'd finally got smart enough to take my purse. It didn't have a lot of tricks in it, but I missed my army knife.

I climbed down off the high bed to check out the windows—a blanket of snow covered the wall surrounding this fortress, and it was still coming down. I didn't see dogs or guards, but it was winter dark and the security lights didn't illuminate all the shadows in the bushes. Monsters could be lurking anywhere.

The room was so padded, I probably couldn't hear a rock concert downstairs, but I listened, just in case I could detect someone outside the door. Not a sound.

I still had no clue why anyone would want to kidnap me. I had nothing anyone wanted. And I was pretty certain they hadn't had a good clue who I was when they took me or they would never have left me untied. I assumed now that they had my ID, they'd learn where I lived and would work from there.

That caused me to fret. Would they go after EG? She would be the only one of my siblings home. They'd have the devil of a time taking Graham. Would he even know I was gone?

By smashing my phone, they'd lost any chance to call anyone else who knew me. I kept the burner phone in my leather jacket, so I was out of luck there, as were they. So what in heck were they doing?

I tested the knob—locked. It's unusual to add locks to the *outside* of a bedroom door. I kneeled down and decided the knob was just on backward, one assumes deliberately? To lock up unnecessary prisoners.

I pulled pins out of my braid and applied one to the little hole in the knob. These modern houses had crap locks. It only took a strong piece of metal to open the tumbler—handy for rescuing the ankle-biters when they locked themselves in.

Holding my breath and praying, I tested the door again. The knob turned, and the hollow panel eased open. I peered through the crack. No one seemed to be stationed outside. The hall floor was as thickly carpeted as the bedroom—really *really* stupid if you mean to kidnap people, or to hear a burglar coming.

I had no idea where I'd go if I made it to the front door. I still wore my fur coat and boots, so I wouldn't completely freeze. But I had no money, no phone, no means of going anywhere unless I found the limo and the keys to it. I didn't have a license, but I'd learned to drive jeeps in war zones.

It might be more fun to find an address and a phone and call Graham. On a good day, he could fly the helicopter over and drop tear gas or smoke bombs. That would be entertaining, but snowstorms made for a bad day. Still, calling Graham seemed a good idea. Maybe I could climb a wall and he could send someone to meet me. I liked that idea a lot better than stealing cars.

No lights illuminated this upper hallway. I cautiously opened doors, searching for phones or maybe old mail with an address. All the rooms were decorated in the same excruciatingly bad taste, as if some designer had been given a percentage kickback on everything she purchased, so she'd bought the warehouse. Massive beds, towering dressers covered in useless doo-dads—empty closets.

No magazines, no phones, no convenient office or study. Movies gave such a false sense of reality!

I found a staircase leading up. If there was nothing on this floor, I figured the upstairs was stuffed with empty servants quarters. But I could hear music below, and the scent of bacon cooking drifted from downstairs.

My stomach told me I hadn't eaten in quite a while. I was even ready to eat that sugary treacle of a birthday cake, had I hung onto it. I hoped that taxi driver had done the honorable thing and carried the presents to Nick. Nick would know something was wrong.

I tiptoed down the edge of the carpeted stairs, avoiding any squeaks. They ended in a marble foyer covered in expensive Turkish carpets. I checked the huge double front doors, but they were bolted with key locks that would require more than a hairpin. That was a fire hazard if I ever saw one.

I bet there was a key somewhere close by, unless the occupants were suicidal, or exceptionally stupid. But I was in no hurry to escape into a snowstorm until I knew where the heck I was. I had hopes I might find some sort of office or study down here—if my growling stomach didn't give me away.

I would find it hard to believe a place this size didn't have a servant in sight, except all the furniture was coated in dust and the marble looked as if it hadn't been mopped in a year. Who bought a gazillion-dollar house and left it empty?

Someone who went around kidnapping people, that's who. For all I knew, the yard was fertilized with dead bodies.

I was trying very hard to concentrate on escape and not what would happen to me when I couldn't provide whatever my kidnappers wanted—whoever they might be.

I poked around the enormous living room—not a magazine or phone in sight. Landlines were so antiquated apparently.

A corridor off the back of the foyer probably led to the kitchen and family rooms. Biting my bottom lip, I tiptoed across the marble and down a side hall instead.

I peered into a dusty dining room with a dozen chairs designed for a castle and utterly no artwork on the walls. Had the designer been fired before she made it down here?

More questionable yet—who installed rugs this thick in every room of the house? Wasn't it fashionable to show expensive wood?

Well, maybe the designer owned a carpet company, along with a feather and cotton batting factory.

Or the owners liked to muffle the screams of their victims.

Okay, not going there, Ana. Keep moving.

I checked the enormous buffet for silverware—*nada*. It was as if someone deliberately taunted their prisoners with freedom and no weapons. I didn't think I was strong enough to break off a chair leg. They were pretty darned substantial chairs. But I knew where to find them if I needed them.

I crept down to the next door—finally, an office, with an enormous, ornate mahogany desk, no carpet, and no curtains. Dang. Light from a security lamp beamed through the uncovered window. I'd have to be cautious. I tiptoed across the wooden floor, avoiding breaking my toes on the furniture, which was miraculously leather and not over-stuffed upholstery. The shelves had a few rows of books with gilded covers. If I had a flashlight, I'd check to see which classics they'd chosen, but they were probably in Russian.

The desk had nothing more than a leather framed blotter, an old-fashioned brass desk lamp, and an ornate brass pen-and-pencil holder. This was getting ridiculous. Not even an envelope opener I might use as a weapon. I tested the heft of the desk lamp, but I'd have to take the brass top off of it before it would be useful as anything but a barbell.

I began pulling on the hundred and one drawer handles. I wasn't certain I could read anything in the dark, but at this point I was so desperate I'd take any paper I found.

Finally! A folder of receipts. Or copies of receipts since they were all printed out on the same size paper. The printer ink was smudgy, making it impossible to read for addresses in this dim light.

I was desperate enough to dare a light switch. I found the one for the brass desk lamp and hit it. Nothing. I checked under the hood. It had no bulb.

This was just one giant dollhouse, wasn't it?

I studied the ceiling, wondering if I could reach any overhead bulbs.

Broken, they might make a fragile weapon. But these were modern sealed contraptions with which I wasn't familiar. I needed to watch more home improvement shows.

I folded the papers and slid them into my coat pocket. I was glad for the fur. The house was downright chilly, and my fear already had me shivering.

Enormous storage closets and a powder room concluded my exploration of this wing. No lovely dangling lightbulbs anywhere. I hated modern houses.

That meant I either had to figure out how to pry open a window and run, or head for the back of the house and see what was cooking.

Since I still had no idea where I was, and I really disliked being cold, I opted for the kitchen.

I traipsed back to the foyer and took the corridor to the back of the house. I checked doors on my way but only found an enormous—empty—coat closet and a sunroom that might have been pleasant had the skylights not been covered in snow. I peered out the windows at snow-covered lumps inside a walled garden. How long had I been unconscious? The white stuff was thick. Maybe it started snowing earlier wherever it was we were? No matter, I decided one wall was the side of the garage and escape wasn't likely from here.

Finding no addresses or weapons, I went back to the hall and checked the next door down. It had a normal lock. I turned it and peered into the hollow darkness of a garage with no car. Worse yet, no tools. Dang. It was pretty darned evident no one lived here except the furniture.

I could see the outline of a door leading into the walled garden—not much escape there. I could probably hit the lighted button beside this door and open the garage, but by the time I slipped out, I'd have guards all over me. And I'd still have nowhere to go. But it was an option I stored for a moment of desperation.

So I strolled into the kitchen to see who was cooking—and nearly fell on my face.

Bill the Bartender.

～

BY THE TIME GRAHAM'S MEN HAD STORED MICHELLE LEE IN A SAFE PLACE, ostensibly for her own protection, Nick and Guy had shown up at the hospital.

Sending curt messages to position more men around Ivan's Chevy Chase mansion while setting others to investigating the Popovs' other long list of properties, Graham almost left without speaking to Nick. He wanted Ana back, and he wanted her now. He had incredible focus when it was necessary, and Nadia and friends were a distraction.

But Nick wasn't the sort to be deterred. He tracked Graham down and confronted him before he could escape to the stairwell.

"We left Juliana with the kids. Will they be safe or do we need to move everyone to the mansion for the night?"

Nick looked less like his affable self and more like an exhausted father. Graham wasn't fond of slick Brits in bespoke suits, but he knew Ana doted on her younger siblings, so he scowled and didn't shove away.

"I have no real evidence of anything except the Popovs are probably trying to kill Nadia. That means she knows more than we've given to the media—whether about Scion or something else has yet to be determined. My concern is Ana. She doesn't know when to leave well enough alone."

Nick nodded agreement. "She'll nail one of them to the wall and the other will take exception, got it. You need to see this. It verifies what we already suspected." He took out his phone and opened his text messages, handing it to Graham.

FIND ANA! POPOV DANGEROUS! BUYS DRUGS WITH WEAPONS. NADIA HAS PROOF.

The message was from Magda. Graham wanted to fling the phone against the wall, but that wouldn't hurt Magda or ease his apprehension. He'd learned anger management the hard way. "See if you can persuade your mother to send us evidence on Popov that we can take to the authorities. We need search warrants to access their accounts and properties. I'm holding one of his minions, but she won't hold up in court."

Graham didn't tell a worried Nick that one of his men had found Ana's phone smashed into the pavement in Arlington. He needed the Brit to keep his act together. Ana's brother appeared on the brink of exhaustion and murder. Keeping Nick occupied and useful seemed the best solution.

Jaw muscles tense, Nick nodded. "The embassy keeps an eye on Magda when they can. I'll check with them." He glanced reluctantly at his phone. "I don't suppose you can triangulate a text message and find her that way?"

"Unlikely." Graham added a number to Nick's phone. "Contact this man if she calls. If you can hold her on the phone long enough, he can trace the area the call is coming from." He returned the phone to Nick, who stuck it in his suit coat pocket.

"Rose is holding an enormous gala and fundraiser downtown tonight," Nick said, seemingly irrelevantly. "I haven't heard that the event's been called off yet."

Graham understood. "Half the crowd will be staying at the hotel, so they won't call it off. Magda could very possibly be there already. I don't suppose you can persuade Patra or Sean to cover the event?"

"I doubt they can get tickets, but I'll let them know and see what happens. I haven't called them about Ana yet. I was hoping you were tracking her." Without his usual smiling energy, Nick merely looked like any worried brother.

Graham had never known close family. He didn't know how to hug any better than Ana's family did. But he offered what consolation he could. "Ana would kill me if I placed a tracker on her. I respect her wishes because I respect her ability to get out of tight situations. Your sister is one tough lady. We just need to find her before she bombs the Russian embassy or something equally disastrous."

Nick offered a brief smile. "Glad you get that."

He walked off punching a number into his phone, presumably for his journalist sister.

Graham might trust Ana, but he didn't trust Magda further than the next rock. And he didn't want Nick knowing that he had men following the twisted genius full time now that she was back on his court. He called the one in charge. "Any news?"

"She just left the Hilton on the arm of Moriarity. They're both dressed to the hilt. The limo we traced to Popov tried to pick them up, but they handed it over to Bill Smith and his wife and took a taxi."

Graham recognized that as a classic Ana move—bypass villains by throwing others under the bus. Her mother had taught her well. He only wished Magda had taught her to stay out of trouble in the first place.

His man unnecessarily continued, "We figure something bad is going down at Rose's fundraiser tonight."

Yeah, that was a total probability.

"The cops tried to get them to call it off because of the snow, but they had too much money tied up in it," his man continued.

Graham dragged his free hand through his hair and wished he could pound his head against a wall. *This* was the kind of work he did—prevent disasters, pass on intelligence, enable the good guys to do their jobs when they were understaffed. That fundraiser should be shut down *now*.

Rose had yet to call in the Secret Service for protection, which left Graham with no one to call except the cops, and they didn't have enough authority in this case. Magda, Rose, and company would have to go to hell on their own. He was going after Ana.

"Give your info to the feds and keep monitoring Magda. I may be out of contact for a while." He clicked off.

Motorcycles made for lousy transportation in snow. The plows wouldn't have completed the surface streets yet. He called Sam, gave him the Chevy Chase address and told him to meet him there if he could get through.

He'd have to find better transportation and pray he and Sam were converging on the right place.

CHAPTER 21

Friendly, flirty Bill the bartender was one of the bad guys? Did that make sense?

I was sure it would if I had time to piece the puzzle together, but I wanted out of this chilly refrigerator, and he was the only key I saw. Bill wasn't big, but he was young and more muscular than fat Popov. I'd need weapons.

Kitchens normally came loaded with weapons, but this house was so miserably barren. . .

Hiding in the shadows of the hall, peering through the open doorway, I spotted the knife rack on the side of the granite-topped center island. I'm not a fan of blood, but if it had to spill, I'd rather it not be mine. The contents of the rack weren't impressive—a paltry paring knife and a bread knife. I glanced over at the counter and saw a more substantial chopping knife on the counter beside Bill. Dang.

The kitchen was too big and empty to conceal me if I wanted to go for the rack. This was the only floor in the place not padded with half-a-foot-deep rugs. My rubber-soled boots might be silent to some extent, but I had nowhere to go even if I wanted to make a run for that back door.

So I sashayed straight into the painfully bright overhead lights, hugging my fur around me. "What are you doing here?" I demanded, aiming straight for the island and the knives.

Bill turned away from the stove, still holding a frying pan. "Ivan lets me stay here when the weather is too bad to drive."

Ivan, right. The Popovs owned the bar. "Then what am I doing here?"

He didn't seem surprised by my presence. Weird, and a little creepy. Did the Popovs often keep kidnap victims here?

Bill shrugged. "I will guess that he wishes to talk to your mother, and this is the only way he can do it. It's not as if he confides in me. He's been bitching about your mother and her anarchist organization for weeks now."

"You know my *mother?*" I asked, utterly astounded by this little speech. How the crap would he know my mother? She'd lived out of the country for decades and had returned only a month or so ago. And what did he mean about anarchist *organization?* My mother could very possibly be an anarchist, but she was a loner, an obsessed one. People like Magda didn't work well with others.

"Want a BLT? I added egg to mine." He gestured at the toast waiting on a plate. "I don't know your mother. I'm just extrapolating from Ivan's curses."

Was that the faintest hint of an accent? I could have been imagining it. "BLT with egg is good. Do you have tea?" If he meant to pretend kidnapping was a normal, everyday occurrence, I could too. I needed sustenance.

He gestured at a cabinet. "Mugs and bags up there. I think Ivan's driver stocks them. I bring in supplies from the restaurant when I come here or there would be nothing."

"Does anyone live here?" I opened the cabinet indicated, produced a colorfully decorated mug and a bag of Russian Earl Grey. Citrus and bergamot really needed steamed milk or some lemon. . . I checked the refrigerator but Bill was right, the fare was meager. No milk or lemon.

"How does anyone live with an empty kitchen?" I asked, playing along with this weirdness. I found the fancy hot water dispenser and aimed it at the mug. I wasn't a tea gourmet or I'd probably have scorned the faucet and hunted a kettle to make real boiling water—but it was becoming obvious the kitchen was only furnished by Bill and the driver. Useful tools were in short supply.

"No one lives here. It's been for sale forever." He handed me his BLT and started on another.

I was predisposed to like anyone handing me food, but something major was off here—starting with rationality. "I had no idea my mother works with anyone, and anarchy doesn't seem like her style. Why would... *Ivan*... curse her?"

"She and her gang are trying to destroy what makes this country great," he said with almost a growl. "Senator Rose is a brilliant man who has the contacts to open the corridors of commerce, provide for every working man, make it possible for anyone to be rich again. Those who oppose him are undermining the fabric of democracy."

Wow, lovely propaganda spiel. I could do so much with it—*commerce*, my foot and three eyes. *Commerce* meant the rich industrialists in Rose's favorite organization, Top Hat. They printed textbooks and media with insane lies to prove their ridiculously unscientific dogma, robbed people of their life savings, stomped on the little man and the middle man and thought women belonged in the kitchen, propagating more little termites. Okay, so I'm good at propaganda too.

But I'd educated myself in Rose's background. I'd followed the money, read the evidence of lies, seen the results, instead of listening to the shiny, exciting sound bites that concealed reality. It looked like Bill was a tool who believed what he wanted to hear rather than study the facts. That made him deluded, but not dangerous. Yet.

"And in your democracy, it's all right for Ivan to kidnap me and try to shut up my mother?" I asked innocently, taking a bite of the sandwich because my tea was too hot. I used the mug to warm my hands.

"Your mother started the dirty tricks. She needs to be stopped before bringing down a good man, one who will make us all wealthy." The gleam in his eyes wasn't promising, and yes, there was definitely an accent beneath his excellent English.

The chicken in every pot promise—how many times did that one have to go around before people realized it was a scam? "And wealth is more important than peace or law and order?" Better to question and see if his upper story worked at all.

He rescued toast from the toaster and slathered it with butter. "One buys law and order with wealth. A strong military ensures peace."

Brainwashed, got it. If he'd been raised in that kind of society, as I suspected, he was totally prepared for that kind of thinking. "Oh yeah, tell that to Iraq and Afghanistan," I said through a mouthful of bread. "A strong military ensures war and might is greater than right, and dead babies don't matter. So let's get back to my mother. What has she done to irritate your boss?"

Bill shot me a look of annoyance. "She talks like you, apparently. What do dead babies have to do with anything? Women just don't have the minds to understand complex matters."

Man, that was guaranteed to get me on his side. Did he *want* to die? I fingered the paring knife—now in my pocket—and wondered how it felt to sink a blade into a gullet.

"Your mother stupidly conspired to bring Nadia here to bring down a successful industry," he continued with a hint of scorn. "Why does she care what Scion did to survive in his youth as long as he turned his life around? It is no more important than Senator Rose's teenage indiscretions. What matters is what they do *now*—which is building strong industry that brings wealth to impoverished nations. She simply wants to embarrass and humiliate strong men."

I didn't think reminding him that despite all the big industry in the world, the poor people were still poor and the only people getting rich were the people who had money. And snakes were no less lethal when they shed their skins. Logic only confused the brainwashed.

I latched on to the one possible fact in his sermon. *Magda brought Nadia here?* Scarily, I didn't even have to ask why. I was starting to think like my mother. She *wanted* Scion to fall. And she meant to hit Rose with Scion's filth. The old—edited—expression *excrement hits the fan* applied nicely.

"Would that strong industry she's bringing down be distributing soma to the masses?" I asked, knowing he wouldn't get it. *Brave New World* wouldn't be required reading in Eastern Europe. It certainly wasn't here that I could ascertain. It ought to be.

He frowned and returned to building his sandwich. He made a mean sandwich. I'd nearly scarfed mine and considered asking for more. Arguing with dangerous idiots apparently made me hungry.

"Nadia once used that term, *soma*. I do not know what it means. Mylaudanix is making many people wealthy. She was wrong to turn traitor and bite the hand that fed her."

Uh oh. "You know Nadia personally?" I tried to sound casual. That meant he probably knew her ex-assassin husband.

He cut a tomato with a vicious chop of the one decent knife in the kitchen. "She was accountant." He hesitated, apparently realizing he was revealing too much. "I knew her husband."

Right. Confirmation that he came from overseas. He knew Viktor only if he'd been in the Ukraine or thereabouts. Viktor couldn't travel here. "He must be worried about his children," I said with what I hoped sounded like sympathy.

In between sandwich bites, I concealed the second knife in my coat pocket. The two sharp blades were tearing the heck out of the lining, but I was never wearing this rag again.

"Nadia's life insurance will be enough to buy back the children. Viktor is not too concerned. You should call your mother, tell her to come get you. We can talk then. Maybe she will understand the wrongness of her ways."

And maybe she'd end up dead or comatose, like Nadia. I fretted that Bill talking about Nadia's life insurance meant he knew something I didn't, but he could just be assuming she would die. I didn't even know where to start with my questions.

"How would I call Magda? I have no phone and have no idea where I am." I finished off the sandwich and eyed the eggs sitting on the counter. I could fry a couple of more on my own, make more toast. . .

He looked surprised. "No phone? You do not have the phone you took from the bar?"

He hadn't been there when I took Tony's phone.

But he and some female had been in the hospital when it had rung in my pocket, and I'd panicked and given it to the security guard.

I did my best to look puzzled. "I picked up my phone at the bar. Ivan stomped it into the sidewalk. I haven't memorized my mother's number or anyone else's. Without it, I can't call anyone."

That was a lie. I had a handful of numbers memorized—the ones in my burner—the important ones, now languishing in my leather jacket.

He scowled and took a gulp of the beer he'd been guzzling along with his sandwich. Wiping his mouth, he glared at me. "Ivan will find her. It is too important that Senator Rose win for us to fail now."

I really didn't like the sound of this. Now that I had him riled, I might as well push him all the way. If I had a 50-50 chance of escaping, I wanted to make it worth my while.

"If your Ivan is stupid enough to think Magda will come because he's holding me, he doesn't know my mother very well. He's failing as we speak."

I sipped my lemony tea and waited. I'd spent years antagonizing people. I could do it with surgical precision when called on.

"He will not fail," Bill said with confidence, slurping his beer. "I have hacked Moriarity's phone and know what they plan."

Filthy foul word. He was one of the hackers? Crapadoodle-doo and other obscenities. I chewed the last of my sandwich and followed that thought to its logical conclusion. By the time I finished chewing, I figured I might as well get the whole picture because I wasn't leaving here alive if it was up to Bill and Ivan.

"Huh, you're the hacker who put that video of Magda and Moriarity on Scion's security camera? That was pretty smart," I lied.

"Hacked Moriarity's kitchen to do it, too," he boasted.

Yup, the male ego was so easy to manipulate.

"My brother is good, but he's not that good." I lied again. Tudor would never have been stupid enough to leave his earmark all over a hack. I fingered the smaller knife in my arsenal. "So that means you probably know about Graham's servers too?"

"I do not know Graham. Ivan tells me the ISP to hack, and I enter and do as he says."

Double dog stupid. "Graham is the guy who infected your computer with malware and blew up the cell tower you were transmitting from," I said as casually as I could. I was a mere woman. Macho Bill wouldn't perceive me as a threat—until I was ready.

He flung his mostly empty beer can at the wall. It bounced off the massive stainless steel refrigerator. "I will *kill* him!"

I guess that answered that.

His once-friendly face darkened. "I am expert shot. I will find him, and I will kill him. No one does that to me and lives to brag of it."

Uh oh. *Expert shot?* That's what Graham had said it would have taken to bring down Scion. Combined with Popov and this kidnapping action—I think I may have just found Scion's killer.

CHAPTER 22

JOGGING INTO THE HOSPITAL PARKING GARAGE, GRAHAM SPOTTED AN enormous Hummer entering, dripping in ice, snow, and salt. Some days, the gods answered prayers. Or the only people insane enough to be driving in a blizzard were people with insane vehicles.

He ran out in front of it, forcing the driver to a halt. Graham held up his security badge, which was meaningless but made him look official. The driver rolled down his window.

Hoping the only person who wasn't in ER coming out in this weather had to be a doctor or other medical personnel, Graham pulled an Ana and lied through his teeth. "We need to bring in stranded nurses. Are you here for a while?" Graham knew all about the need for medical personnel in emergencies. Blizzards counted.

"Who the hell are you?" the driver rightfully asked.

"Security for the president." This would almost be fun if he didn't fear Magda blowing up bombs all over DC while Ana got tortured. "I need your car. I'll have it back before you need it again. Talk to Jackson." He stuck out his hand for the keys.

Jackson was head of hospital security. The driver didn't look any happier, but he apparently recognized the name. He switched off the ignition. "The president? The president is here?"

"His security is. Can't tell you more than that." Graham practically snatched the keys from the driver as he reluctantly climbed out.

Say anything with enough authority, and people listened. Well, it might also help if the doc recognized that Graham was wearing a designer leather coat that cost a few grand. Graham hopped in the driver's seat and left the poor sap standing in bewilderment. He felt no guilt in stealing the car. He'd pay the guy whatever it was worth when it was all over.

Gunning the motor, Graham tore through the garage and out the exit. He dropped his phones in the cup holders and activated his Bluetooth headphones. At the first major intersection where he was forced to halt in line, he punched in the call for his command central.

"What have you got?" He shifted into gear as the line moved.

"Not good," his operative said, sounding worried. "The limo rear-ended the taxi with our duo in it. The taxi stupidly stopped. The M's jumped out and ran but we fear one of the limo thugs caught up with your female. She was wearing heels. The snow isn't bad here yet, but the streets are slick."

His men avoided being overheard but kept names to a minimum as a precaution. He knew the M's were Magda and Moriarity, so the female in question was Ana's damned mother. "What the hell were your men doing?" Graham shouted at the speaker as he roared the Hummer past a line of cars slipping downhill.

"Sliding on an ice patch. They got off a shot at one of the thugs going after your male, brought him down in the street. But your female had already reached an alley. By the time we had feet on the ground, she was gone, out the other side—so was the thug following her."

"Does she still have her phone on her? Are you tracking?"

"She gave her phone to the male at some point. We're taking him on to his destination, and we've picked up his signal heading for dinner."

At the next intersection delay, Graham punched the address he'd chosen into the Hummer's GPS. "Call her number anyway. See what happens."

Magda had given her personal number to her children. He thought she wouldn't have done that if she didn't have multiple ways of accessing it. Installing tracking devices only worked on the physical phone, not the number. If she decided the limo had followed her phone, she'd ditch it pronto, which she had. But he'd bet half his fortune that she'd had the number set up to forward to a different phone.

He hit the Beltway ramp while his man did as told. The snow was coming down harder here, making visibility nearly zero. Gunning the motor, Graham tested the Hummer's tires. They kept traction. He'd have to think about buying one of the gas guzzlers.

"The call went through, but there's no answer, just dead space."

"Like she answered, left it on, but can't talk?" Graham asked urgently.

"Yeah, exactly like that. We've started triangulation. Think it's her and not the guy?"

"We'll know when you follow the signal. If she's smart enough to divert her calls to different phones, she's smart enough to have turned off the tracked phone when she planted it on male M."

Graham kept the connection open and gunned the Hummer past a salt truck and a line of cars that had slid off the side of the road. The address Melissa had given him for Popov was north, in the Chevy Chase area just over the state line.

Scion's house had been further north, in Bethesda. Graham hadn't been in either place in a decade, but he'd grown up in the area of palatial mansions and gated communities. They'd have snow plows out before the city did.

"We have a location," an excited voice said in his ear. "She's traveling north, not on foot. I'd say they've got her."

Graham clutched the wheel so hard that his fingers hurt. Ana and her mother might not get along, but he knew instinctively that they'd fight to the death for each other. He didn't want to waste resources on a woman like Magda who brought trouble down on anyone in her vicinity, but for Ana, he had to try.

"Have someone follow the signal. I'm nearly at Chevy Chase."

He took the turn and prayed.

~

I WANDERED AS CASUALLY AS I COULD TOWARD THE PATIO DOORS AT THE BACK of the kitchen, holding a fresh mug of tea. Was the blizzard letting up? I couldn't tell.

Through the mist of tiny flakes, I could see a walled yard layered in even snow. No trees, no bushes. The garage and drive formed a wall on the right. I couldn't see a door into the garage from this side. Awkward set-up for the cook, but presumably groceries got carried in through the hall door.

If I scaled that wall, would there be help on the other side?

"How good a shot are you?" I asked idly. He'd just admired Scion. Why would he have killed him?

But if Bill had replaced the video in Scion's kitchen with the one of Magda and Moriarity—he had some kind of access. Maybe he'd just hacked Scion's computers.

"Top of my squad," he bragged, pulling another beer from the enormous SubZero refrigerator. "But the military gets you killed. I prefer school."

He'd gone from saying he'd kill my mother to talking like any self-absorbed college student. Minor personality disorder, I diagnosed.

"I never had a snowball fight," I said in my most wistful feminine manner. Which wasn't very wistful or feminine. I'm a good liar but no actress. "Show me your sharpshooting skills with snowballs."

I found the patio door latch and flipped it.

"You have to hit the alarm button or they drop bombs on us," he said, crossing the room to the security box.

I wasn't at all certain he was kidding. I was fine with setting off alarms that brought police to the door—bombs, not so much.

And if Ivan was in the habit of keeping prisoners, I was pretty sure his alarms didn't alert the police.

"Bombs, huh?" I asked, waiting for him to shrug into his down coat. "That's a pretty drastic reaction to burglars."

"Ivan is paranoid. It is how he survived." He hit the alarm code, turning it off.

Cool beans. No bombs. No guards riding to the rescue?

"It probably alerts local security," Bill continued. "They drive around the neighborhood, looking important. But knowing Ivan, it will alert him and his bodyguards as well. He'd be furious if I brought in the locals."

Maybe he really was just a misguided college student. Just because he was a sharpshooter and hacker. . . Naw, I didn't believe in coincidence. Personality disorders, yes, but not coincidence.

I pulled on my furry gloves and hat and strode out the doorway he opened. I breathed deeply of night air and freedom. Could I scale that wall before Bill stopped me? Probably not. I wasn't particularly athletic but he would be.

But I was quick, and I had lied. I'd had royal snowball battles in my inju-dicious childhood. Pity there wouldn't be any rocks in this barren yard. I scooped up a handful of snow, crunched it, and smacked Bill upside the head.

"Cheat!" he cried. "We have not yet declared war." He rolled up a ball and threw.

I dodged. As far as I was concerned, we'd declared war the moment I'd been brought here. I didn't want to gut the kid with my hidden knives, but I wanted out. His snowball whizzed past my head and hit the wall. Good velocity.

I made small balls with my small hands, and I didn't have a ballplayer's arm. But what I lacked in muscle, I made up for in speed and skill. I pounded him relentlessly. He got in a few hard hits—he had pretty good aim, but I was still fast and dodged most of them.

I was no longer shivering, and I had a better idea of how little the yard offered in the way of escape.

He was forming a cannonball-sized nuclear weapon when we heard the garage door open—followed by shots and shouts.

Bill dashed for the kitchen door. I smacked him in the back of the head. He didn't even turn around.

Idly, I made more snowballs and stacked them where I could reach them while I considered the eight-foot, snow-covered wall—my only means of escape from here. I was seriously considering scaling it when one of the shouts sounded familiar.

"Touch me again and I'll skin you alive, toad," the low, feminine voice purred.

The only person alive who can purr with a shout is my mother. Take a moment to think about it—purring in a stage voice.

I mentally said a word I never used aloud. I was pretty certain Ivan didn't mean for us to leave alive. If he did, we'd have the feds down on him so fast that they'd use his head for a bowling ball before he knew what hit him. But I'd seriously underestimated Fat Guy if he'd actually managed to catch my mother.

Or my mother had decided to save me and let herself be caught. One never knew with Magda. She'd play the story to suit her needs later, so there was no point asking questions.

No matter what issues we had, I couldn't abandon my mother.

CHAPTER 23

WITH A SIGH OF EXASPERATION, I SURRENDERED MY FLIGHT TO FREEDOM AND peered into the kitchen—no Bill, no Magda, no nobody. Fine then. I listened and heard raised voices upstairs. I slithered around out of sight of the hall doorway, nabbing the sturdier kitchen knife on the counter. Better armed, I cautiously peered down the hall. No one there.

I debated the wisdom of checking the garage for the limo, but I feared the chauffeur might still be in there, polishing the fenders of snow crud. I didn't think it would take three men to subdue Magda. She's not much larger than I am.

I darted to the empty coat closet and slipped inside, leaving the door slightly open. I once used coat closets as my favorite entertainment, hiding and listening to my mother's plotting or the whispers of embassy employees, depending on where we were. Closets had been my window on the world.

I didn't do them so much anymore, but this one was empty, convenient, and lacked anything useful like hangers that someone might want.

"Such a lovely room," I heard my mother purr maliciously overhead. "Brown and red are such a fashion statement. I must know your decorator."

Ah, the same room they'd taken me to. Was she signaling me? Didn't Ivan wonder where I was? Or did he not care as long as he had his prime objective?

"My wife decorates," the Russian grunted. "You will stay here."

I didn't hear my mother's reply. They must have shut the door on her.

"Where is other?" Ivan asked, quite clearly.

I heard them stomping down the stairs. I leaned back against the closet wall but didn't close the door. I could see the foyer from here.

Bill, the nosy little runt, replied in Russian.

Popov cut him off. "English! You must remember, you are American at all times. It is not good if you forget at the bar."

Bill grunted a Russian crudity I recognized, then said, "Outside playing snowballs. I figure she's freezing her ass off trying to scale that wall. I didn't know your wife lived here."

"She fill place with things to which I am allergic," Ivan growled, sneezing to prove his point. "Then she left. Women are useless. Fix me food and bring it to study."

If I remembered correctly, the room with the desk in it had leather chairs, and no carpet and curtains. Ivan must have ripped them out.

I didn't waste time pitying the asshat. I waited until I saw them descend the stairs to the foyer. Bill turned toward the kitchen, passing right in front of me. Ivan went down the far hall, leaving the foyer and staircase unobserved. Hearing no one else, I eased up the steps, thanking Mrs. Ivan for the lovely thick carpet that disguised any sound from my rubber-soled boots.

Magda was just unlocking the prison-room door as I reached for the knob. We stared at each other for a moment—thirty years of rocky relationship hitting us in the face. But we were family.

If she felt any emotion at seeing me, she disguised it. "Is there a television anywhere?" she whispered.

Those wouldn't have been my first words. "First room at top of stairs. Probably Mrs. Ivan's. I have no idea if there's cable."

I let her go look for the medium while I maliciously entered the prison room for all those lovely feather pillows. I already had the paring knife out. I began slicing them open as I followed my mother down the hall. I'd make darned certain we heard Ivan coming. I shook the last feathers down the stairs.

Did I hear more sneezing below us?

While I shredded a thick comforter all over the stairs and hall, Magda adjusted the TV to her liking. She cackled as she found what she was looking for. "The pigs were genius, if I do say so myself."

"We can probably walk out the front door if we want," I said in disgruntlement at this delay. "I don't know how soon Bill will remember that he turned off the alarm."

"I cannot miss the culmination of a lifetime of planning," Magda said, sitting on the end of the overstuffed bed. "You can trot out in the storm, if you like."

Curiosity is my besetting sin. I turned to watch the TV.

She had the sound off, but the camera shot was entertaining. Michael Moriarity and what I assumed was his entire extended family were walking around a large banquet hall, handing out flyers. At the head table, standing at a podium, was our distinguished presidential candidate, Senator Paul Rose. Even on this crappy TV I could tell he'd turned as gray as the hair beneath his dye job.

Adorable little squealing pigs were running under the tables, down the aisles, sending the expensively-garbed patrons into a panic as they tried to dodge the elusive porkers. Men in suits—some with concealed weapons—were dashing about, attempting to round up the critters. I waited for one to whip out a lasso. It was even funnier when the pigs ran between their legs, and they had to leap and dance around chairs and tables just to stay upright. At least none drew their guns on the adorable squealers. The pigs wore Scion balloons on rose-colored ribbons around their necks.

I'm not sure how many flyers actually made it into the hands of the fleeing guests, but paper fluttered all over the room. News crews were grabbing them out of the air as they filmed each other dodging pigs.

"You do know how to catch attention," I muttered. "What do the flyers say?"

"We had to keep it brief. It's just an outline of Rose's connections to Scion, and Scion Pharmaceutical connections to weapons manufacturers selling to terrorists in Afghanistan, Iran, and Syria. We left the Russian drug-weapon connection to last. Ivan shouldn't be so pissed."

"You spent a lifetime tying Rose to the gun industry?" I asked dubiously.

"Oh, no, when they follow those leads, they'll find the connection between Rose and every other member of Top Hat. And there's a website—hosted in Rumania, of course—where we outline the murders, fraud, and blackmail they committed to get where they are today, plus evidence that Scion was dealing weapons for drugs. The icing on the cake is Nadia's list of all their offshore bank accounts. We figure hackers will empty them before anyone gets that far."

"You're bankrupting Top Hat," I murmured in awe.

Furious shouts erupted below. Guess Ivan had figured it out too. He probably had the sound turned on. News announcers were practically jumping up and down with glee over a boring fundraiser turned ultimate exposé.

Ivan wasn't the sort to keep his ire to himself. I heard doors slamming and shouts and heavy footsteps running.

"Well, time to go." I handed Magda the paring knife.

She happily grabbed the comforter and began shredding it. "Any back stairs?"

"Not unless you want to do the hapless heroine in the attic scenario. Confrontation time." I took the pillows and ripped them open as I ran for the stairs, comforter held like a shield.

A bullet ripped through the cotton and past my head.

GRAHAM TAKES A WRONG TURN

"The limo has turned into Bethesda, not gone on to Chevy Chase," the voice on Graham's phone reported.

He cursed. Calculating Ivan wouldn't be keeping the women in different houses, he swung the Hummer around in an unplowed gas station, and roared back the way he'd just come. "Keep me posted. I need to redirect my driver."

He called Sam and told him to find a good parking place in Bethesda, preferably near the bar. "What are you driving?"

"The Subaru," Sam said with dignity. "I wish to be there when you are."

Graham snorted. "More intelligent method than this one. I'll let you know when we have an address."

For his men, he tried to sound calm and confident. Alone in the dark Hummer, roaring down empty, snow-blanketed highways, he was filled with dread. He wanted to curse the little fool for getting in over her head, but Ana hadn't been doing anything except shopping for birthday presents.

He reminded himself that she was better trained than most to handle daily emergencies as well as major unexpected events. She was the kind of person one wanted at their side in times of hurricane or earthquake.

He could not protect the world.

He *needed* to protect Ana. His world had just found focus.

He hit the Bluetooth button when the phone rang again.

"All hell is breaking loose at the fundraiser," his man on the scene reported. "I think Rose is feigning a heart attack. Moriarity just left with his family by a side door. Want me to keep following him?"

"Keep me entertained. Tell me what's going down." Information was his lifeblood, the reason he got up in the morning, the only reason he was still sane and not dead from a bullet to the head. He couldn't help Ana until he knew where she was, and information would get him there.

He prayed he'd made the right choice in following Magda to Bethesda and hoping Ana was in the same place. Surely even Ivan didn't have enough security to hold two hiding places.

As the story of the pigs and the flyers and the Moriaritys unfolded, Graham wanted to pound his head against the steering wheel. Magda had really done it this time. She'd just incited World War Three. Every thieving bastard in Top Hat would be gunning for her—and her entire family.

He called Nick to warn him to gather all his siblings and their significant others in the mansion.

"Already on it," Nick reported. "Although I think the men in Top Hat are money guys, not action sorts. They will be slow to respond. Right now, they're calling their lawyers, moving their money around in a panic, and ordering up their private jets."

"Moving their money?" Graham hadn't heard that part.

"Zander uncovered all their secret bank accounts from those files Ana sent him from Nadia's computer. He gave them to Magda when Ana didn't respond. She has them posted on that damned website."

Graham whistled—until he realized the retaliation that would result. He didn't mention that to Nick. "You're probably right, but I don't want to have to hunt any more of your family in this storm. I'll send men to secure the house."

He and Max had already made the mansion into a fortress, but it wouldn't hurt to have extra eyes and ears on duty. Of course, Ana's siblings were probably even better—although more unorthodox—at guarding than his trained professionals.

She had one hell of a family. He'd learned to respect their differences.

"Keep your men posted on Nadia's room," was Nick's curt reminder. "She's showing signs of waking. We have one of her friends reading to her, but she's no fighter."

"On it." Graham called the guard at the hospital with orders for extra monitoring.

After he punched out, the phone sputtered again and a brisk voice gave him an address and directions—Bethesda, as expected. "The car stopped, so they're at their destination."

"Is it one of Ivan's properties?" Graham asked after speaking the address into the Hummer's GPS.

"Yep, listed as vacant. Want us to surround the place?"

"You have anyone anywhere nearby?"

"We have two men watching the bar and one keeping an eye on Scion's place."

"Send them over. They may have a chance of getting there before Ana burns down the building." Graham added that to reassure himself. Ana would most certainly burn down a building if it meant getting out alive.

He just didn't know if she was alive.

He gunned the engine, spun the tires, and roared the Hummer past the snow plows.

CHAPTER 24

"I didn't explore the third floor," I said, flinging the comforter down the stairs. It landed smack on the heads of our attackers. Ivan sneezed, setting off another round of gunfire.

Magda sensibly turned tail and ran back down the hall. Close-up weapons like knives and feathers pretty much lost to propulsion explosives.

"Windows," Magda said, heading for the television suite.

It didn't take a lot of deduction to grasp her meaning. I preferred it to jumping from the attic. "Wrong side. That lands in a walled garden. Go for the front and hope there's a pedestrian gate." I ran to the other bedrooms and began gathering comforters and pillows.

Loud sneezes and roars emanated from below. Men are so clumsy when attacked by soft things. Another shot rang out, but I suspected that was Ivan's trigger finger still going off with his sneezing. I would split a few more pillows, but I'd rather use the rest for a warm landing.

Magda tried to unlock the window in the front room, but it appeared to be sealed or painted shut—fire hazard and bad news. No wonder they couldn't sell the place.

Muttering furiously, we both kicked at the modern double-paned glass until the window cracked, then shattered. I almost fell through before I could knock out the remaining glass with a blanket wrapped around my hand.

With the window open, I heard the rumble of a loud motor.

"They've got reinforcements," I said, trying not to panic as I heard a single set of heavy footsteps stumbling up the stairs.

I didn't hear Bill. Although I hadn't seen any sign of a weapon, having a sniper on the loose was Not Good.

"Whoever is coming up that drive is not Ivan's man," Magda said, listening to the roar while shoving comforters and pillows over the ledge to the snow drift beneath the window. "His driver is his only reinforcement, plus whoever that other wretch is downstairs. Piotr is home, sleeping with his dog," Magda said in disgust. "Piotr is a businessman, not a thug."

"That other *wretch* is a sniper who may have shot Scion," I informed her. "And I don't think that's a snow plow coming our way." I dropped out more comforters and pillows. No one shot at them.

I wanted to be home like businessman Piotr, sleeping with a kitty, with my family tucked safely around me.

I didn't want to be caught up in any more of Magda's disastrous escapades. It seemed as if I'd spent half my youth fleeing into the night like this. I just did not want to go there anymore. My fury added extra oomph to my flinging of pillows.

Graham was no better, I realized angrily, although he at least had the courtesy to keep me out of his business.

A glimmer of logic forced me to recognize that Magda hadn't involved me this time—and I'd *still* been kidnapped. I was hanging out with the wrong danged people.

The roar came closer. Something very large and heavy slammed into the iron gates blocking the drive.

"Not any friend of Ivan's," I agreed, playing my role as Obvious Woman. Ivan's thugs would know the code.

We couldn't lock the door from the inside of this room, but it wouldn't have mattered. Ivan applied bullets to the flimsy lock and the door exploded into splinters. Brilliant man was our Ivan.

"Out you go," Magda cried, shoving me from the window ledge into the comforter-covered snow drift below, saving me from Ivan's erratic gunfire.

As I tumbled out, high-powered rifle fire briefly lit the night. Bill, hiding in the bushes. Out of the frying pan, into the fire, as the old saying goes.

I didn't feel it at first. I did my tumble and roll and slid into the shrubbery around the foundation just as I'd intended. The landing had about knocked the breath from me, so I couldn't crawl out of range as quickly as I would have liked.

The ache in my shoulder began as I tried to slither on my belly behind the bushes while forming a snowball. I only managed a few feet. My left arm was reluctant to let my hand grip the snow. All I needed was a distracting barrage to cover Magda. She seemed to be struggling with Ivan in the window. I hoped she put her knife to good use. I had to take the shooter down—*with snowballs*—so she could jump. I got off a single shot.

As I'd hoped, Psycho Boy swung his fire toward the snowball. He couldn't see me behind the snow-draped shrubs, but I could catch glimpses of him under the security light. I made a few less-than-stellar balls. To relieve my aching shoulder, I got to my feet, and battered him as best as I could while zigzagging behind the overgrown shrubbery.

He kept shooting toward the last snowball thrown. Real snipers learned better than that. Despite his braggadocio, he was no more than a stationary target shooter.

I couldn't see behind me but I knew the moment Magda jumped. The gunfire swung back in her direction, giving me breathing room. I fell behind a particularly large evergreen to watch the vehicle smashing through the front gate.

A Hummer. Graham didn't own a Hummer, but I knew with all my heart and soul that it was Graham driving like a berserker in that car. The oversized tank crashed over the tilted gate, grinding it into the drive. Then the Hummer plowed straight through to the front door rather than follow tracks to the garage.

I figured he'd go through the front door if I didn't present myself.

Gunfire erupted again, this time from the upper story window we'd leapt from. Ivan stood framed in the broken glass, cursing and shouting and shooting at anything that moved.

A single shot from the Hummer's window brought him tumbling down.

I hate, loathe, abhor, and despise guns, but for this one moment in time, I appreciated their convenience.

I stumbled from behind the evergreen, trying to wave my arms, until I collapsed in a nice big snowdrift.

~

Raging internally, Graham swung his automatic from the bastard in the window to the stupid sniper who'd shot Ana. The idiot had frozen in place, hiding behind his gunsight as if it were a shield, while he looked for his targets. Graham aimed his weapon, peeled off a few rounds, and the sniper fell.

He shoved open his door to find Ana. His heart had stopped the moment she'd fallen into the snowbank. *Not again. Never again.* He couldn't lose his life's blood one more time while he helplessly watched his world crash around him.

Graham was aware of other cars following him through the busted gate, of Magda dashing toward her daughter, of men shouting. He didn't react to anything but the unmoving crumpled ball of leopard fur.

He got there first, scooping her out of the snow, and she stirred in his arms. He could have sworn she murmured "My very own Rambo" before she fell limp.

Heart now pounding like a kettle drum, Graham held her close. He could feel her breathing against his chest, although not as strongly as he'd like. He shouted at his men to clean up, while he strode back to the Hummer, carrying his precious burden. He wouldn't lose this woman, *couldn't*.

He didn't even growl when Magda opened the back door and climbed in. He couldn't drive and hold Ana at the same time. Magda was definitely not her usual polished self. Her sleek hair had tumbled down around her shoulders, she was covered in mud and snow and blood, and she was missing her high heels.

"I'll murder you later," he said as he deposited her bleeding daughter into her arms.

"Give me your first aid kit," was her response.

At least she had the grace to sound worried.

Finding a solid first aid kit in the back—certain sign he'd stolen the Hummer from a physician—Graham dropped it near Magda, then climbed into the driver's seat. He spun the damaged Hummer until he'd turned it around, then hit the gas. He refused to lose Ana. For the first time in his life, he abandoned the rest of the damned world and focused on the one part that meant more than life to him.

~

GROGGILY, I PRIED MY EYES OPEN. MY LEFT SHOULDER DIDN'T MOVE AND seemed to be covered in a bulky bundle. I took some time to sift through the sands of memory. Ah, yes, I'd probably been shot by Sociopath Bill. Charming.

I didn't feel any pain, but as woozy as my head felt, I figured they'd filled me up with dope. I had a moment of panic wondering if it was Mylaudanix. That woke me up.

I'd already subconsciously accepted that I was in a hospital bed. Now I realized I wasn't alone, but the presence with me didn't seem threatening. *Graham.* Even in the dark, I recognized him. Maybe it was his expensive cologne, but at this hour, it mixed with his familiar masculine musk.

I wasn't sure he was breathing. I shifted my head enough to see the outline of his big body in a recliner beside the bed. The size alone confirmed his identity.

My heart shifted a little. Graham hardly ever left his attic office. He'd once been pretty well known and attracted unwanted attention when he bothered to step out in public. Maybe he felt safe in a hospital. It had been ten years, after all, and nurses had better things to do than follow ancient politics.

I wanted to ask about Magda, but I didn't want to wake him. I probably should sleep off this stuff messing with my head.

That's when I noticed a screen lighting on the stand. My cell, my lifeline to my family—had been stomped. So this must be the burner. I edged up to a sitting position. The stand was thoughtfully arranged on my right side. Graham was at my left. I couldn't reach my wounded arm out to touch him, but I could reach the phone.

Bless my siblings, but they included me in their group texting. Words were flying. Our news mavens, Sean and Patra, relayed news to Nick and Guy as it came over the wires, sparse as it was. It sounded like Ivan's neighbors had reported a shoot-out at the OK Corral but no bodies were found. Graham's men had done a pretty good clean-up job.

I wondered where they'd taken Ivan and Bill, because I was pretty certain they'd been heavily damaged by Graham's automatic.

Scrolling through messages, I could see even Juliana touched base, asking what hospital I was in. I looked at the time. It was still before midnight here. I did a few mental calculations and eventually worked out that Tudor and Zander were probably just getting up from their distant beds. They should be checking in soon.

If I couldn't crawl into Graham's lap, I'd settle for catching up with my siblings. And myself. The answer to Juliana's question showed that I'd apparently been transported to the same hospital as Nadia was in. I'd have to scroll backward to find the reasoning for that.

If everyone was safe, I wanted to know what had happened to Rose, his pigs, and Magda.

Even though I found Magda's name in the group text, I didn't see any responses from her. As best as I could determine by scrolling back and forth, she'd turned herself in to the police once I was operated on and declared safe. A text from Nick said she and Moriarity were well lawyered up.

Creating a public nuisance probably didn't carry a long sentence, once the police realized Magda was too cracked to have done anything sensible like killing Scion. Pigs and balloons, yes, snipers, no. They'd work that one out eventually. Graham had it right when he called her a twisted genius—no matter what havoc she created, she never got caught.

That Magda has actually turned herself into the authorities instead of fleeing into the night caused much consternation among the family, but there wasn't anything anyone could do at this hour.

I thought about letting them know I was okay, but the long stream of information just exhausted me. I had some serious thinking to do, and no one was expecting me to do anything until morning.

No longer sleepy but needing the bathroom, I eased up from the right side of the bed. Graham was totally out of it. Fine protector he turned out to be. I smiled as I thought it, wanting to touch his hair but fearing I'd wake him. I didn't want to imagine what kind of hell I'd put him through. My whole heart swelled just knowing he'd willingly rode to the rescue. I hadn't even had to send a frantic call.

That was part of my problem.

I found a white hotel robe and slippers that weren't mine in the bathroom. Did hospitals provide robes? Fancy, if so. I probably looked like a specter in all this white fluff, but I appreciated their availability. I really didn't want to see my leopard coat again, but now that I'd remembered. . . I located the coat in the closet and fished for the papers I'd stolen: furniture receipts. Big whooping deal, but they had an address on them. I could have used them for escape, had Magda and Graham not roared to the rescue.

I used the facilities, pocketed my phone, and feeling more awake, peered into the corridor.

There was no one visible, so I walked down to the elevator to pay a visit. Earlier, they'd said Nadia might be waking. I didn't want her to feel alone, if so.

Nadia had bravely dumped a dangerous husband, hauled her kids across an ocean, and kept them safe while working for justice and to prevent others from harm. If I was understanding what Magda had done with Nadia's information, Nadia had accomplished what I hadn't—destroying Top Hat. She and the kids had nearly lost their lives in the process.

I admired her courage but couldn't decide if risking her life was the best choice. She probably hadn't known she was in danger.

Which reflected another of my problems—I *knew* information was dangerous. *Acting* on what I knew was even more so, as Magda and I had proven time and again.

Graham remained safe by staying in his ivory tower. I'd done the same from my basement. I just didn't know if I could hide like that anymore.

Nadia's room still had a guard stationed outside. He recognized me and nodded with respect when I gestured for entrance. I had done nothing to garner respect except go birthday shopping and get myself shot.

To my immense relief and delight, Nadia was awake enough to be grog- gily cupping her phone in her hands as if it were a lifeline, even if she seemed to be praying over it more than seeing it. She opened one eye wide enough to note my entrance.

"Guy said you might be awake," I whispered, taking the chair at her bedside. I was feeling a little woozy again.

She lifted her bandaged chin at all the tubes still hanging on her arms. "Not entirely," she rasped with grim humor.

"I'm Ana."

Instead of trying to talk, she flipped the phone to an image of me helping Anika paste the dinosaur, indicating she knew who I was. I hadn't realized EG had stolen my phone to snap that. Nadia's half smile as she lovingly traced her youngest child's face melted all my hardhearted cynicism, and I wanted to cry in relief that she'd be returned to those beautiful children.

"You've been catching up on the news?" I asked, trying not to sink into sentiment. The drugs must have made me weepy.

She flipped the photos back and showed me images of Anika and Viktor blowing out birthday candles. "Thank you," she whispered.

I was glad the cake and presents had made it to them. Children needed to be sheltered with love and happiness and not touched by the ugliness of the outside world until they were strong enough to understand.

"They are great kids," I said. "Someday, they will be very proud of what you've done to make the world a better place."

That was the flip side of my problem. I wanted to say I'd made the world a better place. I just didn't want to endanger anyone but myself while I was doing it.

She grimaced and leaned groggily against her pillow. "Never again. I wish to see them grow old."

There it was, the answer I'd been seeking from her. "Smart lady," I said.

I could hear a commotion in the hall. I stood up and gestured at her closet. "Nick and Guy brought you clothes. Would you mind if I borrow some?"

She looked startled but nodded. "I owe you my life." After the feeding tubes, her voice was hoarse and barely above a whisper, but I took that as a yes, even if I didn't exactly agree with her.

She was taller, but I yanked on her leggings and didn't care if they bagged around my ankles. Sweaters were meant to be bulky and this one covered me to my knees. I needed time to myself. I wished for my furry boots but I hadn't had the smarts to look for them when I'd escaped my room. Nadia's Uggs were large but stayed on.

Dragging on her coat, I peered around the door. There was a stir at the nurse's station.

I turned and waved to Nadia, gestured with a finger to my lips to stay silent, and let myself out, looking like a departing nurse and heading in the opposite direction of the activity.

By the time the elevator had reached the bottom floor, I'd set up my Uber-app on the burner and called for a ride. I had no cash, but my credit card was in their files. My ID and credit card info were stored in my cloud account. With my phone in hand, I could go anywhere.

Whoever had provided this little gem hadn't realized how far it could take me. Or that I would want to go.

Saying a silent regretful farewell, I gave the address of one of my hide-aways to the driver.

CHAPTER 25

Fuming, Graham had the taxi take him straight to his front door. Waking up at midnight to discover Ana had escaped the damned hospital—while under his watch—had not improved his already turbulent mood.

Before he left, he'd paid the Hummer owner for the damage, then abandoned his BMW bike in the garage and paid the taxi an exorbitant sum to take him home. If he wanted to stay alive long enough to murder Ana, he couldn't be doing wheelies on ice. And poor Sam deserved his rest at this hour after helping clean up after him this evening.

The feds had accepted Ivan and his minion with the understanding they'd receive a full report later. They would bandage them up and interrogate them more officially than Graham could. He doubted they'd be hacking any more computers anytime soon.

Mallard could use his rest, too, but Ana's siblings were all congregated in the horsehair parlor despite the early morning hour. Apparently they were comparing notes, while the old general turned butler was having the time of his life. That Mallard had actually allowed food and beverages past the sacred parlor door spoke of his fondness for this eclectic group of young people.

They all looked up the instant Graham entered. As the eldest, Nick spoke first. "We thought you were guarding Ana!"

Yeah, that's what he'd thought too. He'd had some idiot idea that she'd wake up, see him, and feel safe enough to go back to sleep again. Try explaining that to her brother.

"Ana had other ideas. She borrowed Nadia's clothes and fled." He didn't have to explain that he'd fallen asleep on the job. He headed for the stairs.

The group poured from the parlor and followed him.

"For where?" the gentle one called Juliana asked in genuine perplexity. "She did not come here."

Graham had rather hoped she had, but he wouldn't admit that either. "Where's your mother?" he asked instead.

"The cops let her go an hour ago. We have no idea." That was Patra, the tall, dark-haired, buxom reporter. "Why would Ana go to Magda?"

"If she had bothered telling me anything, I'd let you know. I'm going to bed." He was furious, terrified, and not sleeping anytime soon, but he had to leave Ana's family to do whatever they did, while he did the same.

That was how he operated best—alone.

"I'll have Tudor crack Uber," Nick was saying, scanning his phone. "He'll be up by now."

Uber, of course. He'd stupidly given Ana her phone so she could keep up with her family.

Juliana drifted toward him. "We have only just got Elizabeth to sleep," she said softly. "She will wish to see Ana in the morning. Do you not wish to do the same?"

Elizabeth—a royal name for Ana's evil genius of a sister. He'd be delighted if he never saw the whole damned interfering oddball family again.

Mallard studied him, wearing a long face, which hit Graham hard. The old man would never plead. He'd been his only friend these past years.

Ana had become more than a friend. He'd thought she'd felt the same. *Why the hell had she run away?*

That's when Graham realized that what he felt was hurt. He hadn't been hurt in a long, long time. He'd sealed himself off from emotion, lived in the land of logic, and survived.

In these last months, Ana had reminded him of the roller coaster that life could be. Living included Ana in his bed and pummeling him in his gym. It meant enduring her taunts, hearing her wit, suffering her anger, and enjoying the challenges she flung at him daily. If living again meant Ana in his life, then he wanted Ana—even if it hurt, dammit. He was no coward.

He summoned the rusty diplomacy he'd once wielded so carelessly. "I'll find Ana. The rest of you get some rest. The media will be on our doorstep in the morning."

"I'll handle the media," Patra offered.

"I'll look after Elizabeth," Juliana said.

Nick and Sean began tapping into their phones, already sending out support lines. *That* was how family worked.

And they'd apparently accepted him at his word—as one of the family.

He didn't even need to hack Uber. He had Ana's account information. It was almost as if she wanted him to find her.

Graham *almost* grinned at that realization. Ana would never underestimate him.

~

I'D LEARNED FROM MAGDA TO KEEP BOLT HOLES—A ROOM, A STORAGE UNIT, extra clothes, new identity, credit cards, whatever I needed to lie low for a few days. I hadn't had much use for mine lately—money made a difference. But I picked up my Goodwill bag of duds in the storage locker downtown and traipsed over to a low-rent hotel where I paid a monthly fee.

The room was a step above flophouse. I'd lived in worse. But the place was free of bugs, I had my own linens in my Goodwill bag, and a key not requiring a hotel clerk.

My shoulder was starting to ache, and I'd probably be wishing for drugs by morning. So I knew I needed to straighten out my head before then. I couldn't hide from my family for long.

I couldn't hide from Graham at all.

I could, however, leave the country and abandon the whole lot of them to their dangerous games. I'd done it before. I knew how to do it again. The question became—did I want to? Ten years ago, it had made sense. Now. . .

I lay back on the flat pillow and stared at the cracked ceiling. My shoulder throbbed. I could be *dead* right now. Where would EG be if I was dead? I didn't want to leave her alone and devastated. I wanted to be alive.

If I were alive and in China, would she be okay?

I'd lived without family for ten years. I'd *endured*, was a better way to put it. These last six months of having my family around me had made me a better person, in my opinion. I was happy for the first time in memory.

Which had a lot to do with my spy in the attic, which complicated everything. Graham wasn't reckless like Magda, but he took chances. Look what he'd done last night—driven a stolen Hummer through a blizzard to crash down iron gates. Dangerous men hated him for good reason. Powerful men sought his aid. He did not live in a safe or sane world.

Graham and I could never be a cozy family sitting by the fire, books in our laps, dogs at our feet. It just wasn't happening. Even through my pain, I recognized that as truth. The question became. . . I wasn't sure. I'd wanted to work this out before anyone found me, but answers eluded my muddled mind.

I gave up and fell into a restless sleep.

∼

I WOKE UP WITH LIGHT SPILLING THROUGH THE TORN WINDOW SHADE, knowing Graham was in the room again. The instant I stirred, a hand reached under my nose holding a pill.

"Not Mylaudanix," his deep baritone said.

I gratefully took the medication and the glass of water he handed me. I wasn't good with pain.

I wasn't sure I wanted to open my eyes again, but, as mentioned, curiosity was my besetting sin. I looked up.

Graham's square, scarred face looked drawn and weary. He'd shoved back his overlong black hair, revealing the ugly jagged edges of the red scar that was the visible sign of the damage within. Graham had lost his entire world twice—at age ten, when his father had been killed. Again, with 9/11 taking his wife and destroying the brilliant career he'd had every reason to expect.

I probably understood his damage better than any other person around him.

"You care to explain?" he asked, looking around for a chair. Finding none, he settled gingerly at the end of the narrow mattress.

I'd tried to answer my question with research and logic and failed. Seeing Graham sitting there in the morning light, apparently having spent the entire night hunting for me, I knew the answer with my heart.

"I want a home," I told him. "I want a family. I want what Nadia has. I'm not sure I'm brave enough to have that life."

I think I finally managed to shock him.

He rubbed his head some more, then leaned back on his elbows. "I think you need to expand on that."

"That's what I've been trying to do. I can't say I understand it entirely myself." I wriggled up against the lousy pillow so I could admire his broad shoulders. He'd taken off his coat, revealing bulging arms under a fitted fisherman's sweater. "I love my family, even if they are pains in the posterior most of the time. I love you in a different way that has a lot to do with the way you make me feel right now."

That part, he understood. He sat up, prepared to reach for me, but then he remembered my shoulder. He sank back with a grimace. "Lust is different from love."

I kicked him. "I don't lust over just anyone. I lust over people I respect and admire and in your blamed case, love. You are a person worthy of love. Sometimes," I amended. "You're also a grumpy hermit with deplorable social skills. I'm prepared to accept that. If that was my only problem, we'd be home right now."

He sent me the most angelic smile I'd ever been blessed with in my life, and my insides turned to goo. Graham almost never smiled or I'd have been back to being a doormat long ago. As it was, my heart joyously splatted against my ribcage, and I wanted to give up thinking and get back to kissing.

He flopped back against the narrow bed and studied the same cracked ceiling as I had last night. "Okay, I can live with that," he said with what almost sounded like hope. "*You* aren't precisely the most congenial companion, you'll note. But I wouldn't be here if you weren't the companion I want beside me for a lifetime."

A lifetime! That admission really rocked my world. It was the most I'd get from him, I suspected. He was dancing around the emotional words, I knew, but he had me squirming with anticipation. We'd started out on a pretty rocky basis, but we'd learned to work around our differences, usually physically.

So I didn't really need words. Action spoke louder. He'd probably saved my life last night. He'd gone looking for me instead of saving the heads of important countries, as he was wont to do. I had to be very important for him to abandon his superhero responsibility for all these hours.

The knowledge made me feel special, as I never really had before. *I* knew

I was special, but very few acknowledged that a prickly introvert with anger issues could be anything but annoying.

"You just don't want to be saddled with my family without me to act as barrier," I prodded, pushing the threadbare blanket aside to tickle him with my toes. My family owned half his house. He'd have to deal with them even if I wasn't there.

"True," he agreed, disagreeably. "But I'm learning to use them. Patra is acting as family spokesman for the media this morning. She's great at manipulating the story. She's better than you are at handling interference."

I wasn't in the least insulted. The last time I'd dealt with media, I'd smashed all their pretty satellite trucks into each other. "That earns you a gold star I'll repay when my shoulder feels better. She'll have Tudor hacking media email to know what questions to prepare for. Is Juliana looking after EG?"

"Does anyone actually look after EG? Or do does she just let them pretend they are?" He was back to watching me.

"Very perceptive, Sherlock. So you understand some of the magnitude of what I'm saying when I say I want my family. Now think back to Magda. Am I turning into her? Will I be endangering them and you as she does?"

His big dark eyes widened. I swear, his lashes were almost as long as mine. Well, no, my almond-shaped eyes are my best feature. I narrowed them at him for effect. He grinned again. I could get very used to watching him smile, if my heart could take it. It was racing a mile a minute.

"No, the question becomes, will *they* be endangering *us*? Let's face it, Ana, they are not homebodies and never will be. They have your mother's obsessive genes. All their fathers were the kind of men she admired and respected, men who lived dangerously or adventurously—it's in the blood. You tried to escape that life. How well did that work for you?"

Remembering my years of living safely and sanely in a damp Atlanta basement where my one pride was a moth-eaten carpet, I grimaced. "Not well," I admitted. "I've learned a lot these last months. Demanding justice in an inherently unfair world is not a safe or sane life."

"I know, but someone has to do it." He caught my bare foot and rubbed it. "I've been avoiding the complications by not leaving the attic. I really don't want you involved in what I do."

"Which brings us to what you do," I said, not as caustically as I would have liked because I loved the foot rub. "How can we have a relationship when I'm clueless about your connections?"

He stopped rubbing and drew his brow down in a frown. "I work for myself, just as you do."

Well, I kinda knew that, but there was more to it than that. "Your connections are better than the CIA's."

He shrugged. "That's because I'm willing to work with all the agencies, uniting their information while they bicker with each other. *United we stand* is a good motto, if they'd just practice it."

He had once been a presidential aide. He had security clearances out the wazoo. Czar of the underground information network, probably with credentials from every alphabet agency in the world. He really was a spy in my attic—but he didn't run when trouble loomed as Magda had most of my life.

"What we do is irrelevant to this particular discussion," he said, dismissing my distracting concerns. "I don't like what you do either. I want you in my bed where I can see you, not out gallivanting about the city inciting riots. But I know that's not who you are, and I'd probably get bored if it were."

I kicked him again. "You would not. I'd see to that. But I might get bored with you," I taunted, just to baste the gander with the same sauce. As if Graham could ever be boring!

"Come home with me," he said solemnly, twisting my ankle between his hands. "We need you. Mallard would probably leave me if I lost you."

I laughed at that. "If Magda shows up, we can have him hover over her until she cries for air and flees."

This time, he sat up and hauled me into his lap. *Finally.* I leaned into his shoulder and all the aches went away. Or maybe the pill kicked in.

"From the reports my operatives have sent me, your mother went to Captain Freddy, gave him her complete itinerary, and managed to admit absolutely nothing. I don't think they can hold her on suspicion of setting pigs loose at a banquet—especially since she was busy being kidnapped. My men gave the feds your sniper bartender, along with his gun, which happens to be the same one that shot Scion. They'll inform the cops."

"So many questions, so little time." For once, I really didn't care how this story turned out. "Who hired Bill to kill Scion? And can we go get breakfast?" I covered his square jaw with kisses, then crawled out of his lap.

"Even your nosy family doesn't know what I just told you yet," he warned, helping me on with Nadia's coat, which nearly dragged the ground. "You need to keep quiet until the feds have done a sweep of Ivan's offices."

"I can do that. I'll be feeding my face. Text Mallard and tell him I want blueberry raspberry muffins." I impatiently stamped on Nadia's oversized boots. Right or wrong, I was going home. The joy rising up in me said I'd made the right decision, probably for all the wrong reasons since love is irrational.

"Mallard needs to sleep sometime. He was up half the night feeding your siblings. I trust they'll mostly stay in their own homes once assured you're safe." He sounded grumpy, but he helped me tug on the boots and wrapped his big arm around me as if I were a precious object as we went out.

"I'll make my own muffins," I declared in a rash decision that would most certainly dissolve once faced with a search for utensils and ingredients. "Why would Ivan Popov order Scion killed? Isn't that like cutting off the hand that feeds you?"

"This is why the media can't have this information yet." He guided me down the snow-covered street. The plows hadn't bothered with this inner city neighborhood yet. "Bill the Bartender claims his idol Senator Rose ordered Scion removed because he was a liability."

CHAPTER 26

HOLY GUACAMOLE! PRESIDENTIAL CANDIDATE SENATOR ROSE HAD ORDERED A hit on his campaign strategist? They could charge Rose on conspiracy to *murder*? I'd been right and they'd killed Scion for being *stupid*? Then they ought to kill Rose.

Bombshells apparently enhanced my hunger. My stomach rumbled a protest as Graham tossed me into the waiting car.

Graham had dragged poor Sam out of bed to come after me at this ridiculous hour. Today, his multi-talented driver was driving a flashy-looking black Subaru instead of the limo. I didn't want to force Graham into the public eye, but if Mallard wasn't fixing breakfast, I needed food. A Subaru would go through a drive-thru better than a limo.

"Bagel shop," I said. "I'll run in and buy everything." I really was operating on adrenalin and joy.

Graham pulled out one of his ever-present phones and ordered a dozen of everything, delivered, probably from one of the most expensive shops in town if he had it in his contact list.

I really needed to get used to living like this.

I wasn't sure I could.

"Psycho Bill is bringing down Senator Rose?" I said in a hushed whisper after Graham returned his phone to his pocket. "For real?"

"He has nothing left to lose. His sister tried to kill Nadia. She failed with the hit-and-run. The cops found her car after she tried and failed again in the hospital. The feds were preparing to deport her but now she's behind bars. If Bill actually killed Scion, he's up on murder one. A plea deal keeps him from the chair."

"DC has no death penalty," I said, frowning. His *sister*? I was missing a few pieces.

"Maryland still does. Scion died in Bethesda. Wouldn't you rather hear this on a full stomach?" He drew me against him since I was shivering.

"I'm not sure I want to hear this at all. Bill has a *sister*?"

"Computer programmer, calls herself Michelle Lee, hooked on Mylaudanix, will do anything for Ivan and drugs. Bill isn't on the drugs, but he's not quite right in the head. He thinks if he spills everything, we'll praise him, give him money, and he'll be another Scion someday. Delusional. They were checking out Nadia's hospital room the day Tony's phone rang and you handed it to my guard at her door. That's how they guessed you were getting too close—they called that phone and saw you."

"He seemed like such a nice kid," I said. "But I still don't get it. I thought Ivan Popov worked for Scion Pharmaceuticals, and Bill worked as a bartender for Ivan, and how does Rose fit into this anywhere?"

"Keeping in mind this is Bill and Ivan's versions and what little we've had time to piece together from other sources. . . Rose foolishly believed Scion was working for him and for Top Hat, but Scion was and had always been a loose cannon who worked only for himself. He was not a team player."

"It was Top Hat that ordered Tony to kill our fathers, right? Scion wasn't part of them back then," I clarified, afraid the pain pill was making my head woozy again. "Rose was barely a cipher at that point."

"Do you remember when Tony said *the bloody kid snitched*? He meant Rose. Rose was younger than my father or yours, but he knew they were connected to wealthy men like Max, so he insinuated himself into their company. We may never know how he found out that your father was backing out of the arms deal. Rose was the one who informed Top Hat. Scion learned it from Tony later when Tony bought the bombs from him."

I sat stunned. I'd despised Rose because he had the morals of a baboon, but having the actual evidence that *he was responsible for my father's death*? I wanted him flayed within an inch of his life and hung out to dry.

"That was just the start," Graham continued. "Rose talked his father into using the mine for the weapons. Your grandfather wouldn't have known any of this since they knew Max would go ballistic after losing his son-in-law and his protégé. But Rose had been helpful enough to Top Hat at that point that they agreed to support his political career."

"Rose essentially blackmailed Top Hat," I translated, "although I'm guessing he let them think they were supporting a rising politician to help their cause."

"Mutually compatible," Graham agreed. "They're all cannibalistic roaches. Scion had his fingers in a lot of pies. He and Tony were old pals from the same IRA group your father belonged to. That's how he knew about the GenDef people handling the weapons even though he was still in Ireland at the time. Scion eventually went from selling guns to pushing drugs. He was too rough to be part of the Top Hat team, but he had knowledge, and they needed his wealth and eventually, they all worked together to get Rose on the platform."

"Does Top Hat know what Scion was investing his wealth in?" I thought of the weapons manufacturing industries across third world countries, many disguised as pharmaceutical plants.

Graham shrugged. "Some of them would have supported him, but I don't know who had knowledge of what yet. Magda did a good job, but I doubt we'll ever be able to bring down the lot of them."

I could try. But I didn't like thinking like that yet. "So at some point Scion decided he wanted to go into politics and dug his hooks into Rose's campaign?"

"Again, mutually compatible relationship." Graham kissed my hair.

This was a caring side to my spy I thought I could learn to enjoy.

"Scion had Eastern European contacts who would be of use to many of Top Hat's members," he continued. "He had access to a huge untapped market. Rose had the political influence to help Scion push his drugs through the FDA, and open doors for any other schemes he had in mind."

"But my mother began harassing them," I said, working my way through the labyrinth. "And Nadia and Guy slapped that condemning report on the tables of Congress."

"And Scion suddenly became an enormous liability to a campaign that's been losing momentum since you started pulling out their underpinnings. Rose's team had to cut off Scion and his blackmail before any more dirty secrets leaked." Graham peered out the window to see why we were crawling.

But it was a snow day in DC. Traffic was inevitable. I contemplated leaping out and finding food while the car inched along. Or hitting the Metro. Could I keep using the Metro if I settled into life in a mansion?

"I won't have to go to political rallies or fundraisers, will I?" I asked.

Graham sent me one of those mind-bending, eye-blazing looks. "Did you get hit on the head last night?"

Reassured, I beamed up at him. "Just checking." I'd been processing some of his information and tried my muzzy head on guessing. "Scion had Rose squash Nadia's and Guy's damaging report, but that wasn't enough to keep the report from circulating. He had to get rid of them to prevent them from providing reliable witnesses to the media. He knew Tony could handle one, but not both at the same time, so Scion called in favors from Ivan."

"Another mutually compatible relationship," Graham agreed. "The Popovs had given Scion's company access to Eastern Europe, helped him build his sales team. Scion loaned the Popovs money to buy cell towers and businesses that helped them, and Ivan's hackers, in the American door."

"Ivan's hackers—Bill and his sister?" I asked, still trying to pull together the threads.

"Exactly. The feds are questioning Piotr, but he seems to really believe he's running legitimate businesses, pharmacies, pubs, whatever. Ivan is the one who tossed his bar manager's house when he didn't get paid. He employs hackers, assassins, drug pushers, whatever underhanded methods he can summon to expand their territory. He and Scion were peas in a pod."

The car pulled up to our house—*our* house, my family and Graham's. Six months ago I'd arrived on the doorstep determined to build a home for my family—and learned our inheritance from our grandfather had been stolen. I'd blamed Graham.

Since then, I'd learned a lot of truths about myself, about Graham, and our fathers. I had more to learn, but for now, the house was all I had ever wanted—a solid, safe center for my peripatetic family when they needed help or comfort or just companionship.

The brats were all at the dining room table, scarfing down *my* bagels. They waved hands, newspapers, and napkins as I entered but continued stuffing their faces—until they stopped and stared.

Graham entered behind me, his hand at the small of my back. He helped me into the chair I usually took near the head of the table. And he took the chair next to it that Nick had abandoned in favor of sharing texts coming in on Patra's phone.

Everyone put down their phones and papers, eyes wide in expectation.

Graham never sat at the table with us. He was showing me and my family that he knew how to be a team player.

"EG, wing me a bag," I said as nonchalantly as I could manage.

Her bangs were pink today. I'm not sure in honor of what since she despises pink. She pushed the bag she'd been digging into in my direction.

The others pushed *all* the bags in our direction. Not one of the pigs had bothered looking for plates, hence the waving napkins that had been provided by the bagel people.

Juliana jumped up to pour me a cup of tea. I don't know who had the smarts to boil water, but the cup still steamed as she set it in front of me. Sean gestured at the coffee pot he was on the verge of emptying. "Graham?" he asked.

Sean was the son of the other man who had been killed with our fathers. He'd kept his distance from Graham for years, but the two had quit circling each other like dogs since Sean had chosen Patra and left me alone.

Stiffly, Graham nodded acceptance. He really wasn't used to dining with others anymore. He might attend an occasional secret business meeting where coffee was served, but nothing like my family's informality. Mallard had waited on him hand and foot, so I wasn't certain Graham even knew how to fix his own coffee, much less get up and fetch his own food from the buffet.

"Nick made it, so it's pretty foul," Sean offered, delivering a mug. "We kind of told Mallard to take the day off. Hope that's all right."

"I'm amazed he accepted the offer," Graham said dryly, sipping the foul brew without wincing. He rummaged through the bagel bag I offered.

"He didn't," a cool voice said from the doorway. "I ordered him out."

Magda.

CHAPTER 27

REMEMBERING HIS RUSTY MANNERS, GRAHAM ROSE FROM HIS CHAIR AND
pulled out the one across from Ana. He couldn't remember the last time
Max's immense table had held so many people.

Looking far more polished than when he'd last seen her, Magda brushed
past him in a cloud of expensive scent. She pressed a kiss to Ana's head,
then took the chair he offered. Her blond hair had been fashioned in a
casual upsweep and her attire could have graced a runway. She didn't
appear as if she'd spent the night adorning a police station.

He'd gladly throttle her, but that was Ana's privilege. He had to learn
to share.

The others didn't appear surprised at their mother's appearance, so she
must have arrived earlier and spent her time preparing to make a grand
entrance. Wordlessly, Graham helped himself to a bagel and ignored the
woman who would in effect be his mother-in-law.

He hadn't asked Ana to marry him. He wasn't in the least certain Ana
had any interest in legalities. But given the size of the mansion and their
respective fortunes, they'd have to discuss it sometime. He'd better consider
Magda part of the baggage Ana carried. He'd let Ana take care of philosoph-
ical matters. He knew how to deal with practical ones, like Magda. They
would make a good team.

"Captain Freddy didn't lock you up on general principles?" Ana asked, sipping her tea.

"Max helped Frederick's father when he was shot and disabled on the job a few decades ago. It's all about who you know, dear." Magda gazed in distaste at the scattering of crumpled bagel bags. "You might consider hiring additional help. You cannot expect Mallard to wait on pigs."

"An unfortunate choice of words," Graham murmured. "I trust PETA won't be breathing down our backs for last night's incident?"

"You were always an annoying pest, darling," she said dismissively, getting up to pour tea. "Rose should be resigning about now. You need a television in here."

"Over my dead body," Ana said before Graham could. He hid his smile behind his cup of coffee-flavored mud.

Nick got up and found china in the sideboard. Juliana disappeared in the direction of the kitchen stairs, presumably to fetch more tea. Graham admired how they all knew their tasks with a minimum of fuss. He more than admired Ana's refusal to wait on the woman who had benefitted from her daughter's willingness to take care of her children for so long.

Ana was the reason everyone knew their tasks.

Magda floated gracefully back to her chair. "Of course. You all have those annoying little phones."

EG held up her tablet showing an image of a business-suited man being led away in handcuffs. Sean glanced over. "Rose. They arrested him at his office moments ago."

Magda smirked. "It's done. Top Hat has been crippled from the top down. The minor appendages that remain haven't the connections to unite. They'll pour their money into some other rubber-headed candidate like Bill Smith, I suppose."

"And we have your balloons and pigs to thank for that?" Graham asked cynically.

"Well, I did find Moriarity for you, darling," she cooed.

Ana checked her email and showed him one from Ireland. Graham snorted and let her present it to the table. She handed it to Patra, who was closest.

Patra hooted and gave it to Sean, who passed it to Nick. Juliana returned with the tea and refilled cups. She glanced at the email and shrugged. Graham had high hopes for Juliana. She was an idealistic peacemaker disinterested in politics. He'd like to get to know her brother when he arrived. He'd seen Zander's work. The man was brilliant at understanding financial records. The twins' extended family had been absolutely correct to rip them from Magda's carelessness, even if it meant they'd grown up not knowing their siblings or mother.

EG didn't look up from her tablet. That one was an enigmatic puzzle. He might enjoy watching her evolve.

He'd never had family. Could Ana teach him how family worked?

Nick politely passed Ana's phone to Magda. She didn't attempt to read it but passed it back.

"Forgot your reading glasses again?" Ana taunted, scrolling through the rest of her messages. "My Irish contact found Scion's most recent will. It left everything to Rose—which gives Rose another reason for murder. Unfortunately, Scion never bothered signing it. His family will ultimately inherit it all."

"A severe disappointment to Rose's party, I'm sure," Graham said, sipping the abominable coffee.

Ana laughed as she continued scrolling through her phone. "The Moriartys are already holding news conferences saying they intend to dissolve Scion Pharmaceuticals and all its related businesses. Who sent them the financial records Zander compiled?"

"Tudor," Graham said. "We didn't want them to know where the information came from. He offered to pipe it to them under one of his internet aliases."

"I can't wait until he attends MIT next year," Ana crowed. "Just think. . ." She stopped herself and looked up at him.

"What we can do with our very own personal hacker?" Graham finished for her. "Boggles the mind, doesn't it? I might even take some time off, have a holiday."

"You should take Ana. I'll stay here with the children," Magda suggested, delicately applying cream cheese to a plain bagel.

The room erupted in hoots of laughter and very loud protests.

Ana smiled, and Graham reached beneath the table to stroke her hand.

They might fight, but they'd already learned how to handle that. The very best part of having each other was that they would never, ever be bored—or lonely—again. He squeezed Ana's hand and she flashed that breath-taking smile just for him.

ABOUT THE AUTHOR

WITH SEVERAL MILLION BOOKS IN PRINT AND *NEW YORK TIMES* AND *USA Today's* bestseller lists under her belt, former CPA Patricia Rice is one of romance's hottest authors. Her emotionally-charged contemporary and historical romances have won numerous awards, including the *RT Book Reviews* Reviewers Choice and Career Achievement Awards. Her books have been honored as Romance Writers of America RITA® finalists in the historical, regency and contemporary categories.

A firm believer in happily-ever-after, Patricia Rice is married to her high school sweetheart and has two children. A native of Kentucky and New York, a past resident of North Carolina and Missouri, she currently resides in Southern California, and now does accounting only for herself. She is a member of Romance Writers of America, the Authors Guild, and Novelists, Inc.

For further information, visit Patricia's network:
http://www.patriciarice.com
http://www.facebook.com/OfficialPatriciaRice
https://twitter.com/Patricia_Rice
http://wordwenches.typepad.com/word_wenches/
http://patricia-rice.tumblr.com/

ABOUT BOOK VIEW CAFE

BOOK VIEW CAFÉ PUBLISHING COOPERATIVE (BVC) IS AN AUTHOR-OWNED cooperative of over fifty professional writers, publishing in a variety of genres including fantasy, romance, mystery, and science fiction. Since its debut in 2008, BVC has gained a reputation for producing high-quality ebooks. BVC's ebooks are DRM-free and are distributed around the world. The cooperative is now bringing that same quality to its print editions.

BVC authors include New York Times and USA Today bestsellers as well as winners and nominees of many prestigious awards, including:

Agatha Award
Campbell Award
Hugo Award
Lambda Award

Locus Award
Nebula Award
Nicholl Fellowship
PEN/Malamud Award
Philip K. Dick Award
RITA Award
World Fantasy Award
Writers of the Future Award

CPSIA information can be obtained
at www.ICGtesting.com
Printed in the USA
FSHW010712090619
58883FS